My Man's Best Friend II:

Damaged Relations

My Man's Best Friend II:

Damaged Relations

Tresser Henderson

www.urbanbooks.net

Urban Books, LLC
300 Farmingdale Road, NY-Route 109
Farmingdale, NY 11735

My Man's Best Friend II: Damaged Relations

ISBN 13: 978-1-60162-914-2
ISBN 10: 1-60162-914-1

First Mass Market Printing June 2019
First Trade Paperback Printing May 2013
Printed in the United States of America

10 9 8 7 6 5 4 3 2 1

*This is a work of fiction. Any references or similarities
to actual events, real people, living or dead, or to
real locales are intended to give the novel a sense of
reality. Any similarity in other names, characters,
places, and incidents is entirely coincidental.*

Distributed by Kensington Publishing Corp.
Submit Orders to:
Customer Service
400 Hahn Road
Westminster, MD 21157-4627
Phone: 1-800-733-3000
Fax: 1-800-659-2436

My Man's Best Friend II:

Damaged Relations

Tresser Henderson

Before the Results . . .

Chapter 1

Jaquon

My world came crumbling down in front of a yard full of people when I got flashbacks of Zacariah's descent down the road of destroying as many lives as she could. She annihilated everybody tonight and stepped beyond the line of tampering with my life. Not only my life, but she destroyed Kea's, Derrick's, and, possibly, their families' lives. All because she wanted revenge. All because her world wasn't going according to the way she wanted it to go. *Selfish bitch.*

I knew when I saw Zacariah it was going to be a problem. There was never a time when she was around that there wasn't a problem, and this was why I knew I had to do everything in my power to stay as far away from her as possible. The woman came stepping up in the cookout with a grey tank top, black skinny jeans, and grey stilettos. Who comes to a cookout in sti-

lettos? Regardless, she looked nice. I might not
have liked her but Zacariah always had swag.
And she wanted that swag to aid in her getting
Derrick back. Funny thing was, he hardly noticed her. Why would he when he had his eyes on
my woman, Kea?

When I was sitting at the game table, pulling
my money, with Essence by my side, seeing Kea
walk my way, I knew then things were about
to be on and poppin'. I wanted to snap my fingers and be somewhere else in that moment. I
wanted Essence to disappear into another realm
while my life with Kea remained intact. But, that
was all wishful thinking as Kea approached me
and the woman I had been sleeping with for
weeks. Kea didn't know this but she knew my
past indiscretions with other women. I wasn't
the most trustworthy companion to her. Kea
finding out through others about my adulterous
behavior was one thing, but to see me chilling
with the woman I had been sleeping with behind
her back was another.

So like I expected, Kea went the hell off. One
was for disrespecting her. Then, two, for having
the audacity to have my fling there to flaunt in
her face. Of course I denied it but, after Kea kept
pushing the issue, I had no choice but to con-
fess my involvement with Essence. I wished she

would have seen this was innocent. Essence and I were basically done at that point. I was ready to try to make it work with her, especially since it seemed like I was losing her to my best friend. But, as fate would have it, as soon as I was ready to turn my life around I got hit with a cataclysm that ended everything for me.

The expression on Kea's face was seared into my heart forever. The anger and hurt that consumed her delicate features stared back at me with a vengeance I knew was getting ready to be rectified. So her smacking the hell out of me was only the beginning of what I knew was the end of our relationship.

I was busted plain and simple. There was nothing I could do at this point but deal with the repercussions. You would think I would have learned my lesson when she threw that brick through the window of the other woman she caught me with but the dog in me kept humpin' around.

"Would you like another drink?" the red-headed, freckle-faced bartender asked.

I nodded. I was so consumed in my own thoughts I forgot I was in a bar. I didn't even realize a DJ was playing music. That's just how stressed out I was right now.

"Rough day?" he asked.

"Rough can't even describe how bad a day I've had," I said, throwing back the last of the liquid in my glass.

"I take it a woman's behind this?" Freckles asked, setting another rum and Coke before me.

"You can say that, but the troubles I'm going through are my entire fault."

The bartender nodded and went to serve other people surrounding the bar waiting to drink down the hassles of today. For me, this was my sixth drink and I still didn't have a buzz. I guessed sadness fought against intoxication.

I didn't know what I was thinking when I invited Essence to that cookout. Was I smoking something that clouded my judgment? I mean, I had dabbled with weed in the past but this time I hated to say this decision was done with a sober mind. How did I think it would be okay to have my girlfriend and the girl I was sleeping with in the same vicinity? Essence not being there would not only have eliminated my own breakup but it would have also eliminated Zacariah from coming, and eradicated all the mayhem she brought with her.

I wanted so much to blame that selfish, conniving tramp Zacariah for everything that happened tonight but I knew she couldn't take all the blame. Yes, she put everybody's business on

Front Street but I played a part in this debacle too. If I would have stayed faithful, this incident never would have happened. I would have Kea by my side and my best friend sitting at the bar having drinks with me now.

Hell, I hadn't even thought about Derrick. He and I went way back. I'm talking about riding bikes and playing basketball at eight years old. I couldn't imagine my life going forward without him. When it came to friends, he was the best one to have in your corner. He was my friend despite my arrogance and my conniving ways, especially when it came to women. He had never betrayed me, not until he slept with Kea. Up until then, I was the one who demonstrated distrustful behavior. I had stepped beyond the best friend code and slept with Zacariah, which was the biggest mistake of my life. The sad part about it was Zacariah was the only woman Derrick found out about.

This was not my first time sleeping with one of Derrick's women. I hate to admit that but it's true. There were Tamra, Kelly, Monique, Sasha, and Page. I know that's a lot but this goes back over a twenty-year period. Still, I did it. I wouldn't admit it to him, not unless he asked. And even if he did, I thought I would lie and say Zacariah was the only one who I took to bed.

Does that make me the bad guy in this? Hell yeah. I'm deserving of what I'm getting right now. I never thought about any consequences. Who does when they are doing something they want to do? Still, here I sat, consuming another rum and Coke, wishing I could turn back the hands of time. These were my transgressions coming full circle and I was sitting in the middle of this chaos.

Sipping on my drink, I watched the bartender mix a blue liquid into two tall glasses. He then put a slice of orange on the rim and set the glasses in front of two attractive women at the other end of the bar. One was a redbone with long, curly, auburn hair and the other was a deep mocha chick with a short cut. The mocha chick was more attractive than her acquaintance. She must've felt me staring because she made eye contact with me immediately. A smile crept across her face but I just looked with not so much as a smirk on mine. Women and cheating were what had me sitting here, drinking alone, with my girlfriend ready to leave me. Yeah, I could accept Kea and I were over and go holla at Mocha but I really wasn't in the mood. It was time to go pay the piper and face Kea like a man. I needed to go home, but I thought I needed another drink just to deal with what was to come.

Gulping down the last of my drink, I gestured for the redheaded bartender to bring me one more. Scanning the room, my eyes fell upon someone I was not expecting to see. *It didn't take her long to jump back into another man's arms.* It was Essence. She was just with me hours ago and now she was sitting with some punk grinning all up in her face. Seeing this guy with her actually ticked me off. I stood to my feet to go over and ask her what the hell she was doing. I was going to snatch her up and try my best not to shake the hell out of her. Then I halted. She was not my woman. How could I flip out when she was not the one I had a commitment with? Kea was my main priority.

Essence looked my way. The look she gave me wounded my already sunken spirit. She gritted hard on me but why? What did I do to her? Our little fling was just that, a fling. She knew my situation going in and didn't care. Now she was looking at me like I better leave her alone. I guessed she knew what she wanted and I was not it. I was not about to stand in the way of her getting her game on. So I bucked the fresh drink the bartender set before me, tossed four twenty dollar bills on the bar, and left.

Chapter 2

Jaquon

Driving around for a while, I finally decided to go home and face my demons. I didn't know what I was going to hear once I got there and I guessed driving around was helping me avoid the inevitable. I considered buying flowers, candy, and even a diamond ring at this point but I knew none of those things would work right now. It was sort of like buying my way back into her heart instead of being a man and facing my mistakes. But, still, anything to make Kea forgive me I was willing to do.

When I pulled up into a parking space in front of our apartment building, Kea's madness was evident. I pulled up to find all my items scattered about. I got out of my car looking at how Kea made it rain with my clothes, shoes, CDs, and my game systems. She flung all of it over the balcony. To make matters worse, Kea had sliced and bleached some of my clothes. When I saw the new Jordans I had just purchased days ago soaked in the destructive liquid with slashes all over them I really became angry. I knew I had broken Kea's heart and, yes, tonight was the straw that broke the camel's back but come on. She didn't have to stoop to the level of destroying my property. I'd have expected something like this from Zacariah. She played down and dirty. When she came swinging, her blows felt like gut-wrenching punches being thrown by cement-filled gloves, knocking everybody out. Now Kea had adapted to this same method of revenge. I guessed constantly being betrayed changed the sweet woman I knew her to be.

Scooping up what wasn't destroyed, which wasn't much, I tossed what I could salvage into my car. I then headed upstairs, putting my key in the lock to enter. Before I could turn the key, the door behind me opened. I turned to see Sheila standing there half naked in a two-piece black lace nightie. She was always good for coming to the door in something skanky but now was not the time.

"Hey, Jaquon," she said seductively, smiling at me, posing like she was doing a shoot for *Playboy* magazine. "Do you want to come over for a nightcap?"

I frowned at her, asking, "Are you serious? You do know Kea's in here," I said, pointing at the door I was about to walk through.

"From the way she tossed your things out, I figured you two were over," she said.

I thought about Sheila's attempts that did work on me in the past, which landed me in her bed. For a while I maintained thinking it wasn't right to sleep with a woman so close to home. But the day did come where I was too weak to resist sexual attempts. I went over and did what I did best. I tore that ass up and not just one time, several different times, until my cockiness almost got me caught by Kea.

This particular day I was bangin' Sheila down from the back when someone knocked on her door. I snatched my johnson from Sheila and went to the bathroom while she got rid of whoever it was. To my dismay it was Kea, asking Sheila to turn down the music, which was blasting to mask the moans and groans we both were making.

"I know you and your men like to have sex with the music blasting but do you think you can turn it down please? Some of us are getting ready to go to sleep."

"Okay. My bad. I'll turn it down," Sheila said.

As soon as that door closed I came from the bathroom with a limp johnson, stuffing it back into my boxer briefs, knowing this could never happen again. I was playing with fire for sure, cheating so close to my home with Kea sometimes sitting in our apartment while I screwed Sheila. In the beginning it never occurred to me that the neighbors could talk if they saw me constantly coming from Sheila's place, but the dog in me didn't care because my johnson was overpowering common sense.

I eventually put a stop to it. I hated to because Sheila was gifted in the bedroom. Hell, she was gifted wherever we decided to do it. She was the type of chick who sucked toes and licked balls. She even did this thing with Pop Rocks one night that made me consider leaving Kea for good. But she was a straight-up whore. You couldn't turn a whore into a housewife, and Kea was housewife material, so Shelia had to go.

Seeing Shelia standing in her doorway half naked scared the hell out of me because I was afraid Kea was looking through the peephole, watching this freak attempt to lure me back into her corrupted lair again.

"You look a little stressed," Sheila said.

"I have some things going on right now."

"You need some help with relieving some pressure?" she asked, sucking on her index finger.

"No. I'm good," I said, turning the knob, opening the door to enter.

"Holla at me later, boo. I'm here if you need me."

I turned to look at her angrily before shutting the door in her face. I hoped Kea didn't hear what she said because she damn sure said it loud enough for the people on the basement floor to hear. If I didn't know any better I'd think Shelia was attempting to break me and Kea up. I was surprised her trifling behind hadn't told Kea already. *Maybe I should tell her before Sheila does, but right now that will only add gasoline to this inferno.*

The apartment was dark and quiet. I clicked the light on only to find it didn't work. With the light from the moon giving me enough illumination to maneuver, I made my way to the bedroom. The carpet beneath my feet hushed my steps as I entered our bedroom. I clicked the light on in there but it too didn't come on. *Did Kea pay the electric bill?* I wondered. I looked at the DVD player in our room to see the time showing 2:19, which meant we had electricity. I walked over to the television and turned it on. Finally something worked. The TV lit the room and once it did I saw Kea standing beside me. It was like she appeared out of nowhere. I jumped halfway across the room.

"Damn it, Kea," I said with my heart beating rapidly. I wasn't expecting Kea to be all up on me like she was. I could tell from her swollen eyes she had been crying. She looked disheveled but through her madness I couldn't help but to bask in her beauty. I looked her up and down until my eyes fell upon what she was holding.

"What are you going to do with that?" I asked cautiously.

"I'm getting ready to whoop your . . ." she said, not finishing her sentence as she swung the bat at me. "You bastard. I'm sick and tired"—she swung the bat—"of you cheating"—she swung again —"on me. I want you to pay"—the bat came at me again but missed—"for hurting me."

I jumped back, with the bat barely missing me a few times. She swung again, hitting the lamp, smashing it into pieces.

"Put the bat down before you hurt somebody," I said, trying to escape the path of the aluminum weapon.

She swung again but this time I didn't get out of the way quick enough. The bat landed on my lower back, causing pain to shoot through my body. Again she swung, hitting me on my upper bicep. Her next swing was aimed for my head but I turned quick enough to put my arm up to block the bat from making contact. Pain shot through my arm but I bore it. Thinking quickly, I grabbed the bat before she could take it back to swing at me again. I made sure not to let go of it as Kea struggled to try to regain control of the weapon.

"Let go," she yelled.

"Not until you calm down."

We played tug-of-war before I jerked it hard, snatching it from her grip. This made her angrier. She charged for me and began kicking and punching me. It was hard to block with one hand since I was holding the bat with the other. The beast in Kea was unleashing its rage, which had been festering for years. Finally, I threw the bat across the room. She never noticed, still trying to beat me to no end. I went low, scooping her off her feet and throwing her over my shoulders.

"Let me go," she said, punching my back.

I took her over to the bed, slamming her on her back. Before she had a chance to get up, I straddled her, pinning her arms down, making it impossible for her to move or swing at me again.

"Calm down, Kea," I yelled.

"Let me go. Get off me," she screamed.

"Not until you calm down."

"I hate you. I wish I never met you. How could you do this to me again?" she asked as she began to sob.

"Baby, I'm sorry," I pleaded.

"I loved you, Jaquon," she said with tears streaming down the sides of her face. "Why? Why didn't you just love me back?"

"Baby, I do love you," I said, feeling her pain in its intensity for the first time.

"You couldn't have," she said through a cracking voice.

I could feel her body lose its strength as her struggling arms became limp and her outburst turned into inconsolable sobs. I slowly let go of her arms. She didn't swing again.

"Baby, I'm sorry," I tried to say as sincerely as I could.

"All I ever asked was for you to love me, for you to stay true to me, Jaquon, and you couldn't even do that," she said.

I crawled from atop her and sat next to her on the bed, watching her anguish release itself. She placed her hands over her face and continued to cry. I placed my hand on her shoulder but she shook it off. I wanted to wrap my arms around her, letting her know it was going to be okay, but I knew she wouldn't allow it.

"Baby, talk to me, please," I begged, trying hard not to lose it myself.

"What is there to talk about?" she asked sadly.

"Us."

She sat up abruptly and I leaned back a bit, thinking she was going to start swinging on me again, but she didn't.

She said, "There is no 'us.' I'm not even sure if there was ever an 'us,'" she said despondently.

"Don't say that," I said, looking at her.

"I mean it this time, Jaquon," she said, sniffling. "I'm done being your doormat."

"Baby, we have both done some wrong things here."

Her expression spoke volumes. She didn't have to say a word and I knew what I said never should have come out of my mouth. I knew I didn't have the right to throw up her indiscretions when I had been doing wrong all during our relationship together. Fury invaded her and I knew my words were not sanctioned here.

"You have the nerve to bring Derrick up right now," she said irately.

"I didn't say his name."

"You didn't have to. It was insinuated."

I couldn't say anything because she was right.

"I had every right to cheat on you," she said.

"But you had to do it with my best friend. Derrick and I have been boys forever," I said.

She smirked and said, "What better way to get back at you than to screw your boy?"

"But how was that going to solve our issues?"

"Now you want us to resolve things. Now that I have slept with your best friend, that's when you want to make things work," she said, getting up off the bed and walking over to the closet.

"I wanted us to work before all this happened," I countered.

"Well you had a funny way of showing it, Jaquon. I mean really. You invited one of your women to an event you knew I was going to be at. What were you thinking?" she asked.

All I could say was, "I wasn't."

"Do you want to know why I slept with Derrick in the first place?"

I leaned forward on the bed, shaking my head because I didn't want to know, but Kea continued anyway.

"Jaquon, you were never here. You were always making excuses as to why you were sleeping over Derrick's house. So when he came over here to see you because he was upset about Zacariah cheating on him and you weren't here, our emotions got caught up. He needed somebody and I needed him."

Her words were cutting me deep. I didn't ask for particulars, nor did I care to know, but that didn't stop her from spewing the gory details.

"The next morning you come up in here saying you were with him. I knew you were lying because Derrick was in bed screwing me. He lay next to me most of the night. And you know what, it felt good. He felt good," she said with a coldness I had never seen. "Your friend worked my body like it's never been worked before, but it could have been because he was releasing the pain he was dealing with too. Our grief integrated into a night of passion I will never regret," she said, pointing at me.

I couldn't say anything. All the conversations I had with myself didn't prepare me for Kea telling me in detail how she enjoyed getting it on with Derrick.

"I wanted to see for once what it felt like to be you. I wondered what had you out in the streets all times of night. But I guess in the end the joke was still on me," Kea said.

I lowered my head, saying the only thing I could. "Baby, I'm sorry," I said, repeating myself.

She ignored my apology and said, "I only slept with Derrick because he was there for me. He listened to me. He gave me what I couldn't get from you because you were too busy giving it to other women."

I went to stand but a twinge of pain shot through my side, reminding me of what a scorned woman could do with a bat. "Baby, I want us to work. I love you and I don't want to lose you. I will forgive you for everything if you promise not to leave me."

"I couldn't care less whether you forgive me. The fact of the matter is I can't forgive you. I gave you way too many chances with my heart, Jaquon, and you stomped on it. For goodness' sake, you slept with the enemy."

I forgot about that. Zacariah was once my past sexual encounter.

"You did her and her best friend. I don't know what you got. Hell, I don't know what you could have given me," Kea said.

"Baby, please," I begged, finally managing to stand to my feet. I walked towards her, but she held her hand up for me to stay away.

"I need you to leave. Pack your belongings and get the hell out."

"Is there anything left to pack? You threw everything off the balcony, didn't you?" I said, laughing, trying to lighten the mood. It didn't work.

"Then go outside with your crap, Jaquon. I don't want you here."

"When can I come back?"

"Never," she said.

"This is my place too, Kea."

"I don't care. You are leaving here tonight. Go to Zacariah or Essence or whoever else you've screwed. Just leave me the hell alone," she demanded as she went into our master bathroom.

I sat back down on the bed, looking in the direction she'd gone. I knew this was the end of us. I didn't realize how much I loved this woman until now. I was mad at myself for ruining such a good thing.

I stood back up slowly as more pain shot throughout my side. I walked in the bathroom to find Kea standing in front of the mirror. She was just staring at her reflection. I could see her broken spirit and hated that it was me who caused it.

I walked up behind her, looking at her reflection. She didn't make me move. She didn't
scream at me to get out. She just looked at me
with such sadness. I ran my finger across her
cheek, almost whispering in a sympathetic tone,
"Do you really want me to leave?"

The conclusion to our relationship abducted
my voice. I couldn't speak any louder because
the wind was being taken out of my sail.

"Yes," she said, looking into my eyes through
the reflection in the mirror.

I was choked up. I knew she could see how
much I agonized over her decision and wished
she would change her mind. Tears were on the
verge of falling but I tried my best to hold them
back. I guessed that was the man in me. *Maybe
if I dropped down this masculine wall and let
the pressure of losing her spew from every inch
of me, she would consider taking me back. She
would see she's won this battle and I am waving a white towel in surrender because I want
to make this relationship work.* But I couldn't.
I nodded my head as I cleared my throat of any
emotion wanting to escape me. I wrapped my
arms around her for the last time, making our
bodies into a solitary cell. I wanted our molec-
ular components to transform into something
beautiful. As many times Kea played the song

"No Air" by Jordin Sparks, which I couldn't stand to hear, now I understood what that song meant. Kea was my air. And no one could ever fill the span of my heart that belonged solely to her.

I let Kea go and walked back into what was once our bedroom. I looked around at the space surrounding me. *We did have some wonderful times here.* I placed my hands in my pockets, lowering my head toward the floor. I looked back at Kea one last time and I watched as tears streamed down her cheeks. This was really it. I had finally pushed away the woman I loved and right now the only thing I could do was abide by her wishes and leave.

Chapter 3

Zacariah

My stint in the hospital was a short one. I actually got out the next morning with no one to pick me up. For some reason, Essence didn't bother to call or come by to see me today. I called her house and got no answer. I kept calling her cell but she never picked up. That ticked me off. She knew I didn't drive myself here so I didn't have a car. She knew I had no family I claimed, either, so that left her. She was supposed to be my best friend but right now I wanted to pull that title from her. I was there for her when she passed out while she was screwing Jaquon but then she did me like this. I swore if she was with Jaquon while I had to try to find a way home, I was going to go off. I swore I would end my relationship with her if she continued to see Jaquon. It was either him or me, and it was in her best interest to choose me since he was a continuous cheater. "A friend before men" was my mantra.

Since I couldn't get Essence to come get me, I ended up taking the cab home. "Home" was still staying with Essence, since Derrick kicked me out. Not only did I miss him, I missed that house. Don't get me wrong, Essence had a nice home also, but Derrick's was a lot nicer and a lot bigger. Where Essence's home was one story, Derrick had a two story with a finished basement. I missed the walk-in closets and large master bathroom. I missed the fireplace we used to make love in front of and the granite countertops I used to hop up on to sit when I watched Derrick cook dinner for us. I couldn't say Derrick wasn't right for tossing me out on my ass. He did catch me cheating on him. I was still traumatized thinking about him ramming his fingers inside my womanhood and smearing the residue of the other man's semen all over my face. I had been disrespected many times before but nothing like what Derrick did to me.

I expected to see Essence's car sitting in the driveway but it wasn't here. This was surprising since Essence told me last night at the hospital she was going home. Once inside I saw that the house was empty. I went to her bedroom to see her bed had not been slept in. Where was she? I was ready to cuss her out if she was still sleeping but she wasn't here. *No answer on her cell.*

No-show at the hospital and now her not being home . . . I thought this was odd, especially since Essence used Sunday as her relaxation day. I didn't think she got the spirit and decided to go to church, because she never went to church. I didn't know whether to be happy she wasn't here or mad. Where was she?

I picked up the phone sitting on the console table behind the couch and dialed her number again.

"Hi, you've reached Essence. Leave me a message and I'll get back to you when I get a chance. Later."

After the beep, I said, "Essence, this is Zacariah. Where are you and why haven't you returned my calls? Look, I've made it home now so when you get this message, please give me call. And I will try not to lay your behind out when you decide to call me."

I hung up the phone and looked around the space, a little worried about where she was. Then I thought it was actually nice having the place to myself. The quiet was very much needed, so I walked around the table and sat down on the sofa. Laying my head back, I looked up at the ceiling and replayed the events that landed me in the position I was in.

"I told them I would get them back. They thought I was a joke and now look at them. Who's laughing now? They deserve what they get. Little Ms. High and Mighty over here," she said, looking at Kea, who stood with no tears, no expression, just shock plastered on her face.

"And you," Zacariah said, sneering at Derrick. *"I was your woman. I loved you and you cheated on me with her. This serves you right. I bet you wish you would have kept your dick in your pants now. You wouldn't have had to worry about something as sick as this happening. Karma, baby, karma."*

Snapping back into now, I sat up on the sofa and proceeded to get up. I felt sore, like I had been in a battle. Well I had been in a battle. I was just on the losing end of this battle. Walking into the bathroom, I looked into the mirror at my reflection. With black eyes and a busted lip, anger came over me again. I wanted to go looking for Kea to whoop her for what she did to me.

Yes, I had just opened up the Bible and read a verse the nurse recommended to me last night.

Cease from anger, and forsake wrath: fret not thyself in any wise to do evil.

But how do I do that? How do I not be angry about this? It's not in my nature to turn the other cheek. All my life people had turned away and ignored me like I didn't exist. No one ever cared about me. Looking back on my entire existence I had a lot to be angry about. I had been the only person I could trust in this life. I couldn't trust my mama or daddy. I couldn't trust any of my aunts or uncles. I thought I could trust Derrick but he left me too. And today I couldn't even depend on Essence. All I had was me. Who in the hell was doing anything for me?

Tired of wallowing in self-pity I decided I was going to order some take-out and chill for a little while. Deciding to wait and see if Essence contacted me, I took this time to get to know television again. Why not get caught up in something else besides allowing my thoughts to dampen my already sunken spirit? So I clicked the tube on. Too bad the first bit of news I heard was a tragic death, and it was someone I knew.

"An elderly man by the name of Otis Hanks was shot and killed late last night at the Copper Ledge apartment complex in a robbery gone bad," the anchorwoman said. "Sources say the gunman was an African American male looking to be in his late teens. He was wearing black jeans and a jacket with green lettering on the back. If you know any information regarding this murder, please call your local authorities."

I was shocked. Derrick's biological father was dead. I just talked to this man the other day. I wondered if Derrick got a chance to see him before his passing. I wanted to go over to his house to see him but thought better of it. Not after what I had put him through. I did decide to do the next best thing and call him. I knew once his caller ID showed it was Essence's house, he might not answer, but to my surprise he did.

"Hello."

"Hey, Derrick. It's me, Zacariah."

When he heard my voice, he said nothing.

"Derrick, are you there?"

"I'm here."

"I didn't know whether you hung up on me."

"I have every right to, don't you think?" he said impassively.

"Yes, you do, but, Derrick, just hear me out. I want to apologize," I said, thinking this might smooth things over a bit.

"I think it's too late for that."

"Please, Derrick. I'm really sorry. I didn't mean for things to turn out like they have."

"It went exactly like you wanted it to go, Zacariah," he said loudly.

"Yes. No. Derrick, look, baby, I never wanted us to end up where we are now," I said, confused.

"You can't blame any of this on me."

"I know if I never cheated on you, we would still be living in bliss."

"I doubt that," he said coldly.

"Well I think so. I love you."

"You love me so much you were determined to ruin my life. I'm sitting here more unhappy than I've ever been in my entire life and it's all because you couldn't leave well enough alone. All you had to do was let me go on with my life, but because I wanted my future to be with Kea, you couldn't let that happen."

"You're right but, Derrick, I didn't lead you to believe your father was your biological dad. That was your mother. And I didn't rape Kea's mom to produce Kea. That was your biological father," I said defensively.

The next thing I heard was a dial tone. I dialed his number back but he never picked up the phone again.

I was mad at myself for going there with him. I was getting aggressive because he was trying to blame all of this on me but he couldn't. Why couldn't he see his mother, Kea's mother, their dad, and other family members let these lies consume a past all of them were trying to conceal, which eventually turned his world upside down? I was just the one who brought things to the light.

Chapter 4

Zacariah

It was four days later and I still hadn't stepped foot outside of Essence's house. And Essence hadn't stepped foot inside. I thought maybe she had gone to visit with her parents. She was planning this trip before all this drama came up. *Maybe the stress of everything made her leave earlier than she planned.* I was supposed to go with her but if she needed to do this on her own then more power to her. Right now I had Derrick to worry about.

I used these days for my body to heal. And it gave me time to think about how I was going to get Derrick back. Since he decided to ignore my numerous attempts to talk with him, I decided I was going to try to call him from a pay phone. Of all the days he needed me, today was that day, since they were burying Mr. Hanks today.

I dressed like I was about to rob somebody. I had on a black jogging suit with a hood I pulled over my head, and some dark shades to cover my healing bruises. The sun felt good but I was in no mood to enjoy the spring-like weather.

I climbed into the back of a cab, since I still didn't have a car, and asked the driver to take me to the nearest pay phone. He turned and looked at me like I was crazy.

"Did you hear what I said?" I shouted to the African American man.

"Oh, I heard you. But why don't you tell me where the nearest pay phone is because I don't know."

"You drive around all damn day. You never see a pay phone?"

"Ma'am, why would I be on the lookout for a pay phone when everybody on earth has a cell phone? Even my five-year-old granddaughter has a cell phone," he said jokingly.

But I didn't find a damn thing funny.

"And why are you dressed like that? Are you running from somebody?"

"The way I'm dressed is none of your concern. What you should be concerned with is finding me a damn pay phone like I asked," I said angrily.

"And like I told you, ma'am, I don't know where one is."

I sat there fuming. Of all the cab drivers I had to get, I got the one who didn't know nothing about nothing.

"Ma'am, I started my meter already and we haven't budged an inch," he told me and I glanced at the escalating amount.

I asked, "Do you have a cell phone I can use?"

He frowned at me.

"Please. I'll pay you for using it. I need to make an important phone call."

"Is it long distance? Because I don't have one of those plans."

"It's local. So are you going to let me use it?"

He thought about it for a minute before he reached into his pocket and pulled out a flip that looked like it was one of the first ones to come out.

I started to say something but changed my mind when I found the man staring at me. I flipped the phone open and dialed Derrick's number. Putting the ancient device up to my ear, I heard it ringing, my heart pounding at the thought of hearing his voice.

"Hello."

"Derrick, please don't hang up—"

As soon as he heard my voice, he did just that. I knew he had to be mad but he had to be over it by now. Maybe he was acting like this because he was grieving. I knew my boo needed me and I wanted to go to him. I regretted I never told him how sorry I was about him losing his biological dad.

I handed the old man his phone back and sat thinking about what I needed to do next.

"Is there something else you would like me to do, ma'am?" he asked.

"As a matter of fact there is. Can you sit here and wait for me to come back out?"

"Yes, I can, but please know my meter still will be running."

I said, "Okay," and got out of the cab, making my way back into the house. Derrick wouldn't accept my calls. Then maybe he would talk to me in person. It was time for me to go and pay my last respects.

Chapter 5

Zacariah

While the graveside service was going on, I made sure to remain in the background where no one could see me. I had on a black sleek knit dress with side ruching and a black-and-white wide-brim hat with a circumference of twenty-two inches. I made sure to wear a dress that was modest so Derrick could see I was trying hard to win him back.

As the preacher spoke, I felt like I should be sitting with Derrick and his family. Hell, I was practically family as long as Derrick and I were in our relationship. What we were going through was temporary, just as long as Kea stayed out of the picture. Still that seemed to be difficult. Here she sat in the front row with Derrick at the casket. *Sanctimonious trick.* There she was still thinking she could take my place. But it would be over my dead body.

Once the service was over I watched as everyone greeted one another. Individuals lined up to greet Derrick and other family members. I could tell he didn't like this portion of the service. How could he, when he was sitting in front of a casket holding a father he never knew? The pain was evident on his face and for a split second, I regretted that I played a part in his sadness.

As the crowd diminished, it was then that Derrick saw me. The expression on his face was one I wasn't familiar with. It wasn't one of happiness or anger. It was as if he were an empty shell of a man going through the motions just so he could get home. I hoped when he saw my dependability he would see how sorry I was and would let me help him get through everything he was going through.

When I made my mind up to approach Derrick, Kea stepped to him. She caressed his arm gently and a bit of jealousy shot through me. Then annoyance crept in and again I tried to remember the words my nurse said to me. But I realized my anger was a part of me and so was revenge. I wanted to beat Kea down right in this graveyard, burying her under one of these tombstones. Hell, she could share a hole and be buried with her rapist father. But I had to maintain my composure. I had to do it for Derrick and show him I was a changed woman. My body trembled as I tried to hold back the feelings of wanting to lay hands on this trick, but I held strong and remembered I was here for my boo.

I walked over to the two of them carrying on a conversation. I overheard something about getting paternity test results in a few days. Derrick nudged Kea, who turned her attention from him to me. All conversation ceased when I stepped in front of them. I was hoping Derrick would be the first one to speak, and he was, but I didn't like what came out of his mouth.

"What the hell are you doing here?" he asked angrily through clenched teeth.

"Derrick, I wanted to come and show my support. I heard about what happened and—"

"And what? You came to gloat?" he asked.

"No."

"You have some nerve showing your face here today."

"I came here for you, Derrick."

"I didn't ask you to come. Never once did I pick up a phone and say, 'Zacariah, I need you.'"

"But I knew you would," I said, watching Kea sneer and shake her head in dismay.

"Are you happy that the man I never got to know is dead? Or is this some sick way of you seeing Kea and me together, knowing we can never be lovers . . ." He paused.

Just him saying the words "Kea" and "lovers" in the same sentence made me cringe. But I held my ground.

"No. Please. Just hear me out, Derrick," I pleaded, trying to look sincere, but it was hard seeing Kea get satisfaction out of Derrick humiliating me in front of everyone.

"Why should I listen to anything you have to say? You have been the worst thing that has ever happened to my life. I don't even want to look at you right now," he said, walking away.

I watched him head in the direction of his mother, who was glaring at me with disdain. That woman never liked me. *She can jump in the same hole along with Kea.* Treating me like I wasn't good enough for her son, and acting like this Christian but telling lies all along. Oh, she had a story to tell. And it had to be good for her to have Derrick thinking his entire life the man he knew as his dad wasn't his biological father.

"Mentally something has to be wrong with you, Zacariah. You really thought coming here today would be okay with Derrick?" Kea asked with her black clutch in her hand, which matched her black suit. Her hair was pulled back and shades shielded her eyes also.

I still thought I was better looking than she was and couldn't see what Derrick ever saw in her. "I didn't come here for any drama, Kea," I forced out of my mouth.

"That's all you are full of, Zacariah. Everywhere you go there is a theatrical performance with you playing the leading role as queen bitch."

I smiled smugly, trying really hard not to reach out and smack the hell out of this trick.

"And here you are proving my point by reveling in our sorrow at our dad's funeral. Just when I thought you couldn't sink any lower, you somehow find new depths of dirt to throw in our faces. But I guess I shouldn't be surprised since low down is your customary ranking," Kea said.

My heart was beating so fast I thought it was going to thump out of my chest. I felt sweat beads building underneath my clothes and one of my hands balling into a fist.

I said, "I didn't come here in triumph. Does it look like I have a victorious expression on my face? I'm saddened by what has happened and I came here to support Derrick."

"Well how did that work out for you? As you can see he still wants nothing to do with you."

"I completely understand that but I won't stop trying to be there for him. I love him."

I didn't care if she saw how genuine I was because I wasn't here for her. She couldn't comfort him like I could.

Kea removed her shades and looked at me through squinted eyes. "Leave Derrick alone," she said slowly like I was dense and couldn't comprehend her words.

"Excuse me?"

"You heard me. Stay away from him."

"And who the hell are you?" I questioned with attitude, wondering why this female always had to test me.

"Just because you think I'm his sister doesn't mean I will not be in his life. If anything, I'm going to be there for him even more."

"Too bad it won't be in his bed again," I retorted.

"I don't need to be in his bed when I got his heart," she countered.

It caused me to almost choke on the deep breath I took in from her comment. *His heart. I have his heart*, I thought.

"I'm going to be there to tell him to stay as far away from you as possible. You are a manipulative, trifling little whore. If you come near him, I will beat you down like I did before. I warned you and you crossed me once. You see where that got you. I showed you what I'm made of so please try me again. I dare you."

No, this trick wasn't threatening me on the sacred ground of souls resting. The pastor who gave the eulogy stood several feet away, chatting to some of the mourners, but managed to cast some stares in our direction. Clasping my hands in front of me, I played it cool. For once I wasn't going to be the one looking discourteous. Kea was the one getting rude with me. I swore I saw her neck roll and her pointing her little finger at me like I was her child or something. I thought she was trying to provoke me but it wasn't going to work. Not today. So I nodded, smiling slyly.

"You caught me off-guard before, Kea, but don't think I'm going to ever let you get me like that again. You better be glad I'm not sweeping the ground with you now. And some words of advice: don't you ever threaten me again," I said like nothing was going on between us. Just a little friendly conversation was what we were having in everyone else's eyes.

"Oh it wasn't a threat, Zacariah. It's a promise," Kea said before walking away.

A promise. Didn't I just tell her to not threaten me? I chuckled as she made her way back to Derrick and his mom. All of them walked toward the awaiting limousines. I smiled at the pastor, who was still staring me down. I brushed my dress, put my purse under my arm, and proceeded to the awaiting cab, all the while wishing I had jerked Kea by her ponytail and slammed her face into these headstones. But I shook the thoughts off and thought of other ways to get her back.

Taking out my cell phone I found the number for my cousin.

"Hey, girl. Do you think you can stop by and see me today? For what? Don't be questioning me. Just come over as soon as possible. I need a huge favor from you and I can guarantee I will make it worth your while."

After the Results . . .

Chapter 6

Derrick

I loved my mother dearly but I couldn't wait to get away from her. When that nurse revealed that Kea and I were sister and brother, I damn near blacked out. My knees buckled beneath me. The room turned black and the only thing that kept registering in my mind was the fact that I had sex with my sister.

I didn't know if I dropped to my knees. All I remembered was looking at Kea and seeing the same shocked look on her face. Her father had his arms around her.

Leaving that facility, Mom tried to talk to me. Tears filled her eyes and I almost found myself saying, "What in the hell are you crying for? I'm the one who just found out my life was nothing but a bunch of lies." But I said nothing. I stood as Mama pulled me down to where my chin met her shoulder in an embrace. I didn't return the gesture. I just stared at the cars passing. I actually contemplated running into the traffic, hoping a fast, speeding car would take me out of my misery. I felt like my life was over. What I knew wasn't what it was at all. I was second-guessing if the woman who was holding me was really my real mother at this point. Who in the hell was I?

Mama held me, sticking to me like glue. I knew she wanted to help me but I wanted to get as far away from her as possible.

"Baby, I'm sorry," she kept repeating. "I'm so sorry."

You damn right you sorry, I thought. How could a mother do this to the son she claimed to love so much? Didn't everybody know that secrets eventually came out? Why try to hide them? But you see what it is, the older generation doesn't think about the consequences of their actions. They're too busy trying to be respected and loved and keeping their kids from knowing not much about their upbringing. Or should I say they only let us know what they want us to know. This here today was something I should have known about. I shouldn't have found out about it from Zacariah at a cookout given by me at my damn house for all my guests to witness. *What in the hell will they think of me now? I'll always be known as the guy who slept with his sister.*

I gripped Mama's shoulders and pushed myself from her embrace.

"I'm going home," I said blankly.

"I'm coming with you," Mama said.

"No, you are not, Mama."

"Son, you don't need to be by yourself."

"Mama."

"Don't try to talk me out of it. I'm going home with you, Derrick, and that's all it is to this," Mama said sternly.

Anger came over me. I tried really hard not to disrespect her but she was making it difficult for me to keep my composure. All I could say was, "I'm going home by myself."

"Derrick."

"Mama, will you let this go!" I yelled. My sudden outburst caused Mama to jump. But I didn't care. I tried and tried to tell her but she wouldn't listen. "I don't want you or nobody else around me right now. You understand me?"

She stared at me with tears streaming down her face.

I continued to say, "I need to process this. And looking at you right now is doing nothing but making me angry."

"Baby, I'm sorry," she apologized again.

A noise to my left caused me to turn and look in that direction. It was Kea and her dad walking out of the facility. Kea's dad still had his arms around her. Our eyes met and I turned, looking away from her.

"I got to go, Mama," I said, reaching in my pocket and retrieving my keys.

"But how am I supposed to get home?" she asked, reminding me that she rode with me here.

"Maybe Kea's dad can give you a lift home," I said, pointing at him as they approached. I didn't give them time to get close to me. I turned and walked away.

"Derrick."

I heard Kea call but I couldn't stop. Hearing her call out to me was the exact moment that I began to break. Water formed in my eyes as the pressure of the revelation hit me harder than it did when that nurse said, "The test proved by an average of 99.9 percent that Derrick and Kea are brother and sister."

I started walking faster. I heard Kea call out to me again.

"Derrick, wait."

I couldn't be around her now, and like a track star trying to win an Olympic gold medal, I took off running. I was running away from them. I was running away from this result. I wanted to run away from it all because this turned out to be the worst day of my life.

Chapter 7

Zacariah

When a coworker from Essence's job called to see where she was, I began to panic. This let me know that maybe Essence didn't take that trip to see her parents, since she didn't put in time to take off from work. Essence loved her job and wouldn't just up and leave like that. Something wasn't adding up.

Before this call I was getting angrier with her with each passing day, because I couldn't believe she didn't have the nerve to check in and let me know where she was or even find out how I was doing since I was in the hospital. What type of friendship was this? We never went more than a couple of days without talking and now it had been almost two weeks. The phone call from her coworker only put more fear into my heart that something was wrong, but I didn't want to jump to conclusions yet. I had to check with her mother to see if she had arrived. Maybe an emergency caused her to leave so abruptly to the point that she couldn't take off from work or call me to let me know what was going on.

Searching in the console table where the phone was, I found Essence's address book. Flipping to the Cs, I found her mom's number. I dialed it and waited for someone to answer.

"Hello," a male voice said like he was surprised the phone even rang.

"Hello," I said.

"Yeah. Who dis?"

Oh, brother, here we go with the backwoodsness. "My name is Zacariah and I'm calling to speak to Essence."

"Who?"

"Essence."

"Essence don't live here no mo'. She moved to the city."

"I know that. This is her best friend."

"What yo' name is?" he asked.

"Zacariah," I said.

"Who?"

I knew no matter how many times I said my name, he wouldn't get it. So I asked in frustration, "Is her mom there?"

"Yeah," he said, not saying anything else. He could have said "let me get her" or "hold on a minute," but this guy held the phone, waiting for me to say something else, and I knew, then, why Essence hated to go home.

"Well, can I speak to her mom?"

"Oh. Okay," he said, putting the phone down.

I heard some loud voices in the background and some scuffling around the phone. It took awhile before anybody came to the phone.

"Hello," an elderly woman's voice said.

"Yes. Is this Essence's mom?"

"Yes, it is. Who dis callin'?"

"Ma'am, I'm Essence's best friend, Zacariah."

"Oh hey, baby. How you doin'?"

"I'm doing fine, ma'am," I said, loving her sweet voice. "Ms. Clemons, I'm calling to see if Essence is there."

"No. Essence not here. Why? She not wit' you?"

My heart fluttered a bit because now I was worried. Essence was not with her family, so where in the hell was she? And now how was I going to explain not knowing where she was?

"No. She's not here either," I said.

"How long she been gone?" her mother asked.

Here was the question I didn't want to answer but didn't have a choice. I could lie about how long. "She's only been gone a couple of days. She was supposed to be traveling to visit with you. Maybe she stopped to get some rest somewhere. I'm pretty sure she's okay."

"I knew she was comin' home but not dis soon."

"I think she was trying to surprise you," I said.

"Well how 'bout dat. I love surprises."

"Well act like you are when she comes, okay? I don't want to ruin her surprise for you," I said, playing it off.

"I will. My baby is comin' home," Ms. Clemmons said joyously.

"And when she gets there, can you have her call me?"

"I sure can," her mom said.

With that I hung up the phone. Something was definitely wrong. I picked the phone back up urgently and dialed Essence's number again.

"Hey, you have reached Essence. Please leave your name and number and I will get back to you as soon as I get this message. Later."

"Essence, this is Zacariah again, girl. Where the hell are you? I'm worried about you. Please call me as soon as you get this message and all the other messages I have left you. Call me back," I said, hanging up the phone.

This was not like Essence. Somebody always knew where she was. I thought it was time to call the police. What choice did I have? She had been missing for over forty-eight hours so they had no other choice but to investigate.

With the phone becoming my closest companion, I dialed the police station. When I brought the phone to my ear, I heard somebody saying, "Hello."

"Hello, Essence," I said, getting relieved.

"No, this is not Essence."

"Then who the hell is this?" I said, allowing that relief to turn back into my panic state.

"I just called to tell you it's done."

In my irrational state I said, "What's done?"

"It's done," the voice said again and I caught on to what was going on. My panic state turned into one of elation.

"Are you sure?" I questioned.

"Yes."

I didn't even think I said good-bye before I hung up the phone. I did a dance in the middle of the living room floor. Plan "get my baby back" was now underway. I knew Derrick would need some comforting and now was the perfect time to show up and be there for him. I knew his spirits were lower than low right now and I counted on the fact that he wouldn't care who attempted to help him pick up the pieces of his life, just as long as he had a warm body by his side. Finding Essence would have to wait until tomorrow. She'd been gone this long. One more day wasn't going to hurt. I had to go be with my baby. It was about time I got some good news.

I packed an overnight bag with my favorite Victoria's Secret fragrance, Pure Seduction, some lotion, soap, and deodorant. I pulled out my sexy lace panty and bra sets and placed them in the bag along with a couple of changes of clothes. I would keep this in my trunk just in case Derrick needed me to stay over for a few days.

I primped in the mirror, making sure everything was straight. Lucky for me my bruises were finally gone and I was back to looking like the gorgeous woman I was. Thirty-six, twenty-four, thirty-eight were my measurements and I looked fine as ever with my coffee-colored complexion looking like smooth chocolate. I winked at myself for looking so good before exiting the bathroom. I picked up my bag, purse, and keys and headed to my old stomping ground, Derrick's house.

When I arrived, it was around 8:00 P.M. It wasn't quite dark yet but the sun was losing its battle with the horizon. I couldn't tell if Derrick was home. He usually parked in the garage. I parked in the driveway, thinking he was home. Getting out, my excitement was spilling over. I was finally going to get with my baby and I didn't have Ms. Kea here to interfere with that. I went to the door and rang the doorbell. I turned, looking at the brick two-story homes across the street with their immaculate lawns, hoping I would be living back in this neighborhood again.

No one came to the door. I rang the doorbell again and still no one answered. I went to the side of his house, peeking in the window of his garage, and didn't see his car so he wasn't here. For a minute I thought he might have seen it was me and decided to ignore me but lucky for me that was not the case. I wondered where he could be. *Maybe he stepped out for a minute.* It didn't matter because I was willing to wait for him.

My wait ended up turning to three hours. It was now after eleven and still no Derrick. Where in the hell was he? I wanted to call him but I knew as soon as he saw my cell phone number, he wouldn't answer. I wanted to wait longer but I was hungry. My butt hurt from sitting and I had to use the bathroom. So I decided to pick me up something quick. Maybe when I got back Derrick would be home.

Pulling in the parking lot of Wendy's, I practically jumped out of my moving vehicle and ran inside the establishment. My bladder was on the verge of making me look like a fool because I couldn't hold it anymore. On my way, I bumped into some buff dude coming out of the men's restroom.

"Excuse you," I said, still running to the women's door. Once inside I ran to the stall farthest away from the door. I kicked the stall door open, pulled my jeans and panties down, and relieved myself without bothering to shut the stall door. This felt so good. I was so glad I made it in time. A few more minutes and I would have been driving myself home for a shower and change of clothes. I heard the main bathroom door open and pushed my stall door closed, since I still had it wide open, while I wiped and flushed.

When I exited the stall, how shocked was I to see a man standing in the restroom with me.

"Excuse you. I think you got the wrong facilities. The men's restroom is out that door and to your right." I pointed.

"No. Excuse you. You bumped into me and didn't bother to say excuse me."

"Is that why you in here? You want an apology," I said, laughing. I walked over to the sink, squeezing the dispenser for soap. I turned on the warm water, which wasn't warm at all, to wash my hands. I didn't understand why most restaurants didn't have hot water. Who wants to wash their hands in ice cold water?

"So are you going to apologize?"

"Man, I had to pee. You were in my way," I said.

"But that didn't give you the right to be so damn rude."

"Okay," I said, pulling two paper towels and drying my hands off. "If it's going to make you feel better I'll say it. I'm sorry, sir, for bumping into you. Do you feel better now?" I asked, using the same paper towel to turn the water off. "Now can you please let me exit so I can get me something to eat?"

The man hesitated for a second. He stood there and stared at me and that's when it hit me: a flashback from the last bathroom incident. Was this brother about to do something crazy too? What was it with me and crazy damn people in bathrooms? The last girl I talked to in a restroom stabbed herself all because her man was cheating on her with me. She died before they could get her to the hospital. Now I had this thick dude blocking my way just like skinny girl did me months back. I'm not going to lie, I got scared. I almost felt like I needed to avoid bathrooms at all cost since it seemed like every crazy person who existed seemed to enter with me.

"This time I'm being polite. Can you please move out of my way?" I said sternly, hoping this man wouldn't pull out a gun and start blasting. The world was crazy and I didn't put anything past people. I was a little scared but not as much as I should have been being trapped in a women's restroom with a man I didn't even know. He could have been a rapist. But when the guy stepped to the side and allowed me to leave, I knew I was home free.

"Thank you," I said, using that same paper towel to open the door to leave. I didn't want to touch the handle after washing my hands since I knew so many nasty damn women left without washing theirs.

Once I was out I looked back to see the man exit with me. This didn't make me nervous. Hell I guess he figured he needed to leave before another woman caught him in there and screamed. He was a black man and a very nice-looking one at that. They might have thought he was some kind of pervert trying to get his voyeurism on.

I went to the register to be greeted by a tall, scrawny white boy with braces.

He said, "Hi. Can I take your order?"

"Yes, I would like a number six please."

"Would you like to make that a large?"

"No, thank you. I don't need any extra calories."

"Okay, ma'am. That will be $6.45."

I handed the young guy exact change and stepped to the side to wait for my food. The crazy guy from the restroom stepped up to place

his order. Staring at him more I noticed he was
fine as hell. Standing about six foot four at about
240 pounds, the guy had a very nice build. I
didn't notice before either, but he was dressed
very nice. He had dreads, which weren't my
thing but on him it was fitting enough to catch
my attention. By habit I checked out his ring
finger only to see it was empty. His teeth were
white and perfectly straight. His hygiene was on
point because he smelled real good. Must have
been some of that come-and-get-some-of-this
cologne.

For a minute I found myself attracted to him.
No man had had me like this since Derrick. I
mean I had slept around but nobody made my
heart go pitter-patter. Only Derrick had done
that. I didn't believe in love at first sight but, after looking at this guy, I was starting to wonder.
Then again, this could have been lust at first
sight.

The guy ended up ordering the same thing
I did, a spicy chicken combo, but he asked for
honey mustard sauce. When the guy told him his
total he looked over at me and asked, "Do you
got me?"

"Got you like how?" I asked, frowning.

"I need six dollars and forty-five cent to pay for
this. That's the least you can do for being rude
to me."

Was this man kidding me? Me, pay for his food. Hell he should have been paying for mine.

"Hell nawh, I'm not paying."

He giggled and reached in his pocket, pulling out a roll of money. He peeled a fifty dollar bill from the stack and handed it to the young boy.

The young boy noticed the money the man was holding too and looked at me as he stretched his eyes. I guessed maybe he was thinking the same thing I was. He could have paid for my meal, the girl next to me ordering, and probably everybody else waiting to order.

Me being me I said, "You asking me for money and you pulling out a stack like that."

"I wanted to see how generous you were," he said.

"Well I didn't see your generosity stepping forth either," I said, angrily wishing I could jack this punk for his money.

"You don't seem like the type of woman who needs help with anything," he said, grinning at me.

He had a point there. Talk about reading me right.

"Well still you could have been nice and paid for a sister's food."

The young guy set my bag in front of me along with a medium cup for me to get my drink. I grabbed my items and said, "It was not nice meeting you." I walked over to the beverage fountain only to have him follow right behind me. He didn't have his food but he had his cup in hand.

"My name is Fabian. Fabian Hill," he said, holding his hand out to shake mine.

"I didn't ask for your name, nor do I want to shake your hand. I don't know where your hand's been."

Fabian smiled, pulling back his hand. "Okay. Still rude."

"And I think you are stalking me. I mean for real this is getting old."

"A brother was trying to be nice and now I get accused of stalking. Just allow me to get my drink and I'll be out of your hair."

"Get your drink then," I said, putting the top on my Pepsi.

"Beautiful but still unladylike," he mumbled as he put his cup under the dispenser to get ice.

"Unladylike," I snapped.

"You heard me," he said, now getting some Sprite.

"First of all, you don't know me. Second, I ought to slap you for being so damn ill-mannered."

"Do you think I should have slapped you for being ill-mannered?"

My mouth fell open at his words.

"You started this entire thing. I was minding my own business when you practically bum-rushed me. The only thing I wanted was an apology."

"Which I gave you!"

"Which was also condescending. You act like one of them angry sisters. You know the ones who are uncouth for no damn reason and think their beauty is all they need to get away with such a stank attitude. I don't know who has hurt you in your past but you need to let all that resentment go so you can be nicer to people, and stop thinking the world revolves around you because it doesn't."

With that the man walked away, leaving me standing there with my mouth still open. He walked up to the young boy, who handed him his bag. Fabian took it, looked back at me, shook his head, and walked out of the restaurant.

I was fuming. *How dare he disrespect me like this? And, in front of people.* The young white boy was gawking at me. Once I made eye contact with him, he turned his head real quick.

I stormed out of the restaurant. Once outside I searched the parking lot for this asshole. I saw

Fabian getting into a black Charger with tinted windows. Before he could shut the door, I was there holding it. He turned to see what was hindering him from closing his door and saw me.

"You owe me an apology," I demanded.

"For what, telling you the truth?" he asked, snickering.

"You were being an asshole back there."

"And you were being a bitch. So I guess we are even."

"Bitch. I know you didn't just call me a bitch."

"Yeah, I did," he said calmly.

It made me snap. I peeled the top off my drink and tossed my beverage in his face. The drink was dead on, not only hitting him in the face but also hitting his ride.

"Now, that's a bitch," I said, slamming his door and walking away.

Chapter 8

Derrick

I found myself sitting at a table in the corner of this bar, holding my fourth drink. I gulped down my Hennessy and Coke, watching the basketball game that was playing on the TV mounted up on the wall. I was trying to drown my sorrow, hoping it would erase the image of my body touching Kea's. Every time I closed my eyes, images of her hands caressing me invaded me. I envisioned her lips placing soft kisses on me and then the act of me penetrating her.

I tossed back the rest of my drink, wishing to forget but, no matter how hard I tried, I couldn't get Kea out of my head. I wanted her so bad right now but knew I had to obliterate her from my mind. I wanted to expunge the feeling of loving the woman who I just found out was, indeed, my sister.

"Is this seat taken?" a woman asked me as she sat across from me in the booth, not giving me the opportunity to answer.

"It is now." I looked at her hesitantly. I didn't feel like this now. Company was the last thing I felt like entertaining but even in my state of mind I didn't want to be rude.

"Drowning your troubles I see?"

Isn't that obvious? I thought, looking up at her.

"It can't be that bad," the beautiful woman said.

"I promise you it is," I retorted.

She smiled and ordered a drink when the waitress came back to my table with my fifth drink. After ordering the woman started watching the game with me, but the only thing I was interested in viewing now was her.

Ms. Bohemian was what I wanted to call her. She was dressed in an earth-tone dress, with gold bangle bracelets jingling from her wrist and wooden hoops dangling from her ears. Her long, curly hair was pulled atop her head with some strands draping her face. She was striking. She smiled, pausing to pay me some attention before returning her eyes to the game. I took in her full lips and face without any shadow of makeup on it, just a hint of lip gloss and a scent that resonated with fruit. Leaning forward with both arms on the table crossed in front of her, I could see a tattoo decorating her right arm, her left wrist, and the nape of her neck. She was sexy.

And what really drew me in were her eyes. They were aqua blue and didn't quite match up with her golden, caramel features but in a weird sort of way they did. It was like looking into the clear waters on a tropical island. I had to wonder if they were hers, or if she was just like most women thinking it's sexy to wear fake contacts. Something told me that as real as she seemed, so were her eyes.

"Have you finished ogling me?" she asked flirtatiously.

I nodded.

"You don't talk much do you?"

I nodded, bringing the glass to my lips as I savored the burn of the liquor on my tongue as it slid down my throat.

Holding out her tiny, manicured hand, which was dainty yet strong like she appeared, she said, "My name is—"

I held my hand up, stopping her. "Please. No names," I said, shaking her outstretched fingers.

"Okay, I will respect that."

"Names make things official and I'm not ready for that right now."

"I understand," she said tranquilly.

I motioned for the waitress to bring me another while I sipped on the last of my drink. Ms. Bohemian looked at the several glasses that adorned the table but didn't say anything about them.

"You look like you could use some company tonight. Would you like to come to my place?" she asked boldly.

My glass paused in midair and I looked at the confidence in her face. "You don't look like a woman who picks up random men and invites them back to your place," I said.

"I'm not but it's something about you that I like."

"You don't know me. I could be a rapist or mass murderer."

"Well are you?" she asked.

"If I was, do you think I would tell you?"

Ms. Bohemian giggled, saying, "My gut tells me you are none of those things. I get a good vibe from you even though your spirit is in turmoil."

"And you can sense all of that?" I asked.

"Well it doesn't take a genius to figure out something is wrong, with the way you are throwing back those drinks."

Now there were six glasses in front of me and I didn't realize I was drinking them so fast. I turned to look at her.

Our eyes met and she said, "No names. Just some fun."

Needless to say I took her up on her offer and went to her place. I didn't feel like being on my own tonight anyway so the company would be good.

Her home was a replica of herself. Exquisite art, fresh, clean scents, and everything neat and in its place just like she was.

Her living room was a muted pea green with floating shelves with pictures of what I considered to be family on the walls. A caramel-colored sofa and two armchairs sat on top of a beige and wine-colored area rug. A mocha coffee and end tables completed the space. Golden full-length panels hung from the windows as dimmable wall sconces allowed for a romantic, mellow mood.

We basically said nothing as I admired her home. I was so caught up that I forgot she was in the room. I turned to her looking at me. With her finger she gestured for me to follow her. And I did.

We entered her love den. The huge dark bookcase was the first thing you saw as it played backdrop to her king-sized bed. The room was dark and I couldn't tell the color on the walls. It almost looked like chocolate with its pops of red from the bookshelves, which housed crimson vases and picture frames. Books and other knickknacks also filled the shelves.

Ms. Bohemian took my hand into hers and led me over to the velvet bench positioned in front of her bed. She turned me to face her. Placing her open hand in the middle of my chest, she pushed me to sit down. She then gripped my chin, pulling it upward for my eyes to meet her deep blues. She asked, "Are you ready?"

I wasn't sure if I nodded or said yes but the next thing I knew, Ms. Bohemian started taking off her clothes. I watched as she gave me a slow strip tease until she was standing in front of me naked. She fingered for me to come to her and I went to her. I kissed her deeply. She was definitely a great kisser. If this was any sign of what was to come, I knew I was in for a real treat.

Our lips disconnected. Ms Bohemian smirked and walked around me. I turned to see her sit down on the bench. Again she motioned with her finger for me to come to her. I obeyed her command. Standing before her, she looked up at me. She then looked forward to be greeted by my hard erection aching to be freed. She reached out and caressed it. Rubbing it gently, her strokes caused chills to surge within me. I kept looking down at what she was doing. I loved to watch. Evidently she did too because she stared at my reaction.

She began to unbuckle my belt. She then undid my pants, pulling them down slightly in the front. One layer kept her from being skin to skin with me. But as thin as the layer of my boxer briefs was, it looked as though my manhood was about to pierce through the lightweight material.

Pulling the front of my boxers down, she reached in and pulled out my johnson. She smirked again.

I smirked also and asked, "What are you going to do with that?"

Her answer was in her action. She inserted my rod into her mouth and began sucking it. Deep down her throat she went as her other hand fondled my ball region. Stroking and sucking, she made me feel good. I didn't know how much more I could take after about ten minutes. I stepped back from her, breathing deeply. She took the back of her hand and wiped the wetness from around her mouth.

"Why did you move? I wanted to you to cum," she said.

"Oh, I'm going to cum. But not like this."

"Why don't you let me taste you?" she asked.

She dropped to her knees and moved toward me. Moments later her mouth was back on my johnson. The slurping sounds she was making was like erotic music to my ears. The more she slurped, the closer I came to releasing.

"I'm cumming," I told her, expecting her to pull back, but she didn't. She kept stroking and sucking me. I tried to pull back but the grip she had on my johnson let me know she was not about to let me step back again.

"I'm cumming," I told her again as a warning. She deep-throated me. The tip of my manhood touched her tonsils and that was my cue to release. I burst my sweetness inside her mouth with her never stopping her stride.

Jerking and seizing, she finally let go of me. With the release of my manhood, I felt like I was going to collapse to the floor. She literally sucked all the life out of me. But I stood strong with my legs trembling from my explosion.

Ms. Bohemian got up and sat back down on the bench. She said, "You taste good."

I giggled, still trying to regain my composure. Pulling strength from my reserve I said, "Now it's my turn."

With my johnson still free, I fell to my knees. I gripped a handful of her thick mane, jerking her head back, exposing her neck. She moaned with pleasure. I kissed her down her neck, then to her breasts, squeezing one while my tongue teased the nipple of the other. Her head fell back, enjoying the pleasure. Slowly I kissed my way down her stomach, making the muscles jump with each peck. Her legs began to loosen as I snaked my way down her body. I stopped at her belly button. A silver ring looped its way through her skin. My tongue began to tangle with it. She giggled, caressing my head as I made my way farther down until I met her bliss. I looked up at her looking down at me near her territory of pleasure.

Once in the zone of indescribable gratification, I plunged my tongue into her nectar, enjoying the sweetness of her sap. Ms. Bohemian was laid all the way back now with both of her legs draped over my shoulders. She pushed her hips into me, twirling them with the rhythm of my tongue. The more my tongued dipped deeper into her kitty, the more she twirled. Wanting to take this pleasure to another level, I slid two fingers inside of her, causing her to sigh, "Oh, shit."

I knew from the jerking of her body she was cumming. The more her body jerked, the more I increased my sucking and fingering until she couldn't take it anymore and pushed herself away from me. I had indeed pleased her. I came up for air, standing to my feet and wiping her juices from my drenched face. I looked down at her seizing body as she breathed heavily. I hoped she didn't think this was over. My johnson was hard as a rock and I needed to get mine now. I was getting ready to give her the second half of this session. The first part was just the synopsis. Now it was time for the full-length story.

With one swift move my johnson was free to explore the depths of her abyss. She was a moaner. With each inward stroke I gave her, Ms. Bohemian let out a sexy moan, almost taking me to the place of releasing earlier than I wanted to. A couple of times I had to pause, kissing her neck, while I tried to calm myself from discharging too soon. She wrapped her long caramel legs around my waist and thrust her body upward to meet my manhood. She didn't like it when I paused. She yearned for my thrust and that excited me more.

"Please don't stop," she begged, trembling as she continued to thrust her body into mine. I happily obliged and I slowly ground my body into hers. The more I hammered her, the less her legs could hold on to me.

"I'm cumming," she squealed. "I'm cumming."

I pushed my way deeper into her punany as her body tightened.

"I'm cumming. I'm cumming. I'm cumming," she screamed as she released her warm sap all over my johnson.

Now it was my turn. I had made her cum yet again and now it was time for me to revel in my victory. I stroked her eagerly, waiting for the moment when the tingles surged into a climax for me. It didn't take too many strokes before I was also exploding. But instead of leaving it in, I pulled my way out of her and shot my semen onto her stomach.

I looked over at Ms. Bohemian lying next to me, who was sleeping peacefully. She was a beautiful woman and looking at her thick, busy mane and smooth body convinced me this was why I did this. Her loveliness was enough to mesmerize me for a night. Weeks with a dry spell and she came along to bring water to my desert. Just looking at the dip of her back leading to her ample behind was making my johnson hard all over again. I didn't know if I should wake her for another round or leave. Turning away from her I knew I had to get home. I couldn't stay here another minute.

In that short moment Kea's face crept into my mind and I felt guilty for what I had done. I felt like I was cheating, but how could I cheat on my sister? Getting up, I started to pick up my scattered clothing and began to get dressed.

Sliding on my shoes after getting dressed, I heard Ms. Bohemian's smooth voice say, "So you were going to leave without saying good-bye."

She never turned in my direction. If I didn't know any better I would have sworn she was talking in her sleep.

"You are not going to answer," she said, turning to look at me as she pulled the crumpled sheet around her naked body.

"I didn't want to disturb you," I said.

"You have been looking at my body for a few minutes now. I know you wanted to go again, so why were you too afraid to ask?"

How would this woman know my thoughts?

"You look puzzled."

"I am. I'm trying to figure out how you knew that," I said.

"Call it women's intuition."

"I had a great time with you."

"I'm glad you did. I had a good time too," she said, smiling.

Silence filled the space as each of us waited for the other to speak.

"Well I think I'll be going now," I said, turning toward to the door.

"Who is she?" she asked, causing me to pause.

"Excuse me?" I said, turning to her in confusion.

"Who were you thinking about when you were having sex with me?"

I couldn't answer. I didn't want to answer. Ms. Bohemian stared into my frozen eyes.

"You didn't think I would be able to tell that I took the place of a woman you loved. I wondered who she was and why you were here with me instead of being with her."

"Things happen."

"But love is eternal."

"So is drama and heartache," I said irritably.

"Life is what you make it," she countered, propping herself on her elbow as she pulled the sheet around her breasts.

"And sometimes the actions of others interfere in the life you are trying to make."

"True, but if you love this woman, you should go after her."

"It's more complicated than that. We can never be together again. Case closed, and I would appreciate if you left the subject of her alone," I said, getting ready to walk out of her room again.

"I'm sorry. I was trying to help."

"Please don't. People have helped me enough and they helped me into this misery."

"Well I can be of help in your pretending if you like. Come back to bed and let's get to know each other one more time before you go," she said, smiling and patting the space next to her. "I don't mind."

I wanted to leave but the offer was topped with her crawling to her knees. She let the sheet fall from around her body, revealing her magnificent physique. The offer was opened to me again and I was ready to close it. So I went to her, pretending that she was the woman I loved.

Chapter 9

Derrick

I kissed Ms. Bohemian on the cheek as I attempted to sneak out of her bedroom for the second time. This time, she was knocked out unconscious as I made my way out. As good as our time together was I really wasn't in the mood to wake up to any conversation that could lead back to my reason for being with her in the first place. The time with her did help take my mind off what was going on in my life, but I wasn't comfortable talking to her about it.

When I attempted to pull into my driveway, I was surprised to see a car already sitting there. I pulled beside it, looking into the vehicle to see a sleeping Zacariah. Lines appeared in my forehead as irritation filled me. I hit the garage door button and maneuvered my car into my space. I guessed the noise from the garage door woke her up because the next thing I saw as I got out of my ride was Zacariah getting out of hers. I acted like she wasn't there as I made my way to the entrance of my home. Before I could put the key in the lock Zacariah started questioning me.

"Where the hell have you been, Derrick? I have been sitting outside your house all night long waiting for you," she asked fretfully.

The audacity, I thought. I giggled for a second before allowing my irritation to return. "Who in the hell told you to come over here anyway?"

"I was trying to surprise you."

"Surprise me with what, another sister? Or this time would it be another dick up your behind? Which is it, Zacariah? None of your surprises have been good ones. Did you not understand me when I told you I didn't want to have anything to do with you ever again?"

"But—"

"And do you not remember I also told you that you were the worst thing that has ever happened to me?" I said, raising my voice.

"You didn't mean that."

"Yes, I did."

"Please tell me you weren't with her."

I snickered at her boldness. Was she for real?

"Which 'her' were you referring to?" I said, crossing my arms across my chest.

"What do you mean which? I'm talking about Kea," she said, looking perplexed.

"No, I wasn't with Kea," I said in a tone that hopefully clued her in on me being with someone else.

"So you were at your mother's, right? She needed you to do something for her and you decided to stay the night, right?"

I could see the hope on her face but Zacariah was not a stupid woman. She got the hint and I was about to burst her bubble.

"Wrong."

"What do you mean wrong?"

"You heard me."

"Then where were you?" she asked, raising her voice this time.

"Not that I have to explain anything to you but just so you are clear we are over, I was with another woman," I said coldly.

"What woman? Kea was the other woman," Zacariah said.

"No. I have another beautiful female in my life," I taunted her. I was enjoying inflicting this pain on Zacariah. Seeing her trying to register that another woman was in the picture made this day turn out to be even better than Ms. Bohemian made it.

"Who is this woman?" she asked angrily.

"Some female I met at the bar," I said nonchalantly.

"So you picking up random chickenheads now?"

"If that's what you want to call it."

"Did you sleep with her?" Zacariah questioned.

"Yes, and it was damn good, too. I ate her pussy and everything," I divulged, hoping my words ripped through her heart like her revelation of my relationship with Kea did me. I could see the hurt in Zacariah's face immediately and I smiled. "She tasted like sweet candy."

"How could you do this to me? Why, Derrick? I'm here for you," she said, with tears starting to form. "You could have come to me."

"I don't want you," I said uncaringly.

"Yes, you do," she snapped.

"Why would I want to touch you? Who knows how many other men's fingers been touching you?"

"Like you knew how many men touched this female you were willing to sleep and eat the first time you met her. How is she any different than me?"

"The fact she's not you made everything perfect from the beginning. Zacariah, I used to love you. Make sure you catch that. I said 'used to.' We were in a relationship that required the both of us being faithful to one another. Not one, but both, but you reneged."

"Why can't you forgive me already? I've apologized numerous times and you keep pushing me away. Why can't we go back to the way things used to be?"

"Because I'm not that man anymore. The Derrick you knew is long gone."

"Come on, Derrick. What we had was good. Don't you remember?" she said, coming toward me.

"It was good until I found out it was built on untruths."

"Besides all that, Derrick. I know you are grieving. I know you needed someone to be there for you and I was here."

"You have to be a damn fool if you thought I was going to fall into your arms in my time of grief, asking you to come back into my life."

I could tell by her expression that's exactly what she thought would happen.

"After what you did to me, that will never happen," I said, walking closer to Zacariah. "Your love is like acid to my skin. It eats away at me until there is nothing left. I have nothing else left for you, Zacariah."

"Please don't say that to me, Derrick," she said, softly whimpering. "We are meant to be together. Look how fate has worked. Kea is your sister for goodness' sake."

"You made all this drama happen, Zacariah."

"I had nothing to do with you being blood related to Kea. That was your mother and father's doing," she said in frustration.

At that point I wanted to wrap my hand around her throat.

"Don't you ever talk about my mother or my father, or my family for that matter. Do you understand me?" I screamed, getting in her face, trying to control the rage aching to be released. I felt like I could become a woman beater as bad as I wanted to beat Zacariah down. I found myself balling my fist like I was going to hit her but the gentleman in me refrained from assaulting her. A car riding by brought me back to sanity and I backed away from her. It was my neighbors from across the street pulling into their driveway. As they got out, they waved and I waved back, watching them go into their home.

As soon as they were out of sight I said, "Get the hell off my property, Zacariah," dismissing her.

"I understand your hostile behavior, but come on, Derrick. I sat outside all night."

"I didn't ask you to sit out here. That was your choice."

"Can't I come in so we can talk?" she pleaded.

"We're done here," I said.

"We are not done damn it. You need me. Especially after the results."

I paused. I didn't know if my motionless state lasted for seconds or minutes as I deliberated her words. "Results? How did you know about the results, Zacariah?"

She nervously went from one foot to the other. I could tell she knew she had said something she shouldn't have, but why? Her eyes were moving from the ground, to the house, to the window, to the neighbors' home next door.

I asked again, "How did you know about the results?" I moved closer to see what she was going to say. This caused her to back up. The more I approached her the more she backed away from me until we were standing outside of my garage and near her car.

"I don't know. I heard it from somewhere I guess."

"That's confidential information."

"I don't know," she said uneasily.

"Those results were only told to three other individuals besides myself and I know they wouldn't mention it to a soul," I said, visualizing me, Kea, my mom, and her dad. The only ones present besides us were the doctor and the nurse.

"I heard it from Kea's mother."

"How did she—"

Zacariah cut me off, saying, "Kea's father must have told her."

"And what reason would you have to keep in contact with Kea's mother?"

Still nervous she said, "I guess we connected somehow."

"I don't believe you," I said.

"It's the truth."

"You know nothing about truth, loyalty, love, or respect. You are a sorry excuse for a woman and I regret the day I ever let myself fall for you."

"Derrick—"

"Hear me and hear me good," I said, pointing at her. "I hate you with every morsel of my being. Stay the hell away from me before I have a restraining order issued against you. Now get off of my property before I call the police."

Her tears fell as I stepped back into the garage. I turned and said, "I know you are lying about something, Zacariah. And if I find out you have been messing with my life more than what I know about, you will regret it," I said, hitting the button for the garage door, closing it with her on the other side of it.

Chapter 10

Kea

I looked at the roses on my desk as my best friend, Terry, put on her best rendition of the R&B greats singing "Happy Birthday." I laughed at her weak attempt to put on the performance of her life as she squealed into the phone line.

"Girl, you need to stop," I said, laughing hysterically.

"Girl, I can sang. You did notice I said 'sang' and not 'sing.' That means I gave it my all."

"I caught that," I said, wiping tears from my eyes.

"Didn't I sound like Patti LaBelle?"

"More like being in the bottom of a barrel. You know you and nobody else on this earth walking sounds like Ms. Patti. She is the queen of her craft."

"So I didn't sound good?" she asked.

I laughed, which felt good since I hadn't laughed much lately. It had to be Terry to take me to the point of tear-jerking laughter.

"Terry, you sounded okay but don't quit your day job. I appreciate you trying. It's the thought that counts."

"And here I was thinking I could get a second job being a singer."

"No way. You better stay where you at," I said, and we both chuckled.

"Let me get back to work. I just wanted to wish you a happy birthday, Kea. I'm coming back home tomorrow and I can't wait to see you. I'll take you out, that's if you can find a moment to pry yourself from up under your punk of a boyfriend," she said in disgust.

So much had been going on that I forgot I hadn't let Terry know about me and Jaquon. She didn't know about me and Derrick, about Mr. Hanks, and she didn't know about my issues with my mother. Hell, she didn't know anything that had happened within these past couple of months since she had been working in Los Angeles. She had business to attend to on some high-powered case defending some celebrity she wasn't at liberty to disclose due to confidentiality. I respected that. She could say it paid her big money. I was proud that she had made it. Even though it was work for her, it was like a vacation with all expenses paid. I was jealous a bit. While she was living it up, my world came crashing down. I knew I couldn't tell her everything now but I could tell her about me and Jaquon. This news would make her day.

"Terry, I kicked Jaquon to the curb."

"Since when?" she questioned.

"It's been over two weeks."

"Why am I just finding out this wonderful information and what made you finally come to your senses?"

"It's a long story," I said.

"Talk. I got time."

"But I don't. I'm at work. Plus I don't want to get upset here. I've cried enough rivers. I'm not trying to flood this place."

"Damn. What happened? I knew I shouldn't have gone out of town."

"Well you had money to make and defenders to support."

"You still could have called me," Terry said.

"I didn't want to bother you with my problems. Besides, it was nothing you could do about it anyway."

"Okay, but you know we got to get together so you can catch me up," Terry said.

"We will."

"Now we got two things to celebrate, your birthday and now you leaving that bastard Jaquon. Girl, you have made my day. I'm ready for us to get our drink on. And don't tell me you don't want to drink because we both are going to get hammered," Terry said with glee.

"I'm not trying to get drunk."

"Maybe you should. Alcohol can make any situation look great. Ask the last guy I slept with. When I turned over and saw his face that next morning, girl, I almost jumped up and ran for my life."

I burst into laughter again.

"Those drinks made dude look like Denzel but the next morning he looked like a gazelle."

"Shut up," I said, leaning back in my seat, laughing uncontrollably.

"I'm serious. My drunk self remembered him having a close cut but the next morning, Kea, he had predator hair. Alcohol can make anybody and any situations seem majestic."

"What happened to the guy?"

"I kicked him out. I told him he had to go."

"And he just left like that?" I asked.

"He didn't have a choice when I pointed my pistol at him."

"Stop, Terry. No, you didn't pull a gun on dude."

"Hell yeah, I did. Homeboy tried to insist he needed some more of my sweet stuff. He was lucky I was drunk enough for him to get it the first time. Sober sex was out of the question, especially when I had to look into his unattractive face."

"But a gun, Terry."

"You damn right. I tried to get out of bed and he called himself playing by pulling me back in the bed after I said no. Girl, I thought he might try to rape me. I managed to get loose. Then I reached in the drawer in my nightstand and pulled out Mr. Pistol. He almost pissed himself when he saw me point my gun at him."

"Terry, you wrong. You rocked that man's world. He just wanted some more of your stuff, girl," I said, laughing.

"More hell. I wanted to rewind that mistake and get my dignity back. Dude was ugly as hell."

"Girl, I'm getting off this phone with you. Call me later," I said, still laughing at my crazy friend.

"Okay, girl, but remember we got to get our drink on when I get back. I'm trying to forget about my indiscretion."

"Sounds like you had enough alcohol already," I said, giggling.

"Which is why, again, I need to get drunk to forget."

"Love you, Terry. Bye," I said, cutting her off because I knew we could have gone on for an hour if I allowed it. It was so good talking to my friend. Terry always seemed to cheer me up.

I hung up the phone and stared at the gorgeous arrangement that was sent to me for my birthday. I thought about the sweet message in the card:

> To the woman I love and will always love for the rest of my life. I promise to always be here for you.

The card had no name on it. I had to wonder if Derrick sent it to me. I did tell him I was getting ready to turn the big 3–0. *Maybe he remembered.* Thinking of him made me smile.

Moving the arrangement to the side, I giggled, thinking about how its vastness was blocking my view of people. But I didn't mind. It was too beautiful. Everybody couldn't help but notice the extravagant piece, whose luminescent color lit up the office.

Many of them came by saying, "Somebody must really love you," and "Girl, what are you doing to get flowers like that?"

I smiled, wondering the same thing. Whoever it was had indeed gone overboard sending me three dozen long-stemmed peach roses mixed with baby's breath. The wide-mouthed clear vase held them as each petal reached toward the light. I pulled one out of the vase, bringing it to my nose to sniff. The scent was heavenly as I closed my eyes and thought of Derrick.

My phone rang.

"Kea Fields speaking. How may I help you?" I asked, still trying to sound professional.

"Hey, baby girl. Happy birthday."

"Thank you, Daddy."

"How's my girl's day going so far?"

"It's been a good one thanks to Terry. You know I haven't had too many of them in recent days so I'm going to take this day for what it's worth."

"I hear that. I sent you a little something in the mail. You should get it today hopefully."

"Daddy! You didn't have to do that."

"I know but I wanted to."

There was a slight pause and I knew Daddy had something else on his mind but he wasn't saying it.

"Daddy?"

"Yes, baby girl."

"What's wrong? I can tell by the tone of your voice it's something."

"I don't want to ruin your day," he said.

"Spit it out, Daddy. I'm a big girl. I can handle it," I said, hoping I could. I felt like I couldn't take any more bad news but I couldn't let Daddy know this.

"I'll tell you some other time. It's your birthday—"

"Daddy."

"Okay," he said, sounding defeated. "Has your mother called?"

As soon as he asked me that question my stomach churned. I did wonder if she would call to wish me a happy birthday, because I was still her daughter. But I knew she wouldn't. Why would she? She hated me, and all because I was the child she birthed from rape. I wished she would see it wasn't my fault. I guessed looking like the man who took her innocence overpowered the love she had for me.

"No, she hasn't called me," I answered.

"I'm going to call that woman and cuss her out. She can't keep treating you like this."

"Let it be, Daddy. She's living her life and she chooses to do it without me in it."

"But she acts like Emory is her only daughter. That ain't right and I know it has to bother you."

It did bother me. As much as Emory and I were trying to become closer, I still couldn't help but wish Mother loved me as much as she loved my sister. Even though Emory moved away, we talked at least once a week. It used to be three times but now that she'd had the baby, her life was full of her husband and my little nephew, Jacob. I only fit into that picture through words spoken via telephone. I guessed I could make an effort to go see her but I was afraid to. Yes, she was my sister, but she was also the favored daughter. I envied that about her. I wanted a mother too, but our mother chose her and not me, so resentment still lay within me.

"Kea, remember that I love you and I'm always going to be here for you no matter what, okay?"

"I know, and I love you too, Daddy."

"You enjoy your birthday and maybe we can get together this Sunday and go out for lunch or something. Or maybe I'll come by and make you that jambalaya."

"You know I'm going to have to invite Terry, because if she finds out you made jambalaya without inviting her, she's going to flip her wig."

Daddy laughed. "Well, baby girl, I'm going to let you get back to work. Happy birthday again."

"Thank you, Daddy, and I love you."

"I love you too," he said before we both hung up without saying good-bye.

***

I wondered if I should take the bouquet of roses home, but as big as it was, I didn't think I wanted to try. Plus, leaving them at work would give me something beautiful to look at each day for a little while.

When the sun hit my face I was happy I was free for another weekend. It was Friday, payday, and my birthday. *Can this day get any better?* I thought as I made my way home.

Walking into my apartment my feet were met with a wide assortment of what looked like rose petals. When I looked up, I found that more roses filled the room. Pink, white, red, yellow, and more peach took over the space. My living room looked like a flower shop. Smooth jazz played in the background and I wondered who was in my place. The aroma of food tickled my nostrils as my stomach began to growl at the scrumptious scent.

Shutting the door quietly, I gripped my keys and dropped them into my purse. With each step taken, my steps were hushed by the carpet and rose petals beneath my feet as I made my way to my kitchen. Getting closer, the aroma of succulent food led me. When I turned the corner, there was no mistaking who was in my kitchen, since I had been with him for years. I saw Jaquon standing at the stove, stirring something in a pot.

"What are you doing here?" I bellowed.

He turned, startled by my voice. "Happy birthday, baby. I'm cooking you dinner. I hope you are not tired of seeing flowers," he said, smiling that devilish grin of his. An even bigger surprise was the fact that Jaquon had cut his hair. The cornrows were gone and now he had a close cut edged up to perfection. As long as I had been with Jaquon I had never seen him without his hair braided up or pulled back when no one could do his hair for him. He actually looked like a grown man now. I didn't think he could look more handsome but Jaquon was sexier than ever. For a split second I felt a heat rise up within me that made me want to have sex with him right then. Damn he was still fine. Dark skin and all. And the wife beater didn't help as his muscles bulged from beneath the thin material. I almost ran over to Jaquon and planted my lips against his but I didn't. The fact he was a low-down, dirty cheater stopped me.

"Kea, are you okay?"

"I'm just noticing you cut your hair."

He rubbed his head, asking, "Do you like it? You know I've had my hair for several years now. It feels kinda weird."

"It looks good on you," I said, thinking it looked more than good. "So it was you who sent me those flowers today?" I questioned.

"Yes. Who else could it have been?"

My look gave him the answer and he turned his attention back to the stove with a hint of jealousy, which crept up in him. I looked around to see that the table was nicely decorated with a golden cloth draping it. Cream-colored candles were lit and white square-shaped plates adorned it, with silverware and napkins surrounded by a gold holder. Champagne and flutes sat among the grandness as more roses played center.

"I didn't ask you to come, nor did I ask you to cook for me, Jaquon. I didn't ask for the flowers, either."

"I know you didn't but I wanted to do this for you."

"You didn't do this when we were together but now you decide to do this once I've kicked you out and our relationship is over. Don't you think you have this thing ass backward?"

"You are right, Kea, but it's never too late," he said, placing some Spanish-style rice into a casserole dish I purchased two years ago.

"It's too late for us. I dumped you, Jaquon."

"I know this. And I'm doing this as your friend."

"Exes can't be friends. Too much hurt and pain resides here."

"But maybe we can set a new standard."

"I don't want your friendship. Honestly I don't want anything from you. Well wait a minute. I do want one thing. I want you to leave the keys to this place and never come back."

"That's two things," he said, grinning.

"I don't care," I said angrily.

"Are you getting this angry because I'm here or because a part of you is loving what I did for you? No matter how much you try to tell yourself, Kea, a part of you still has to love me just like I love you."

His words caught me off-guard. I hadn't examined my own emotions but I didn't think I had to. I hated when he twisted my mind up like this. My heart did flutter at the sight of him and he did look so good. And I knew he was right because no one can just turn love off, no matter how bad their mates treat them.

I wished I would have been smart enough to change my locks. Then I wouldn't be dealing with this right now. I had to wonder, did a part of me want him to return? He probably thought that when his key worked, I hoped he would come back to me and give him confirmation I still wanted him.

"At a loss for words, I see. I gave you something to think about, huh," he said, opening the oven.

"Jaquon," I called, admiring his biceps as he lifted the fish from the oven and put it on the stove.

"Kea, I'm not trying to ruin your birthday. I'm here because I think you deserve this. Does it matter if all of this came from me?"

"Yes, because I think you are using this as a way to get back with me and I don't want you."

"Baby, if you want me to leave, I will. I will place all the food I prepared on the table and let you enjoy it without my company. I don't mind. As long as you are happy, that's what matters to me."

He gazed at me with sincerity and I wished he didn't. I wished the smug, cocky Jaquon would emerge and make this easier for me, but the man standing before me was someone I wasn't familiar with. Yet it was the man I fell in love with. His face was the same and he definitely had the same body, but not the same attitude. It wasn't even the same attention because this Jaquon was interested in being with me.

I watched him place the completed food on the table and place the reminder of dirty dishes in the dishwasher. After wiping down everything, he wiped his hands on my apron he wore and placed it on the counter.

"Everything is done. In case you don't want to drink champagne, I picked you up a two-liter orange soda. I know it's your favorite."

Damn it! Why was he doing this to me? He was really making this hard. He slid on this crisp white collar shirt that looked good with his dark denim jeans and white sneakers. I caught a whiff of his cologne and he even smelled good. That was Jaquon: always dressed to impress and smelling good enough to eat.

He continued to say, "It's an ice cream cake in the freezer, too."

Once he buttoned his shirt, Jaquon stared into my face.

I stood defensively with my arms crossed, not being able to say anything.

"I'm sorry I intruded. Happy birthday and I hope you enjoy the food," he said, brushing past me to leave.

"Jaquon," I called out in reluctance. He came back into my view. "You . . . don't . . . have . . . to leave," I said hesitantly.

He smiled, asking, "Are you sure?"

"This doesn't mean anything. I just can't eat all of this food by myself. You did go out of your way to prepare it," I said like I had a mouthful of taffy with my words wanting to stick and stay within my mouth.

"Thank you, Kea," he said, walking over to my chair and pulling it out for me to sit.

"And I want the key to this place when you leave," I said.

He nodded, giving me that smile that made me want to forget about eating and drag him straight to the bedroom for some birthday sex.

Chapter 11

Jaquon

"What the hell are you doing here?" was the first thing out of Terry's mouth when she pushed her way into the apartment.

"Kea! Kea, girl, where are you! Where's Kea?" She scowled. "And where did all these damn roses come from?" she asked loudly, looking around at the assortment. "This ain't no damn flower shop."

"Will you keep it down? Kea is sleeping," I said as she looked me up and down, with attitude of course. Terry and I didn't get along at all. And it wasn't because we slept together either. It's because we didn't mesh well together. Upon first meeting me years ago she had no qualms about not liking me, which made me not like her. She'd never had anything nice to say to me. And now her big mouth woke me up from a sound sleep. It was like awaking abruptly out of a scary dream only to find the monster standing over you. I was barely dressed, with only my boxer briefs on, showing my morning hardness. I had my hand over it but it wasn't like I was doing a good job hiding it. The last thing I wanted was for Kea to think I was trying to get with her best friend.

Terry glanced at my stiffness and then focused her attention on the living room to see covers on the couch and my clothing on the chair.

"Kea!" she called out, screaming. "Kea, where in the hell are you!"

"I told you she was sleeping."

She threw me a wicked glance, which meant "shut the hell up," and I shook my head at her outrageousness.

"Kea," she continued to call, now moving to the bedroom, knocking at the door. "Are you okay?"

I went over to the chair and grabbed my jeans, sliding them on. I sat down on the couch and watched crazy Terry go into her screaming fit. The door to the bedroom finally opened.

"What? Why are you yelling?" Kea asked sleepily.

"I've been calling you forever. You didn't hear me?"

"I hear you loud and clear now. What is it? Is everything okay?"

"Hell no," Terry said, looking at me. "I should be asking you are you okay. Why the hell is Jaquon here?" Terry asked, pointing at me. "I thought you told me you kicked his trifling behind to the curb."

Kea looked at me. She rubbed her eyes and yawned as she clenched her pink robe closed. I was able to get a glimpse at her breast before she pulled it closed, which instantly turned me on.

"Are you going to answer me?" Terry asked impatiently.

"Are you going to answer me first? Why are you here so early? It's 8:11. You know I like to sleep in on Saturdays, Terry. I don't like waking up until noon."

"I came back early so I could take you to breakfast since I couldn't get with you yesterday on your birthday. I tried calling you several times last night but you never answered your cell," she said, giving me another evil glimpse. "Now I see why."

"Couldn't this wait until later?" Kea questioned, walking into the living room, sitting in the chair where my clothes were draped. Terry followed her, still giving me the stank face.

"Breakfast is usually consumed in the morning, which explains my presence now."

"Brunch could have worked too," Kea said.

"So you are not happy to see me."

"Yes, Terry, I'm happy to see you. I'm always happy to see you. You just caught me off-guard. I was sleeping good," Kea said.

"Please tell me you didn't sleep with this fool because I—"

"No," Kea stressed.

"That Negro done burned you way too many times for you to give him any more of your pum pum."

Kea laughed, saying, "Nothing happened, Terry."

"Good. I'm glad I showed up when I did. Ain't no telling what would have happened this morning. The punk greeted me at the door with a salute I didn't want to see. I probably interrupted him stroking himself so he could sneak in your room and get you to help it go down."

"Terry," Kea said.

"Is she for real?" I finally said.

"You damn right I'm for real. Now I got to go home and drop alcohol in my eyes from seeing his damn-near-naked ass. I thought a third arm was pointing at me. Now I know why he has your nose so wide the hell open. He's laying more pipe than an average plumber."

Both Kea and I burst into laughter. I couldn't believe she was talking about my johnson like this. I didn't know whether to feel flattered or violated since it was coming from Terry. And I hoped Kea wouldn't think something was going on between us. By her reaction, she didn't.

"Why are y'all laughing? Ain't a damn thing funny. The man was pointing at me like an arrow on a sign saying 'go this way.'"

"First of all, I wasn't naked," I said, explaining to Kea. "I had on my boxer briefs. It's early in the morning, Kea. You know how I am," I said, trying to look like I wasn't trying to get with her friend. Terry was one female Kea never had to worry about me getting with.

Kea looked down at my area and then back at my face. I couldn't tell if it was a look of disgruntlement or contentment.

I went on to say in my defense, "I opened the door because she was pounding on it like she was the police."

"I am the police," she belted.

"You may work with them but you are not the police," I disputed.

"Don't make me call them on your trifling behind now for trespassing," Terry bellowed.

"How am I trespassing?" I asked.

"Okay. Okay. Y'all two, stop it," Kea said, waving her hands in the air.

"Tell him to leave," Terry demanded.

I sighed, wishing she would. Everything was fine before Big Mouth arrived.

"Look. Jaquon, I know how you be in the mornings."

"Thank you," I said, looking at Terry.

"Which was why I had an issue with you staying out all night," Kea continued.

Terry looked at me like, "Now what, punk?"

"I always wanted you to come home to bring that to me but you had that elsewhere," she said, pointing at my johnson.

That comment caused me to slow my roll. Kea knew I was always ready. I woke up ready. So if she wasn't around, there had to be someone around to help ease that aching hardness. I kept quiet and let this rest before it developed into another argument. This conversation about my private area was a bit uncomfortable anyway. Who knew the day would come when I would be uneasy about women talking about my package? Hell, throw Terry in the mix and I might not ever get hard again. That's how much I despised her. She was nothing but a cock blocker and a hater.

"I still don't understand why he's here," Terry yelled.

"Terry, please calm down. Your loud mouth is starting to make my temples throb," Kea said.

Terry never stopped her bellowing as she said, "I can't believe he has wiggled his way back up in here. You haven't even had an opportunity to tell me why you kicked him out in the first place."

Kea looked at me and some anger began to resonate within her. Terry was too busy talking to notice but I did.

Kea said, "You will get the full story on what happened."

"That still don't explain why he's here now."

"If you must know, Terry, even though I'm a grown woman who does not have to report to you, Jaquon cooked me a birthday dinner last night."

"And the food was so damn good that he had to stay here last night. You know this was just a ploy to get you back and get in them panties again," Terry said, frowning like bile was rising up in her mouth.

"Terry, nothing happened. We were both drinking and it was late—"

"You sure he didn't take your pum pum while you were sleeping? You know you can't handle your liquor, Kea. If you are like me, liquor makes you horny."

Kea laughed, saying, "That's enough, Terry. Haven't we heard enough of your ranting for one day?"

"Kea's right. You haven't been here twenty minutes and you got everybody's blood pressure up," I said irritably.

Terry turned her rage to me. She walked closer, pointing her finger in my face, saying, "Don't you ever talk to me like that. You came here with a motive and I know it. You want Kea back."

"And I'm not going to deny that. I do want her back," I said, looking at Kea trying to see what her reaction was to my statement.

"I was right about your trifling behind when you cheated on her the first time, too. But you kept cheating again and again and again," she said, counting with her fingers until she was holding up at least seven.

"We get your point," I said.

"Now you realize how much of a good thing you lost. Now you want to try to make it work," she said, stressing the "work" part.

I stared at Kea's eyes, loving the way she was cuddled in the seat with her feet beneath her. She looked gorgeous, but the weight of Terry's words was affecting her.

"Would you be satisfied if I said you were right again? Will you shut up if I admit that?" I asked.

Kea chuckled and Terry whipped her head around to her.

"You are going to take him back, aren't you?" Terry asked Kea and I couldn't help but want to hear the answer to the question.

"We haven't talked about us, Terry."

"The only person who has brought up us is you," I said.

"Did you let him get some of your birthday goodies?"

"No," Kea said, laughing. "You just asked me that."

"To me, it sounds like you might be a little jealous," I said, sitting back on the sofa.

"Jealous of who, Kea? Please. She's my best friend. What you are witnessing is my concern for her wellbeing."

"But if you had your own man, I guarantee you wouldn't be over here waking us up all early."

Again Kea giggled.

"Don't be laughing at him, Kea. I'm trying to take up for you."

"Well he's right. I know you don't like to hear it but you know what Jaquon is saying is the truth, about the man part I mean. I didn't mean about you being jealous of me because I don't believe that."

"I got a man, for both of y'all's information."

"Does he buzz or did you have to blow him up?" I asked jokingly.

Terry's forehead knitted even harder. Kea tried her best to hold back her laughter.

Ms. Attitude crossed her arms and asked Kea, "Are you coming to breakfast or not?" changing the subject.

"Where are we going?"

"It's your choice."

"You are going to wait for me to shower and get dressed?" Kea asked.

"Damn right," she said, looking at me. "I don't want you to make another mistake getting with this bastard."

Kea stood, stretching as her mouth opened with a yawn. "I can't believe you woke me up this early. I was sleeping so good."

"I wonder why."

"Not for what you think. But let me get dressed so we can get out of here before things get even uglier. It shouldn't take me long. I got somewhere else to be anyway today," Kea said, leaving the room.

"Can I join you?" I asked teasingly, knowing it would make Terry angrier. "I can scrub your back."

"I got this, Jaquon. Thank you anyway," Kea said from the back.

"What you need to do is put your clothes on and leave," Terry said, looking at my exposed chest. I could have sworn she glanced at my manhood again. Even the thought she did made my skin crawl. Yes, I was a ladies' man, but this was one lady I loathed with a passion.

"Do you mind if I finish getting dressed?" I asked, standing. She sauntered to Kea's room, closing the door. I heard it open again and Terry yelled, "Lock the door on your way out," and slammed the door back shut.

I picked up the cover and folded it, placing it on the arm of the sofa. Shaking my head, my other plan had been ruined. I was planning on cooking Kea breakfast this morning. The dinner went so well that I wanted to serve her in bed but Terry the Terror had immobilized the situation. She always got under my skin but this time I found her erratic behavior funny. I saw it as her being envious. I didn't think she wanted me, but you never knew. I was a good-looking guy. I also knew the only woman I wanted in my life was Kea. Maybe Terry liked the fact that Kea was single now and they could start hanging out more often. I didn't know. All I knew was I had to get her back.

At least Derrick was out of the picture and Kea was open for me to reclaim as mine again. I loved her and last night was enjoyable, despite us not becoming intimate, but that made our time more special. I hadn't done that in a long time with her and forgot how good it felt to just chill by her side. I hoped this was the start of us reconnecting our relationship. But if it was up to Terry, Kea and I getting back together would never happen.

Chapter 12

Kea

Terry's mouth never stops, I thought as we cruised down the boulevard to go get some breakfast. It didn't take me long to get ready, especially since a very hungry Terry was rushing me. She probably spent a lot of energy telling off Jaquon when she caught him in my place. I don't know why I'm saying "caught" because it wasn't like I was hiding the fact Jaquon stayed over. Just like I told Terry, one drink led to another, which led to a very sensual kiss, and I knew then it was time for me to go to bed. As bad as Jaquon had treated me I wasn't going to let him leave after drinking, which was why I let him stay on the couch. I considered letting him in my bed and he even joked about it but I knew I couldn't do that. Not now. Don't get me wrong, I wanted that man bad. My body needed him but I couldn't. I felt like I was slipping back into the old Kea and it was time to let the new me emerge.

"Do you hear me talking to you?" Terry asked, jarring me out of my thoughts.

"I'm listening, Terry. Your mouth hasn't stopped running yet."

"I still can't believe you let that bastard stay with you last night. I mean really, Kea, what were you thinking?"

"Oh my goodness, will you leave this alone already?" I said, putting my elbow on the door and hand on my head because it felt like any moment a migraine was going to start. And I had never had one.

"You know he was there to get some pum pum."

"Hell, I wished he would have," I said.

"What?" Terry asked, stopping at the red light.

"Girl, I know we are not together but once that wine got to flowing through my system—"

"See. I told you. You know what alcohol does to you, and me for that matter. That's why I figured you slept with him."

Terry didn't know how much I wanted to. A woman's got needs and Jaquon being there could have filled it for at least one night. I knew I would have been taking a chance because of my feelings being involved but I wanted some good dick and I knew Jaquon could deliver. He couldn't deliver like Derrick but he could hold his own.

I wanted him so bad that I dreamed about him. I dreamed he snuck in my room while I was sleeping and crawled in the bed behind me. *I was buck-naked, making it easier for him to take me. His warm breath tickled the nape of my neck as his hardness rested against my cheeks. The thin cotton material kept him re-strained until he reached down and pulled his johnson through the hole of his boxers. A warm rod probed me as I faked like I was still asleep.*

I could hear Jaquon lick his fingers. He moved them between my thighs from the back and started to push his fingers through to help wet his way for his johnson to enter me. When his fingers penetrated me, I would wake up, asking him what he was doing, knowing good and damn well what the hell was going on.

Jaquon shushed me as he stroked my inner nectar until it became soaked with pleasure. I turned on to my back and opened my legs wide to welcome his fingers deeper inside me, bring-ing my body to the brink of climaxing. Just when I got close, Jaquon removed his fingers. My body trembled I was so close. He gripped my left breast and began to suck on my nipple as my inner thighs ached for him to pierce me. He knew this turned me on. He was teasing me and I couldn't take it anymore. I begged for him to put his johnson inside me. He smiled as he climbed on top of me to give me what I was asking for. As soon as the tip of his johnson touched my outer pleasure, I sighed before he could push into my interior. He teased me with the tip for a bit before thrusting himself inside me. I loved it rough. I loved that first entrance as I arched my back, receiving such a wonderful thing.

"Kea, girl, did you hear me?" Terry asked, breaking me out of my thought about the dream I had. And just like this morning, Terry interrupted my wet dream for a second time.

"What?"

"Did you just moan?" she asked.

"No, I didn't."

"Yes, you did. Girl, do I need to turn this car around and take your behind back home? Because you are not here with me. Your mind is elsewhere and I pray it's not on Jaquon."

"Well if somebody wouldn't have woken me up so early, maybe I wouldn't feel so tired," I said, trying to play my absentmindedness off. "Now repeat what you said. I'm listening now. You have my undivided attention."

"How was your time with him last night?"

I giggled at my crazy friend and said, "Jaquon was the perfect gentleman. He wined and dined me. He then ran me a bubble bath with candles lit, and cleaned the kitchen while I soaked in the warm bath waiting for him to come and lather me up," I said seductively like I was back in that moment. I almost moaned again.

"Don't be sitting here getting all horny with me, because I can't do nothing for you. I'm strictly dickly."

I laughed at my friend.

"You still have to catch me up on why you two broke up in the first place. Wait a minute," she said, holding up one hand. "Let me guess. He cheated on you again."

Her words hurt. Just the fact that she said "again" was enough to make me want to crawl in the back seat and get into the fetal position. "You remember when I told you I was going to Derrick's cookout."

"Yes."

"And you know Derrick and I was doing our thing."

"Yeah," Terry said.

"Well, after everybody ate and had some fun, Derrick and I left for a minute and had our own little fun."

"Get out."

"Girl, he rocked my world," I boasted.

"And nobody missed you two being gone?" Terry asked, still driving to our destination.

"We both left at different times so it wouldn't look obvious, but once we came back, Zacariah approached us like she knew we were together."

"Hold up. I thought Derrick and Zacariah were broke up."

"They are."

"So what was the trick doing there?" Terry asked.

"I still don't know to this day. I guess she called herself crashing the party. And crashing she did."

"Girl, you have to speed this thing up. You got me about to palpitate over here."

I laughed as I went on to explain more. "Evidently the girl Jaquon was seeing happened to be Zacariah's best friend. Her name was Essence I think. Girl, when I walked into that back yard, she was sitting beside him like Jaquon was her man, totally disrespecting me."

"Did you snatch the bitch up?"

"No. I played it cool. The one I dealt with was Jaquon because he was my man," I said irately, getting mad all over again.

"You should have snatched that bitch up anyway, but go on," Terry said, getting angry.

"Jaquon and I got to arguing and Zacariah decided to put her two cents in by exposing me and Derrick. The funny thing is Jaquon already knew about us."

"Get out of here," Terry said, enthralled in my unraveling soap opera.

"I was wondering why he started coming home and being attentive all of sudden. But, Terry, here's the kicker. Zacariah and Jaquon slept together too."

"Get the gun."

"I wanted to. If I had a piece, I swear I would have got to cappin' in that back yard. I don't know who would have got shot first, Zacariah or Jaquon."

Terry laughed, pulling up to another red light.

"Everybody knew about it but me. Evidently this had happened over a year ago."

"Even Derrick knew?" Terry questioned.

"Even Derrick, which hurt me the most. But Zacariah had one more trick up her sleeve. She revealed to Derrick and me that we had the same father."

Terry turned completely to me like she was sitting on the sofa in my apartment. She forgot we were at a stoplight and was quickly reminded by the blaring of the driver behind us blowing their horn.

"I'm moving," she yelled, putting her hand out the window and throwing up a middle finger.

"Stop doing that. You know people crazy. The middle finger can get you jacked up."

"Well I'm crazy too. They can step if they want to. They are going to find their ass full of lead," she said, turning right. "Now back to what you were saying. You lost me. You have to back up and repeat that last thing you said," Terry said, confused.

"Getting dirt on me from my mother, Zacariah found out who my father was. She went to see him, only to find a picture of Derrick when he was a teen with a message on the back from Derrick's mom. Something about 'here's a picture of your son,'" I explained.

Terry turned into a gas station abruptly. I looked at her gas hand and it was on full.

"Why are you stopping?"

"Kea, I had to pull over before I wreck this car. I need a minute to take all this in."

I smiled at my friend, who was in disbelief. She leaned against the door, turning my way to listen more.

"I can't believe this, Kea."

"You. Derrick and I were devastated."

"So this means," she said, doing calculation with her finger in the air, "you slept with your brother."

When she said it, it sounded so nasty. I said, "Yes."

"Oh my goodness. But how do you know Zacariah was telling the truth? The woman is a conniving bitch."

"That's true, and we didn't know, which is why we had a paternity test done."

"And? Don't leave me hanging," Terry said, eager to hear the results.

"The test proved we are indeed related."

Terry sat there with her mouth open, shaking her head. "I can't believe you have been going through all of this and you didn't tell me. I'm surprised you're not sitting in the corner of a rubber room taking sedatives to get your mind off of all of this."

"Believe you me, I've cried enough tears to last me a lifetime. Besides, growing up with a mother like mine made me strong enough to deal with heartache like this."

"So what now?" she asked. "Are you and Derrick done?"

I frowned, saying, "Of course. That news divided us forever. Derrick can't even look at me without getting upset and I feel just like he does."

"Have you gone to see this man who's your dad?" Terry asked.

I forgot that piece of the puzzle.

"I tried to do that first thing, Terry, only to find out the night of the cookout when all this mess

was going down, he was shot and killed by somebody trying to rob him."

"You know what, I don't know if I want to hear
any more of this madness. I didn't think it could
get any worse, but I see it has," she said, turning
back toward the steering wheel like she was going to pull off, but she didn't.

"And guess who my father ended up being,
Terry."

"I don't know if I want to know," she said.

"The old guy who I used to take breakfast to
who lived on the first floor in my building."

"Are you talking about that man who sat outside all the time smoking?" Terry asked.

"Yep. That was him."

"So all this time you've been talking and chillin'
with your very own father."

"Crazy right," I said with tears forming in my
eyes. "I wish he would have known who I was
before he died."

"Aw," Terry said, leaning over and wrapping
her arms around me. "At least you still have a
dad who loves you. You have more than some."

"I know," I said, wiping my tears from my
cheeks.

Terry leaned back, looking at me, and asked,
"Are you sure you are okay? This is a lot for one
person to deal with."

I smiled and said, "I'm good. I try not to think about it because when I do . . ." I pointed to my face.

"It's going to be okay. You know I'm here for you no matter what."

"I know."

Terry sighed loudly and said, "I hope you know all of this catching up has made me lose my appetite."

I laughed, wiping the tears from my face, saying, "Well I'm still hungry. I need to eat something before I go to this will reading today."

"What reading?"

"Mr. Hanks, the man who's my father, put me in his will."

"How ironic is that? Even though he didn't know you were his daughter, he still loved you enough to put you in his will," Terry said. "That's a happy ending to this tragic story. I swear if you weren't sitting here telling me face to face, I would think you read this out of a magazine, or book, or something."

I laughed, saying, "Hopefully this reading will give me some closure when it comes to Mr. Hanks."

"Some more closure you need to deal with is closing your heart off to Jaquon."

I rolled my eyes, saying, "Terry, please don't go back to him again."

"I'm just saying, Kea. The man wants you back and that's evident. Why should you give your heart back to a man who crushed it when he had it? You've been through this with him too many times. Let him go. That's one less issue you have to deal with."

I nodded as Terry put the car into drive to continue to our destination. I thought about what she said and knew she was right. I did need to exclude Jaquon from my life completely. I wasn't sure if I wanted to. Being with him last night confirmed I still had feelings for him. He was trying, but I wasn't sure how long this nice, affectionate Jaquon would last.

I couldn't have Derrick anymore. I hadn't been single in forever. And the fact of the matter was, after last night, I was already considering giving Jaquon another shot. I hadn't told him and I damn sure wasn't going to tell Terry. I needed to see where these days were going to take me. Hopefully some clarity would come into play to make me see the next step I needed to take.

Chapter 13

Derrick

Urgency was a factor due to ingrates looking to score it big. My real father's body wasn't even cold in the ground yet, before many of his so-called children came crawling out of the woodwork, fighting over assets they thought they were entitled to. Honestly I didn't feel entitled to anything this man had since I hadn't known him as my biological father. How could I now claim what was his? If it weren't for me being convinced by Mama to come, I wouldn't be here now. Hell, I still needed time to wrap my mind around what was going on in my family and how the father I thought was my real dad actually wasn't. I hadn't gotten the nerve to ask my parents, yet, how all this happened. I thought I was scared of the answers. I wasn't sure if I was ready to hear the truth. That "truth shall set you free" crap doesn't work all the time. I felt in my case it could be a hindrance on how I proceeded in my life. Especially if it was something more extreme than what had already occurred.

I entered the room for the will reading, which seemed to be a tight fit. Even with several people already here, Kea's face was the first one my eyes landed on. She looked more beautiful than ever. She had cut her hair, which looked great on her. I wondered what my reaction was going to be when I saw her again and I could feel happiness fill me. Then the reality of our relationship set in quickly as my joy turned into grief, knowing this woman I loved deeply was my sister. It was in this moment I wished I never came to the reading of my so-called father's will. From the spectacle of people who showed up, I almost turned and walked out of the facility.

I thought Kea sensed my presence. She turned in my direction. Her eyes met mine for a moment and she smiled at me, instantly causing me to feel at ease. She motioned for me to come over to her but I didn't move right away. I wondered if being near her was a good idea. She saw I didn't move and motioned again for me to come over to her. Before I could make my way over to the chair near her, someone plopped herself next to her. She looked at the woman and then back at me. Kea hunched her shoulders and I held my hand up, letting her know it was okay.

I looked around to find somewhere else to sit and found an empty seat away from her. I wanted to go over and put my arms around her small waist but I knew it would just stir up emotions within me that only existed in the deepest of hick towns. There could be no more incest here. Not that it really felt like incest, because we didn't know we were siblings. Our sexual encounter was a mistake made by us not knowing we were brother and sister, but I wasn't about to pretend to overlook that factor just to be in her arms again. I considered it many times, thinking we could run away from all of our family and live where no one knew us, but that was my imaginary world.

I looked over at her again but she wasn't looking at me. She was talking with the young woman next to her in an orange and white sundress. I leaned down and gripped my head, wishing the thoughts I was having about her would go away. I wanted to be with her so bad but she was my sister, for goodness' sake. Any feeling I had for her had to be drawn with a line of kinship. That line that was once crossed could never be stepped over again.

I looked back up. I was happy she wasn't watching me gawk at her like a high school kid with a crush. I fell into her smile, which was calling me to kiss her sweet lips. I, again, shook off thoughts of her that deepened with each glance her way. I knew the person next to me had to think I was crazy by the way she kept looking at me sideways, snarling at me. I did hear her say to somebody on her cell, "This fool next to me looks like he's about to lose it up in here."

I ignored her and kept my head down to the floor. There was no one else in here I wanted to deal with besides Kea. And let me tell you with all the different types of personalities in the facility, hers was a welcome delight. These people here were a cross between *Good Times* and *The Boondocks*. Some I had seen around, but never did I imagine we could possibly be related. Most were an embarrassment, to say the least. I hoped my face wouldn't show my dislike for them.

The 160-pound chocolate crusty woman sitting next to me kept running off at the mouth. I almost told her to mind her own damn business and go find some soap, water, and lotion to go on her stank, ashy body. Her ankles, feet, knees, and elbows glistened with white flakey matter I only saw as skin wishing to escape her body. And the funny thing was if she washed, fixed her hair, and put on some decent clothes, she might actually look nice.

"Yeah, girl, I'm here to get my money so I can go out tonight," she said to someone on her phone. "And half these people here don't deserve to get nothing. I'm the only one who cared for that man."

I ignored Crusty and eagerly waited for the man to come through the doors for this reading. I hoped he would bring in fresh air because the air in this room was putrid. The woman beside me, using her outside voice, did her part in adding to the unneeded funk of armpits, unwashed behinds, and stank breath. Some smelled like they hadn't showered since this time last month.

I couldn't take this anymore. I got up to leave but an African American gentleman entered the room with a folder filled with papers. He scanned the space, looking at the many unsavory individuals who, I assumed, were asked to come. I sat back down since it was about to begin. I was here so a few more minutes shouldn't hurt.

"This meeting will come to order," he said loudly.

Some kept running their mouths like he didn't say a word, including the woman sitting next to me who was too busy talking about what she was wearing to the club later.

The man repeated himself, this time elevating his voice with authority. I looked at the woman next to me.

She said, "Girl, I got to go. They are getting ready to get started. Wish me luck and hope I come home with a fat check," she said, clicking her phone off.

"We are here to hear the last will and testament of a Mr. Otis Hanks."

"Can you please hurry up? Because I got somewhere to be," a female said with her arms crossed. "We have been sitting here too long already so just give me my money so I can go."

"I heard that," another woman boasted. "I got to go home and cook."

"You know you don't cook," said the guy sitting beside her, as they entered into a battle of words. "The only thing you know how to do is boil water and add some hot dogs to it," the guy said, laughing, causing many around him to laugh also.

I wasn't feeling it. I was ready to get this thing started so I could get the hell out of here.

"Please, everyone. Can you calm down so we can get through this? I will try to hurry, and it will go a lot faster if you all would not interrupt me while I'm trying to read his will. This shouldn't take long."

"It better not," another woman said.

Instantly, I could tell she was from the wrong side of common sense. 90 percent of the people in here represented not having too much upstairs. Especially when I saw a woman who looked like she still had on her nightgown. I mean bedroom shoes and all. And her language was awful. I thought even this Ebonics dictionary they created needed to be redone with some of the words coming out of her mouth.

The man said a few things and then began to read the last words of the man who helped in my creation. "I, Mr. Otis Hanks, being of sound mind, do herby leave my life's fortunes in this order. To Rhonda, Malequa, Shaquala, Precious, Charity, Darryl, Lloyd, Roscoe, Sonny, and Ethan, I leave you money in the sum of ten thousand dollars—"

The woman next to me jumped to her feet, screaming, "Ten thousand dollars. I'm getting ten thousand dollars."

Others began to cheer until the man reading the will said, "Excuse me. I wasn't finished reading. Can you all calm down and let me proceed?"

The woman sat down, smiling from ear to ear. All she had on her mind was that $10,000 she was about to get. That was until the man continued with what he was going to say.

"To Rhonda, Malequa, Shaquala, Precious, Charity, Darryl, Lloyd, Roscoe, Sonny, and Ethan, I leave you money in the sum of ten thousand dollars to be split evenly among you all," the reader said.

"Split," the woman next to me said. "What do you mean split? We are not getting ten thousand apiece?" she asked.

"No, ma'am," the guy said, visibly irritated.

"What that equal to?" one of the other women asked.

I shook my head at their ignorance.

"Man, what does that mean?" a guy wearing a black baseball cap asked, not giving the reader an opportunity to respond.

The reader paused and said, "Ten names were called. Ten thousand divided by ten would leave each of you one thousand dollars."

"One thousand dollars," many blurted in disbelief.

"That's it," another one yelled.

"I thought this man had hundreds of thousands of dollars and he leaves us a thousand dollars."

The reader continued without commenting on their reaction. "Shanna, Nathan, Tony, and Hope, I leave five thousand dollars apiece," the reader said, angering the ones who only got $1,000.

"How come they get more than me? Why didn't we get the same amount?" Crusty, sitting next to me, said.

"He ain't got no land or some cars to leave me?" one guy asked, standing with a toothpick in his mouth.

"What about some vacation homes or artwork we can sell?" another one asked.

The reader looked on without saying anything. Really he couldn't because the room had erupted into utter chaos again.

"You called me way down here to tell me that sorry excuse for a father only left me a thousand dollars," Crusty beside me blurted. "It's going to cost me that to pay my rent and put gas in my gas guzzler of a car. He could have at least left me enough money to buy me a new ride," she said. "And they get five thousand. I want to over-rule this reading."

"Ma'am, you can't overrule the reading. This is not court. If you do have a problem, what you can do is contest the will."

"Well I'll do that then," Crusty said.

I looked over at Kea, who was looking in aston-ishment also. We both made eye contact before smiling because we knew what the other was thinking: *these ungrateful individuals and they could be some kin to us.*

"The man ain't never done a damn thing for me and he pays me back by leaving me nothing," another woman yelled.

"Well I got five thousand so I'm good," one said, angering the ones who received less.

Many were on their feet, screaming at the gentleman reading Mr. Hanks's last words.

"I want some more money," a few of them shouted.

"You can alter his thing and distribute that money evenly. It's only fair, man," a guy told the reader.

"Settle down please." He motioned for them to sit but no one listened. He tried to explain to them that the man gave a reason why but no one wanted to hear it. Their dreams of living the good life had vanished with the speaking of three words: "one thousand dollars."

"He can't explain nothing to me. I don't want to hear nothing else this man has to say to me," Crusty next to me said. "Give me my check so I can go," she said, getting up and fanning that awful odor around. "If I wasn't broke, I would tear this check up. But maybe I'll go find his grave so I could spit on it. I think that will make me feel better."

She walked up to the man, demanding her check. That ended up with the reader passing out checks to those ready to leave, which was the majority. I thought he was supposed to wait until the reading was over to pass out the money, but

I knew he was ready to get some of these people out of his face in order to continue. I knew he did this so he could continue in peace.

Many exited with Crusty, including the woman wearing her nightgown and slippers. One guy was so mad about his thousand he kicked one of the chairs, causing it to bounce off the wall. But none of them were mad enough to not take the money. All that talking and all that unnecessary ruckus, when they were walking out of there with more money than they came in there with. Talk about ungrateful.

When I looked around the room there were only seven individuals who remained, and they were me, Kea, Mama, my aunt, and three other women. Seeing my mama and my aunt threw me for a loop. I didn't see them enter, but how could I when they were standing at the back of the room?

Once they noticed I saw them, both of them came over and sat next to me. They could sit now since some chairs were available.

"Mama, what are you and Aunt Henny doing here?" I asked, looking at both of them with a questionable stare. I hadn't seen my Aunt Henny in over a year.

"Derrick, baby, how are you?" Aunt Henny asked, giving me a big hug.

"I'm good, but what are y'all doing here?" I asked again, this time looking at Mama.

"We are here for the same reason you are," Mama said.

"And you didn't bother to tell me you were coming."

"Baby, I had to wait on Henny to get to the house first before we came."

"But you still could have told me."

"I know, baby, and I'm sorry."

"So both of you are in the will?" I questioned.

Aunt Henny's eyes shifted before she said, "Yes. I guess. I was called too."

"So how did you know him?" I asked my aunt.

"I grew up with Otis. You know I know him from your mama hooking up with him back in the day," she said, laughing.

I frowned at the thought of my mother hooking up with anybody. "Is hooking up how I was conceived?" I asked Mama, but neither of them found that to be funny. I knew the annoyed tone I used didn't help matters.

"Derrick, my sex life is none of your business," Mama said.

"Mama, it was made my business when I found out, from Zacariah no less, that the dad who I thought was my real dad isn't, and that this man whom I've never met is. I'm still waiting for you to explain that one to me," I said angrily.

"I will, but not now," she tried to say quietly as the reader tried to bring order back into the room to continue the reading of Mr. Hanks's will.

I swore if I wasn't confused before I got here, I was certainly confused now. What the hell was going on and why wouldn't Mama tell me why she lied to me all my life?

Chapter 14

Kea

To my surprise Derrick's mother and a woman who looked a lot like his mother were sitting next to Derrick now. He didn't seem happy about seeing either of them as they conversed. Whatever was being said I could tell Derrick didn't like it. The way he was clenching his hands clued me in. His mom glanced over at the woman with a worried look. I did wonder what that glimpse was about.

The man continued to read Mr. Hanks's last will and testament. $10,000 was left to two of the remaining people, who also retrieved their checks and left. One was satisfied but the other was angry that she didn't receive more. Both were women and I couldn't tell if they were his children or his baby mamas. Either way, both collected their checks and got out of there.

The next recipient was the lady who used to bring meals by for Mr. Hanks. He left her with $20,000. She dropped her head in appreciation as tears streamed down her cheeks.

"Thank you, Lord," was what she said as she cried tears of joy. She also got up to leave.

"To Henrietta and Shirley, you two are a hoot." This caused both Derrick's mom and the woman sitting next to her to chuckle.

"Y'all know why y'all a hoot but I'm not going into that right now. I want to thank you for being there for me. Shirley, I want to thank you for the gift of raising such an awesome son. Derrick is the son I've always wanted even if he didn't know anything about me. Still I appreciate you keeping me informed of how he was doing. It made these last years worth living knowing I had my blood running through such an amazing man."

Ms. Shirley looked over at Derrick, who was looking down at the floor. She took his hand into hers like a proud mother as she continued to listen to Mr. Hanks's last words.

"Henrietta, I leave you twenty thousand dollars and, Shirley, I leave you with fifty thousand dollars. This isn't much but I hope this can somehow make up for all the trouble I've caused in your life."

Ms. Shirley began to cry as the woman next to her wrapped her arms around her. I couldn't understand why both of them received money, but who was I to try to comprehend this situation when I was sitting here getting ready to receive a gift from Mr. Hanks that I didn't think I deserved?

The reader asked, "Would you two ladies like to get your checks now and leave also?"

Ms. Shirley looked at Derrick as he said, "You two can go, Mama."

"We can stay," Ms. Shirley said.

"I'll be fine. It's almost over so you two leave and try to enjoy one another. I'll be over soon, okay?" Derrick said with a forced tone.

Ms. Shirley kissed him on the cheek and she and the other woman gathered their checks before leaving the room. Now Derrick and I were left. How ironic was it for us to be the last two standing? We peered at one another. I wanted to go over and hold his hand. We were in this together and I wanted my reaction to reflect that but I didn't move. I continued to sit as I awaited the final results of Mr. Hanks's will.

"To Derrick: I'm leaving you one hundred thousand dollars."

Derrick's eyes almost fell out of his head when the man spoke those words.

"Can you repeat that?" Derrick asked surprised, as we both chuckled. The reader repeated the amount to him. Derrick stared in astonishment.

"He had an explanation if you want to hear it," the reader said and Derrick nodded.

"I guess you are wondering why I left you this amount of money since we never had a relationship."

Derrick nodded in agreement to Mr. Hanks's words, with his hands clasped in front of him and elbows on his knees, leaning in like a child waiting to hear something bad.

"Well, son, I loved your mother. At one point in my life, I loved that woman more than I loved myself. I still love her."

Derrick's eyes glistened and I knew these words brought twinges to his heart. I knew he wasn't going to let a tear fall but he was moments away from it happening. His mother was his life regardless of the secrets she harbored from him.

"Your mother never knew my sordid past and she didn't care. Shirley was the type of woman who would forgive anything even after all the wrong someone like me has done. I let a good thing go with your mother but I'm happy she found love in someone who I knew accepted you as his own child. I couldn't have asked for a better father for you. He was a better man than me. Your father never tried to keep me from you. It was I who made the choice to stay away once I saw how happy your family was. I didn't want to interfere with that. So I let things be. She always let me know how you were doing and when your games were and sent me pictures every chance she got. I loved her for that and she was the only mother of my children who went out her way to do so. You have grown into a wonderful man. You are a better man than I am and I know that's due to your dad and Shirley. I wasn't there to help you then, not that you needed it, but I can help you now. Maybe this can make up for some of the heartache I have caused. And I have no doubt in my mind you will continue to be great. Hopefully I will be that angel looking over you if God permits me to enter heaven's gates. It can go either way but still I'm thankful to call you my flesh and blood. I love you, son."

Derrick nodded in agreement, choking down as much emotion as he could.

I, on the other hand, was crying like a baby. Those were the words coming from our biological father and I knew it hit the core of Derrick's feelings. I got up and went to him. I sat down beside him and took his hand into mine. I could tell by the look on his face his unanswered questions were now answered, at least from this end. I wasn't sure about his mother's end but I did know a weight had been lifted from Derrick and the peace of knowing showed through him. I laid my head on his shoulder. I felt his lips kiss the top of my head and I closed my eyes in contentment.

"Thank you for being here with me," Derrick said through choked-up emotion.

I lifted my head and said, "I will always be here for you."

We both looked at the reader and the man continued. "Last but not least, Kea. You have been more like family to me than anyone ever has besides Shirley."

I felt bad knowing he died not knowing I was his daughter.

"You helped make my last days special and for that I'm grateful. You brought sunshine to my gloomy days and for a young person, you can throw down in the kitchen, girl."

I chuckled at his words.

"I'm going to miss the food you used to bring me and our conversations on the stoop. Don't let anyone interfere with the great person you have become. I know life is hard but don't let anyone change you. That's as good as the devil wants. You have such a kind heart and I pray no one changes that. I love you, Kea, this is why I'm leaving you one hundred thousand dollars."

I looked over at Derrick who had his hand over mine now. My mouth was open in amazement.

The reader continued to read but I didn't hear anything else after $100,000. This figure kept echoing in my head, and it was in this moment I was happy it was only Derrick and me sitting here to hear this, because everyone else might have jumped us in rage.

The reader continued. "Kea, I hope this money brings you happiness. And don't spend it on that lowlife, Jacobi."

I giggled, knowing Mr. Hanks called him by the wrong name on purpose. That's just how much he disliked Jaquon.

"Don't let that man spend up all your money or I'm going to come from my grave and haunt you. Anyway, Ms. Kea dear, keep striving to make every one of your dreams come true. I love you as if you were my own."

Tears streamed down my cheeks as I wished he did know I was his own.

"Congratulations, Kea," Derrick said.

"I can't believe this."

"Believe it," the reader said. "Mr. Hanks thought a lot of you, Kea. More than you could ever know."

"But one hundred thousand dollars? I knew the rumor was true about his lottery winnings but I never thought . . ." I said, choking on my words.

"Mr. Hanks was private about his funds. He knew if it really got out, all those ingrates you saw today would have come with their hands out while he was living. After paying all his back child support he had, he banked the rest and lived the life like a man who hardly had any money. He knew neither of you were like that. Today is proof. You saw his children and family only wanting what they thought they deserved, only to get disappointed. If you ask me, it felt great to see their reaction."

"Oh they were a trip," Derrick said.

"Count this as another blessing," the reader said, getting up to leave. "Here are your checks," he said, passing Derrick and me each a checked filled with more zeros than I had ever seen on a check. I was going to count this as a huge blessing and pray to God that Mr. Hanks was up there with Him. Regardless of his past I knew he could repent for his sins. I just prayed he had time to do that before he died. I knew I could pray for his soul, and hoped when my time came, I was going to heaven to see him again. Until then I knew I had to do my best to live the best life ever here on earth.

I just wished those days could have been spent with Derrick.

Chapter 15

Derrick

Walking out of the building, I held the door open for Kea, who was behind me. Once we were outside both of us paused. I took a moment to take in how good she looked. With a black shirt-dress and heels, Kea looked so sexy. Her legs looked like they went on for miles and I loved they way they glimmered.

"Crazy day, right?" she said, putting her shades on to block the sun.

"Crazy wasn't the half. I can't believe we are related to any of those idiots."

"Me either. And I hope none of them hear about our money and try to establish a connection just so they can get close to it."

"They can try but it's not going to happen."

"Well I guess I better get home," she said, reaching into her bag drooped in the crook of her arm for her keys.

"Kea, do you think we can go somewhere and grab something to eat?" I asked, wondering where my words were coming from.

"I . . . don't . . . know," she said hesitantly, finally finding her car keys in the enormous bag.

"It's just lunch. Nothing more. Just because we can't be together don't mean we can't act like siblings for real. Besides, I haven't had a chance to do anything for you for your birthday."

"You remembered," she said, smiling.

"I'm a day late with it but I knew I would see you here today."

I could see the wheels in Kea's head turning as she looked at the passing cars driving to their destinations.

"Okay. I don't see any harm in that," she said, smiling. "But where are we going?"

"Krispy Kreme," I blurted, and she hit me on the arm, laughing.

"Ha ha, very funny."

This was funny because this was the spot where I really got to know Kea when she came to me about my ex-best friend, Jaquon. She suspected he was cheating, which he was, but at the time I didn't feel it was my place to tell her. From that day on our connection grew.

"I'm just joking. We can go anywhere you want. It's your choice, birthday girl."

"Well they do have this new soul food restaurant that just opened up downtown. I heard the food was good. Have you been there yet?"

"I can't say that I have."

"I have a taste for some wings."

We ended up getting some grub and talking like old times. I hadn't felt this good since the hours before my cookout. I soaked up her cheeriness. She was talking about what she may do with the money and how she would like to go back to school or write a book about her life. I listened intently, not saying a word. My nods let her know I was hanging on her every word. I missed Kea's company so much. She made everything around me seem tolerable.

"You are not saying much, Derrick."

"I'm listening to you."

"I can tell something else is on your mind," she said.

"I'm enjoying your company. I haven't been this happy since . . ." I paused.

She took a sip of her water, nervously running her fingers through her hair. "I was wondering when we were going to get back to that. You know we can't pretend that the last few weeks haven't happened," she said.

"I know, but I want to forget it. It's too much for me to deal with," I said, watching her dip her French fry into her ketchup.

"Where do we go from here? How do you see our relationship continuing?" she asked.

I looked down, not knowing how to respond. *Do I lie or tell her the truth?* Lying would entail embracing the fact that we were siblings and saying we could never be, but the truth was I wanted to forget about what had happened and love every inch of her. I shook my head in confusion. A battle between common sense and what would make me happy consumed me. She noticed my struggle.

"Derrick, I can tell you are not okay talking about this."

"I'm not. I can't find the words to say," I said, leaning back in my seat, looking down at my food that looked so good but I didn't have the appetite to eat.

"Just say what you feel. You have never had to hide your feelings from me so don't start now. I'm your sister."

I winced at her words and said, "That's the problem." It came out in a higher tone than I meant it to.

"I see," she said, sitting farther back into her chair, wiping her greasy fingers on a napkin.

I stared into her eyes, deciding to lay it all out on the table, and leaning forward with my hands clasped together I said, "Kea, I still love you."

"I love you too."

"No. You don't understand. I love you," I stressed, looking at her. "I love you in the sense of wanting to be next to you. I want to caress you. I want to kiss you. I want to make love to you, Kea."

Her demeanor was that of a brick wall. I couldn't tell if she was disturbed by my revelation, or if she was glad. I couldn't read her at all. I sat waiting for her to respond but she didn't. She just looked at me sincerely. I decided to say something to break the silence.

"I can't stop thinking about you in that way. I can't grasp the fact we are siblings. I don't believe it. No one can convince me of that. Not even a paternity test. Something is not right here and I know it. And I'm going to figure it out. I don't think destiny would bring me to the woman I was meant to spend the rest of my life with, only to turn around and be faced with this issue. It's senseless to me."

"I know, but the test said—"

"I know what the test said, Kea, but my gut is telling me otherwise."

She lifted the napkin from her lap and placed it on the table. "I don't know if I can deal with this right now, Derrick. I thought I was ready. Hearing you say this and thinking about the test and how it has ruined our relationship is hard for me too. But how can that test be inaccurate? You heard the results just like I did. How can it not be true?"

"I know it's wrong. Look, Kea, tell me you don't feel the same way I do. Something's not right. If you don't feel that way then I'll never speak of this again," I said confidently.

"There is something that's not sitting well with me either but—"

"Exactly. Kea, I don't think we are related. And that's why I'm going to ask you to come home with me."

She shook her head no.

"Please."

"I can't do this, Derrick," she said, getting up from the table.

I stood with her.

"I have to go. Lunch was nice," Kea said, grabbing her bag, and out of the restaurant she went.

I reached into my pocket, pulling out my wallet, and tossed three twenties on the table before going after her.

"Kea, wait," I called out, but Kea kept walking.

Once we were outside in the parking lot I caught up to her, saying, "Please wait."

Kea stopped and turned to me. "I'm not going to your place, Derrick. What is that going to solve?" she asked feverishly.

"I want you to come with me," I said, grabbing her hand. "We can just talk some more. That's it."

She looked at my hand touching hers and looked back up at me. Her fingers were limp within my hand and I grasped her hand tighter, glad to have this contact with her.

"Please. Come with me."

Chapter 16

Kea

Why I agreed to meet Derrick was beyond me. It didn't hit me until I was walking into his home, looking at the area where we made love after having a picnic in front of his fireplace. I paused in the doorway before entering deeper into the space. All that talking I did to not come here with him and here I was at his house. I knew this was a big mistake but I couldn't help myself. I wanted to see where this was going to go.

"Please sit down," he said, gesturing to the sofa, but I decided to sit in the chair away from him.

"Okay. I'm here. Explain this conspiracy of yours."

"Straight and to the point, huh."

"We have to be, Derrick. Especially with you admitting your feelings for me."

"And you don't feel the same?" he asked.

I didn't respond. I did feel the same as he did. Seeing him created flutters within my stomach that wouldn't stop. The warmth between my thighs made me feel guilty also. Sitting in his living room, picturing our bodies meshing as one as the flicker of the fire's flame helped tickle our fancy pushed my level of desire for him to an all-time high.

"This is a mistake. I can't do this," I said, getting up abruptly to leave. Derrick jumped in front of me, blocking my path.

"Do what?"

"This. Being here with you. I thought I was strong enough to do this but I can't," I said, backing away from him in frustration. "Sitting in this room only brings back times we can't have anymore."

"But who says we can't?" Derrick disagreed.

"I do. You do. Society does. Siblings don't procreate, Derrick!" I yelled.

"Baby, something is not right about this. I know it. You know it. We are not related," Derrick said convincingly.

"How do you know?"

"Look. Sit down for a minute and let me explain."

I pushed out air from my dispirited body and sat down, this time on the sofa. Derrick sat next to me.

"Zacariah was here the other night."

"For what?" I asked, frowning.

"She said she thought I needed her."

"For . . . ?" I asked.

"Something about how she heard about the results."

"What? Those are confidential."

"I know. I said the same thing. But she said something about hearing the news from your mother."

"My mother," I said, placing my hand on my chest to make sure I heard Derrick correctly.

He nodded.

"How would she know?"

"She said your father must have told your mother and that's how she found out."

"That makes no sense at all, Derrick. Especially since my parents no longer live together and hardly have a kind word to say to one another. Why would Daddy tell her? And my so-called mother said she wanted to have nothing else to do with him either. He had no reason to contact her."

"I thought that too. So I got to thinking. What if Zacariah had something to do with the results?"

"How? Why? Well I know why. But how?"

"Maybe she knows somebody within the office. You never know."

"Zacariah having people working in a medical facility; I find that hard to believe."

"We don't know any of her people," Derrick said.

"Still, would someone want to risk their job like that?"

He hunched his shoulders.

"Of all the offices around she knows the one person in the one we go to. It sounds farfetched."

"True, but do you want to take that chance? I think you and I need to have a second test done somewhere else."

I looked at him skeptically.

"No one needs to know about it. Not even our parents. Just me and you. It's worth a shot, Kea. Zacariah is a conniving, manipulative person. I wouldn't put anything past her."

"She is vengeful."

"Let's do this. If not to prove her wrong, let's do it for us," he said, believing in what he was saying.

His strength and excitement put hope in my heart. "But what if—"

"I'm not thinking about that. I'm thinking about being your man again."

"We have to prepare ourselves just in case the results were accurate."

Derrick leaned in and kissed me. My face was cradled in the palms of his hands as his tongue explored my orifice. I wanted to pull away but I didn't. Our breathing was sporadic as we tried to suck up each other's essence. My hands joined in our unification, pulling him by the collar of his shirt closer to me. It was minutes before either of us came up for air.

"What are we doing?" I asked, looking into his eyes.

He kissed me again, pushing his lips with vigor on mine as he laid me down until I was completely horizontal with the weight of him on top of me. I could feel his swollen pleasure adjacent to my thighs throbbing to be unrestricted. The beast wanted to be disciplined and I was the only one who could conquer the monster.

Through kisses I whispered, "This can't happen, Derrick," but the more I objected, the more he persevered.

"Let this happen," he moaned, thrusting his manhood farther into my mound. His tongue relocated to my neck as I arched with the ease from him making me feel fulfilled.

"This isn't right," I whimpered, but it further fueled his craving. He tore my dress open, exposing my breasts. I could hear buttons hitting the floor. Derrick gripped my breasts. His hands felt splendid on them as he squeezed enough to make me feel a twinge of pain.

"Please stop," I whimpered like a weakened life form not able to fight the passion raging between us.

"You don't want me to stop," he said, moving farther down south.

"Yes. Please. Stop, Derrick," I said as his hot breath finally made it to my center. He pulled my lace panties to the side and, without any hesitation, Derrick dove into me, causing me to grind vigorously into him. He was insatiably devouring me. It didn't take long before my body was convulsing from the pleasure his tongue was giving me.

Derrick freed his girth and pushed it deep into me before I had a chance to push him away. His manhood caused more tingles to captivate my body as he moved vehemently, pushing in and out of me.

"Don't stop," I found myself saying as Derrick mesmerized my body to bliss.

I wanted control. I wanted to run the show for a while so I threw Derrick to the side and climbed on top of him. He grinned with satisfaction as I slid down his length, causing him to now sigh with pleasure. I moved my hips back and forth, then circular, then back and forth and then up and down, grinding deep, bringing my body to another peak of fulfillment. Derrick was right there with me, not able to sustain his climax any longer either. The more I bucked, the more his pushes strengthened as his hands clasped themselves around my waist, pulling me down harder on him. Each stroke was stronger than the last and the next thing I knew both of us were exploding.

Chapter 17

Zacariah

Who knew I would have company standing in my doorway? And, no, it was not Derrick even though I wished it were. The man standing before me was Fabian. Yes, it was the man from the restaurant who I threw my drink on. I thought that incident would be a one-time encounter but to my dismay it wasn't.

"What are you doing here? Better yet how did you know where I lived?" I asked with attitude.

"Your wallet," he said, holding it out to me.

And there it was: my wallet. I searched high and low for this thing, wondering where in the hell it was. I knew the last time I had it was the night I went to see Derrick, which happened to be the same night I met Fabian. Since I couldn't locate it, I considered it lost or even stolen. Lucky for me the only thing I had in it was my license and some cash money. I wasn't worried about the money so much as I was worried about my license. I did not feel like going to the DMV to sit in there half the day to try to get another one. I hated that place. So me being who I was I had been driving around without a license for the past few days.

"How did you get this? Did you steal this from me?" I asked suspiciously.

"If I stole your wallet, then why would I return it to you?"

"I don't know. Criminals do crazy things. Maybe you needed to see if it was more you could steal," I said.

"Are we going to stand here and argue about this or are you going to let me in?"

Frowning, I said, "I don't know you. You're making me think you are really stalking me now."

"You look like a woman who can take care of herself. Besides, look at me. Does it look like I need to stalk women?"

He ain't never lied because Fabian still looked fine as hell. He might've looked better today than he did the last time I laid eyes on him.

"Good-looking guys stalk too. Maybe it's some type of ego boost and it excites them to have that control over a woman."

"Are you going to let me in or not?"

I stood there for a moment as he stared into my eyes. I stepped back, waving my hand for him to come in. Call me trusting or just plan crazy. I leaned more toward me being crazy.

Shutting the door, I said, "I'm going to let you know if you are thinking about taking advantage of me, I carry a weapon and I have no shame in my game about busting a cap in your ass."

Fabian giggled, saying, "How did we go from me returning your wallet, to me being a stalker, and now you busting a cap in me?"

"I'm just saying. Don't get any ideas."

"The only idea I had was doing a good deed."

"Well it's done. Now what?"

"Look I'm not here for no drama. Here's your wallet. I'll be on my way. Damn. This is what a guy gets for trying to do the right thing," he said. He shook his head and headed for my front door.

"How did you say you got this again?" I asked.

He sighed before turning and said, "After you threw your drink in my face, I went back into the restaurant to get some napkins to clean myself up along with my ride. When I entered, the young man behind the counter told me you left it there. I told him I knew you and would return it to you."

"But you don't know me."

"So you wanted me to leave it there. Again, I was trying to help. A thank you is all you needed to say."

"I didn't ask you to return it."

"You know what, I don't have time for this," he said, sighing. "You are a trip and a half."

"Now I'm a trip."

"What do you call it? Here I am still being considerate even after your drink toss and I'm still getting my ass chewed out by you. Just like in the restaurant everything has to be about what I'm doing wrong but not what you are doing wrong."

"I can't help it if you are stupid," I said.

"Next time I'll keep my kindness to myself and leave your damn wallet in the restaurant."

"Well it won't be a next time," I blurted.

"Good. Is that a promise?" Fabian asked.

"You damn right it's a promise. And to show you I can be nice about this situation, let me give you some gas money for your troubles," I said, reaching into my wallet for some money. To my surprise all my cash was still there. Nevertheless I pulled out forty dollars and said, "Here you go. Is this enough?"

Fabian held up his hands and said, "I didn't ask for your money, Zacariah."

"But you are making such a big deal about this."

Again he sighed and said, "You are the most exhausting person I've met in my life. Are you really this unhappy? Is everybody so malicious toward you to the point you can't see when somebody is treating you with some compassion?"

Damn, he sounded like Derrick for a minute. I usually didn't notice when people were trying to be nice because all my life it was always about what everybody got for themselves. Even my own parents didn't care about me like they should have, so why would I expect anyone else to care? My mentality was get them before they got me. It was all I knew.

"Whatever has happened in your life I hope you get that resolved so you can see when someone's being genuine."

Fabian turned to leave again and for some reason I didn't want to see him go.

"Wait . . . Fabian."

He turned, putting his hands in his pockets, but he didn't say anything.

"Look, I do want to thank you for bringing my wallet to me. I'm also sorry for coming off so harsh," I said undauntedly.

He smiled and said, "You are welcome. I accept your apology."

"See, I can be nice when I want to be."

"How often do you choose to be? My gut is telling me only when you want something from that person," Fabian said.

"Don't piss me off now by trying to play psychiatrist," I said to him.

"I'm just saying. You are a very feisty woman and I'm usually attracted to your type. But you take that feistiness to a whole new level."

"I knew you liked me. It was the way I threw that drink in your face, wasn't it?" I asked jokingly.

"You are an attractive woman. Even in your rant at the restaurant I couldn't help but notice your beauty."

"Boy, you know how to lay it on thick."

"No. I call it like I see it. And right now I see a woman who I would like to take out to dinner," he said, smoothly slipping a date in.

"Dinner?" I questioned.

"Or lunch. Either one is fine with me. I promise not to take you to Wendy's since our last encounter was so terrible."

This caused me to laugh. "You know I have a man, right?" I said.

"Well is he here?"

"No, but he will be here shortly," I said, lying through my teeth.

"I'm not about to break up a happy relationship. Disregard my request then," Fabian said, backing off.

"You give up way too easy."

"I'm not giving up. I'm respecting your relationship."

"Well I'm not really in one. Just trying to see where your head is."

"Still playing games," Fabian said.

"Not really. Part of what I'm saying is true. I had a man and I'm trying to get him back. He wants me but he hasn't figured that out yet."

Fabian nodded, saying, "Oh that's it. He doesn't know it yet."

"Yes, but I will still go out with you. I need something to keep my mind off of things going on."

"If you are okay with this, we can meet up tomorrow. Say around seven. I'll pick you up if that's okay with you."

I paused, pretending to think about whether it was okay, but really I didn't care. I needed a change of pace. Maybe me going out with another guy would jar Derrick into jealousy. Maybe this would be what it took for Derrick to realize I was the woman he wanted in his life, and he couldn't let another man come in and swoop me up.

"Seven is good. I'll see you then."

"Then it's a date," Fabian said. "And if you don't mind, I will take this money," he said, snatching the money from my hand. "You did cause me to have to pay to get my car cleaned."

Chapter 18

Jaquon

I knew Kea was a huge Tyler Perry fan and his new movie, *Madea's Big Happy Family*, was coming to DVD today. Since we didn't make it to the actual movie I decided I would buy it for her to watch at home. Even though I respected Tyler Perry for all he had accomplished despite some of the hardships in his life, I really wasn't a big fan of his movies. I was more into martial arts movies and anything with a lot of action. Tyler Perry's movies were made more for women. Call me a man's man but tonight I was willing to sit next to Kea and watch this movie ten times if it meant getting closer to her.

After picking up the movie, I found myself standing in front of the video games. I was deciding if I should buy me another one to add to my growing collection. Well it was a growing collection before Kea destroyed some of them.

When I saw *God of War III* I thought about Derrick and the time we spent playing part two together. We couldn't wait for this version to come out. We used to spend hours on end playing not only this game but many other games. We would pick up some beer and snacks, making it a day of nonstop battling to see who was better. He won some and I won some. It was probably why our battles lasted so long: because we were each other's competition. Neither of us was better at any game. We really were almost equal when it came to winning. Our battles would last until the sun rose again with neither of us having gotten a wink of sleep. Those were fun days that I missed. Now I was looking at a game I knew neither of us would play together. How ironic was it for our competition to be over a woman?

I had wanted to call Derrick but I didn't think he would want to hear from me. Even if he considered talking to me I wouldn't know where to begin in our conversation. The one thing I knew for sure was Derrick couldn't stand betrayal of any kind. Our bond was compromised by both of us but I had no one to blame but myself for the demise of our friendship. I slept with Zacariah first, which started this snowball effect of "what comes around goes around." Yes, he slept with Kea, too, but if I would have kept my dick in my pants, all of us would be in a good place right now. I felt my love for sex clouded my judgment over actually being in love with Kea and my friendship with Derrick, which was why things were so messed up right now. My cheating ways caused these dominos to fall and here I stood, wishing I could set the chips back up and start everything all over again. What we had going on right now was some grownup shit I wished I never stirred up. I wished a "How you doing, man?" or "What's been up with you?" could begin the healing process of our friendship, but I knew better than that. It would take a higher power for real for Derrick to ever consider being my friend again. Thinking about the demise of our friendship brought back memories of the day I crossed the line when I slept with Zacariah for the first time a couple of years ago.

"Yo, Dee man, where you at?" I asked, busting my way through the door of Derrick's home like I always did without knocking. Zacariah was curled up on the couch.

"Don't you ever knock?" Zacariah asked with her usual attitude. "I'm sick of you busting up in here all the damn time like you pay mortgage up in this piece."

"Girl, shut up. I was doing this before Derrick got with you and I'm going to continue to do it until he gets rid of you."

"Well I guess I got to learn to lock the door then."

"That's fine. All I'm going to do is use my key," I said, showing it to her.

"Aw. I can't stand you."

"And I don't like your trifling behind either. Yo, Derrick man!"

"Stop screaming. Derrick's not here. He had to take his mother to visit with his aunt."

"Dag, that's right," I said, remembering he told me yesterday he was going out of town.

"So you can leave now. And like I said before, learn how to knock. I could have been coming out the shower or something and I don't want you gawking at me."

The visual of Zacariah naked wasn't hard to imagine since most of the clothes she wore were revealing anyway. She sat there now wearing some cut-off shorts and a white tee tied in the back, showing off her tiny waist and voluptuous breasts. Just the thought of checking her out like that made me want to throw up in my mouth but my body betrayed me. A chain reaction started and before I knew it, I couldn't control the rising of my manhood. I quickly put my hand in my pocket like I was sticking the key back in it as I turned away from her.

Zacariah looked at me sideways, asking, "What the hell is wrong with you?"

"Nothing."

"It doesn't look like that to me. You didn't think I notice the old hand-in-the-pocket-to-hide-a-hard-dick trick," she said, smirking. "You must like what you see."

"Please. You wish."

"Boy, please," she said, getting up from the couch and sauntering past me with a leisurely stroll to the kitchen. "I know I look good and I don't need you to tell me that."

She did look good and I couldn't help watching her fat ass gyrate its way out the room. As hard as I tried to calm myself down, the harder it felt like my manhood was getting. Zacariah came back moments later with a glass of juice and she had the nerve to be drinking out of a straw. This sent my mind into even dirtier realms as I thought about Zacariah's lips sucking on the tip of my manhood, too. Hell, I had all the juice she needed.

"You still here?" she asked, taking a gulp of her juice before sitting back down on the sofa.

Even the tightness of her thighs as she folded her feet beneath her turned me on in this moment. What the hell was going on with me? I couldn't find any words to say. I was known for talking mad game but right now I was speechless. My manhood was pulling blood flow from my brain. I had to be delusional to be hard over my best friend's girl, and one I didn't like at that. But my manhood liked her a lot.

"You still try to calm yourself huh. All this," she said, pointing at her body, *"got you tripping,"* she said, giggling and looking at my crotch.

"How you going to walk around all the time damn near naked? It's like you like dudes checking you out."

"Jaquon, I'm at home. I can sit here with nothing on if I wanted to," Zacariah said. *"I decided to chill today. I was getting ready to cut the television off and read my book. This peace is a great welcome. Well, that was until you stormed up in here."*

She placed her juice down on the coffee table. She then cut the television off and picked up her book as she threw her feet on the sofa, lying back to start her reading. The silence was awkward as I watched her long, smooth legs cross at the ankles, which stretched out, leading to where her shorts tucked their way between her thighs. Feelings of doing Derrick's woman trampled on how wrong this was but my body was telling me to go ahead, that this was exactly what Zacariah wanted.

Zacariah peered over the book, saying, "Why you standing there staring at me? You don't have anything else to do?"

"I do," I stuttered.

She laid the book down across her abundant breasts, and I wished I were the pages making contact with the thin cotton hugging her melons.

"Jaquon," she said, snapping her fingers. "Why am I making you so nervous?"

"I'm not nervous," I blurted. "I was thinking about what I was going to do now that I don't have my boy to hang with," I said, playing it off as much as I could, but I knew I was doing a horrible job at it.

"You have a girl. Go be with her. Better yet, go be with all them other women you choose to slum with," she said boldly.

"I don't slum," I said defensively.

"Tell that lie to somebody who might believe you. Your first name should be lying, second should be cheating, and last should be dog."

"I bet you want to catch some of my fleas," I retorted confidently. "I've seen how you've looked at me too."

"No, thank you. I don't want any itchy and scratchy here," she said, pointing to her camel's foot.

"*You can't sit there and tell me you haven't wondered why the ladies love me so much,*" I said.

"*I thought they were stupid. They see a cute face and lose their damn mind.*"

"*So you think I'm cute.*"

"*You all right. Derrick, on the other hand, is fine.*"

"*I would like to think both of us are good-looking men,*" I said with assurance. "*I don't hang with unattractive people. I guess I should leave because I'm in the presence of one now,*" I said, laughing as I walked to the door.

"*Ha ha,*" she said. "*Keep letting those women swell your head up. One day it's going to burst.*"

"*Please, Zacariah. You act like you haven't whored in your day. I know your past reputation too and if the opportunity arose, you would hop on the first dick you saw.*"

"*I'm looking at one now and I ain't hopping,*" she countered.

"*But you want to.*"

"*Please,*" she said, picking up the book to go back to pretend reading.

"*Admit it, Zacariah. You are curious about me,*" I said, walking back toward her. "*You have to wonder if my manhood is big. I do wear a size thirteen shoe.*"

"Boy, I have seen men with your shoe size still swing something the size of my pinky so you better shut up about that. Shoe sizes don't matter," she said, holding up her pinky.

"In my case it does. I'm swinging real low."

"I didn't ask you. I can ask you this: why don't you admit you have been goggling over me since you got here?"

"I'll admit I was checking you out. I had never viewed you this way before."

"And what way is that?" she asked, looking around the book.

"The way that made me rise up, wishing I could get a piece of you."

Zacariah got up, placing the pages of the book down on the sofa to hold her spot. She got up and walked over to me. "You know I'm going to tell Derrick you made a pass at me."

"No, you're not," I said, moving closer to her until her breasts were touching my chest.

"How you figure?" she asked daringly.

"Because your craving for me is too deep for you to pass up the chance to hop on this," I said, looking down at my hardness.

"You're crazy," she said softly, looking at me seductively.

"And you know you want me," I teased.

We started kissing ravenously and Zacariah didn't bother to push me away. She dove into the abyss with me, pulling me into her until no space occupied the distance between our yearnings.

Next thing I knew I was inside her. She was bent over the back of the couch while I banged her from the back doggie style. I had to admit Zacariah had that good good. It was all nice and wet for a brother. I could have sloshed around in her for hours but I couldn't. I had to get in and get out before my boy got home and saw me drilling his girl. Even though he was supposed to be out of town, my man Derrick could have been telling Zacariah this to catch her in a compromising situation. And I didn't want to be the situation he caught her with.

That one incident led to several until Zacariah told me she was pregnant with either my or Derrick's baby.

"You're what?" I stared at her in disbelief.

"I'm pregnant and I don't know if the baby is yours or Derrick's."

"I can't believe this. You weren't on birth control pills or something?"

"Yes, but it's not a hundred percent. You act like I got pregnant on purpose. I don't want a baby right now. I'm not even sure if I ever want kids."

"*So what are we going to do? You can't tell Derrick you're pregnant.*"

"*I know this, Jaquon. Derrick wants kids more than anything. If I tell him this and this baby end up being yours, it would kill him. But not before he kills you.*"

"*So what now then?*" I questioned.

"*I think our best option is for me to get an abortion.*"

I never once argued against her getting one either. I was hoping she was going to say that. It was bad enough I slept with her but to get her pregnant on top of that, this had to be some type of double violation. I always told myself I would never let a woman get rid of a child of mine but in this case it was necessary. I knew I didn't want to lose Derrick as my best friend or ruin my relationship with Kea. Hell I didn't want Zacariah to be the mother to any of my kids so this had to be done. It was a choice we both came to easily.

I admit I had some doggish ways but never had I been dumb enough to get another female pregnant. Not until Zacariah. Still, our secret was out in the open, even though it was not in its entirety. I hoped it never came out. Derrick and Kea might think Zacariah told everything there was to tell that night of the cookout but little did they know we both had that secret. I hoped we both would take it to our graves. The pure fact that baby could have been Derrick's would be a good enough reason for him to go over the edge. Killing his baby was the ultimate betrayal. Now we would never know if that child was his or mine.

I thought that's why my hatred for Zacariah grew. She was the one woman who made me cross that line of friendship, and getting pregnant with possibly my child only fueled resentment I had. I knew I couldn't only be mad at her; I had to be mad at me. I should have learned then how karma came back to bite but I kept pushing the limits and ended up losing Derrick and Kea anyway.

Chapter 19

Derrick

I felt a light tap on my shoulder as I stood trying to figure out which blank DVDs I wanted to purchase. I turned to see who was trying to get my attention. I thought it may have been a salesperson until I turned to see it was Jaquon. A smile popped on my face briefly until I remembered what he'd done to me and that's when it dwindled. It had been awhile since I had seen him. The last time I saw him was the night of my cookout.

"What's up, Dee," Jaquon said, holding his hand out to shake mine, but I looked at it, not returning the gesture. Jaquon lowered his hand, saying, "Okay, I see you are still angry with me."

"You think?" I said, turning my attention back to the DVDs.

"Look, man, I have wanted to call you so we can talk about this."

"And tell me what? I thought everything that needed to be said was said the night of my get-together."

"We never got the chance to discuss it," he tried to say sincerely but I wasn't trying to hear it.

"I can't believe you betrayed me like that, Jaquon," I said angrily.

"Derrick, I'm sorry. I've wanted to tell you that but—"

"You were my boy and you played me. Me of all people," I stressed by putting my hand on my chest. "We're like brothers, thick as thieves. How could you do me like that?"

"Derrick, man, please hear me out."

Pointing at him, I said furiously, "I was here for you. Every time you needed me, I was there. You practically lived at my mama's house when we were coming up because you didn't want to go home to your own damn family," I said, thinking about how tough his home life was. He came from a single mother who tried her best to raise him the best way she knew how. In doing so she worked three jobs and was never home. His father left when he was a baby and his grandmother died when he was eight, which was around the time we started hanging out together. So, the only place he had to go was my house. As hard as his mom worked, she still found it hard to keep food on the table. My mom helped by letting him stay with us. Mama even offered for his mother to stay when their lights got cut off one time. They might not have had a lot but he knew he had looks and he played on them all the time. That's why he was the player he was and that same player ended up playing me in the end.

"I know I hurt you, Derrick," Jaquon agreed.

"I helped you move into your new place. I helped you get the job you got now. And let's not forget how I was your alibi when it came to you cheating on your woman. Yet your doggish ways couldn't resist sleeping with mine," I said, hurting at the fact I'd lost my best friend over some ass, some trifling-ass at that. Sure, I could disregard and be his friend again. I could let friendship override betrayal since I found out Zacariah was a skanky trick anyway. But Jaquon destroyed our trust. I wasn't sure if I could get over that.

"Derrick, man, you did all those things for me and I will never forget it. You are my brother, man. Blood doesn't make people family. The fact someone is here regardless of whatever goes on and loves you in spite of is reason enough for me to know you are my family, Dee."

I looked at his genuineness and knew he meant what he was saying, but it couldn't alleviate the sting of it all. He fractured our bond.

"Derrick, it didn't go down like that with me and Zacariah."

"So you saying you never slept with her."

Silence was his answer.

"Like I thought. If penetration was a factor, then so was you corrupting whatever alliance we had."

Jaquon shifted with uneasiness, looking around at the individuals who started to stare at our squabble. I knew my stance had bristled to the point of cage-match status. I had to try to calm down but I was furious. It was at this point I didn't give a damn about these people standing and gawking. Just thinking about Zacariah and Jaquon together sent me into a rage. One fist was balled so tight, my nails embedded themselves into the palm of my hand. Jaquon looked at my demeanor before speaking.

"Derrick, we have been boys forever and—"

"Exactly! That's why you never should have taken it upon yourself to sever that."

"You didn't have a problem returning the favor when you slept with Kea," he snapped. The look on his face told me he wasn't prepared for those words leaving his mouth, but just like Jaquon he did things without thinking about the consequence. And right now I wanted his consequence to be a beat down.

"Derrick, I don't want to argue with you. Nor do I want to fight you," he said, looking at my fist.

"Then we can end this conversation and continue with our day," I said, trying to walk past him. Jaquon grabbed me by my arm, stopping me. I didn't jerk away. I just turned to look at his hand on me. I then looked at him like he had lost his mind.

Jaquon let me go.

Out of the corner of my eye I saw one of the department store employees acting like he was putting some merchandise on the shelves, all the while gaping at us. Then I noticed a little boy who looked to be about eight with blond curly hair with a video game in his hand. He ran to his dad with excitement, saying, "This is the one I wanted, Daddy," holding a Mario game up.

Everything around me was going on like things were great and here I was ready to punch my ex-best friend dead in his face for disrespecting me in more ways than one.

I eyed the skinny, redheaded employee, causing his eyes to shift from me and back to the merchandise he was handling. I thought about asking him what the hell was he looking at but I knew I couldn't take my frustrations out on him.

I told Jaquon, "You are lucky we are in a public place."

"Derrick, I know my actions haven't proven loyalty to you. I am willing to do whatever it takes to get back to where we used to be. Come on. Look at where we are standing. We always came here to purchase the latest games to play, man. We used to play until our eyes burned," he said, punching at me playfully, but I didn't want to buy into it. Jaquon paused to see if I was going to say anything but I looked at him to continue talking.

"You and Kea are the two individuals I want back in my life."

Why in the hell did he go and say that?

"Kea," I blurted. "After all you did to her, you expect her to take you back."

Jaquon looked stunned at my reaction.

"I know I have hurt her but—"

"And now you realize the error of your ways. I tried to tell you that when you were sleeping around on her but you wouldn't listen."

"Man, I know. And I'm trying to get her back. I know she's a good girl."

"Get her back?"

"Yes, I'm trying to get Kea back. Like for her birthday I sent her flowers and cooked her a nice dinner. She wasn't happy at first but she came around. She let me eat dinner with her and we talked without arguing. She even let me stay the night."

"On the couch, no doubt," I said arrogantly.

"Yes, but I was still near her," he said confidently.

I had to wonder if this was his arrogance being rubbed in my face on purpose, showing me he could get her back if he tried. Talk about throwing salt in my wound. Now it was time for me to return the favor. "That's funny. Kea never mentioned being with you when she was with me."

He frowned and asked, "When did you see Kea?"

"I was with her last night. We had some um, things to talk about," I said slyly.

Jaquon grimaced even more at the way I said it but I didn't care. I enjoyed seeing him squirm for a change. It didn't feel good when somebody was messing with his girl, or should I say ex-girl.

"She would be a fool to take you back," I told him.

"Maybe, but I'm not going to stop trying to get her back. I'm hoping you will give me a chance to get our friendship back on track, too. I will do anything to make us right again, man. You are my boy for life. What is it going to take? Just tell me."

Chapter 20

Zacariah

I was getting ticked off at the pudgy blond police officer sitting behind the desk, pretending to be working. Awhile ago she told me to, "Have a seat and someone will be with you shortly." That "shortly" turned into a hell of a long time with thirty-seven minutes passing. I was sitting on this hard bench with my legs crossed, bouncing my foot angrily. Her fellow coworkers walked by, looking at me like I had two heads. Maybe it was my low-cut top revealing cleavage that caught their attention, with my five-inch stiletto heels. A couple of the officers walked by, smiling, never making eye contact with me but with my breasts. No one bothered to stop, yet they were peering down at my breasts like they wanted to nurse them. A "Hi, can I help you?" or "Would you like a donut?" would have been nice but I got none of that. I wished these puppies helped me get some assistance a lot quicker.

I looked over at the three other people waiting with me. One woman was filing her nails, wearing a purple and orange dress. She looked busted. Her hair started to resemble a bird's nest. Her weave should have come out weeks ago. Another was reading her Bible. She seemed like a grandma probably here to bail out her son or grandson. She was an attractive lady with grey hair to her shoulders and it was so pretty. If I ever got grey, I would want my hair to resemble hers. It had so much shine. As good as she looked, the worry in her face was obvious. I almost felt sorry for her. Then there was a man, sitting with his legs crossed better than mine. When I looked at him, he waved like he knew me. I looked around to see if anybody was beside me but this sugar-coated brother was waving at me.

"I like those shoes, girlfriend," he said, pointing at my onyx and grey stilettos with a chrome heel.

"Thank you," I responded.

"Where did you get them from?" he asked.

"To be honest I don't remember. I bought them over a year ago."

"What size are they?" he asked.

"It's a nine."

"Too bad. I wear a thirteen."

I thought even if they were his size, he wasn't going to get my shoes.

"Honey, I was going to buy those babies from you right now. Those shoes are hot to death. They match this outfit I just bought to enter this contest."

"What contest?"

"Child, I'm competing in Ms. Dragalicious honey and I'm going to bring it at the show," he said, twirling his neck and pointing like he knew he was the sexiest diva walking. "I was willing to pay a nice grip for those beauties," he said, looking at my shoes again.

Curious, I asked, "How much grip you talking?"

"At least three hundred. I know they are name brand just by the way you sitting here G'd up in this nasty police station. You look like a sista coming with nothing but the best, honey. You are a fashionista who is rocking it."

Three hundred dollars, I thought. *I know I didn't pay more than a hundred for these shoes, if that.*

I smiled at this compliment and said, "To be honest, I like my labels, but these babies aren't name brand."

"Shut up," he said with his mouth open. "That's even better."

"Now don't get it twisted, I like to look good wherever I go but I don't have to rock names all the time either. If you got it like I do, you can make anything look good," I told him and he snapped his fingers, laughing.

"You go, girl. That's how I get down too. I just wish I could find those shoes in my size," he said.

I wished these shoes were in his size too because I would have taken them off my feet and sold them to him, making a couple hundred off the deal. I always kept a spare pair of shoes in my car so I was good there.

Getting tired of the small talk I decided to find out what was taking so long. Life was short enough without the po-po stealing more of my precious time. I got up off that hard bench, waiting for the feeling to return to my butt cheeks. I walked back up to the same female officer who told me to wait.

"Can I help you?" she asked, looking at me like I was disturbing her.

"Yes, I would appreciate if you would get someone out here to help me."

"Ma'am, please have a seat and someone will be with you shortly."

"Do you not remember my face from earlier?" I said, pointing at my well made-up face. "I heard this same rehearsed speech over fifty-five minutes ago. Just because I'm black don't mean we all look alike," I spat with frustration dripping from my words. My tone got the woman's attention.

"Ma'am, if you have a seat someone will be—"

"I'm not sitting and waiting," I said loudly, causing her brows to rise a bit. "I've been more than patient. Now my tolerance has run out. You call somebody on your little phone and get them out here now," I demanded.

She eyed me like she wanted to come around that desk, handcuff me, and throw my behind in jail for making her day worse than it already was. I hoped she wouldn't try because, as mad as I was, I would get arrested for assaulting an officer.

"I'm sorry for any inconvenience but as you can see, we are busy around here."

"And my time is valuable too. I've been sitting here long enough to see many of you, including yourself, take time out for some damn coffee and some casual conversation. I see you all found time for that. Now if you don't get someone out here now I swear I will complain to the highest authority I can on how unprofessional you people are, including you Officer Reynolds," I said, reading the name on her badge. "Don't think I didn't notice you sneaking and eating donuts.

Do your damn job and get me somebody to talk to before I have your damn job!"

A slight redness came upon her face. A dark-haired, exotic-looking man walked up, wearing black-rimmed glasses, asking her if everything was okay, like he was going to do something. *Now somebody wants to find out what's going on.* I was pissed.

"Everything is fine," she said, squinting her eyes at me.

"Everything is not fine. I've been here waiting for some help. I need to talk to somebody, preferably in the next minute, about my missing friend. I know a missing black woman may not be on your list of priorities, but I would appreciate some assistance, even if it's only to make you all look like you are doing your jobs," I said, tapping my freshly manicured nails on the desktop.

"Go Ms. Thang. You tell them because I have been sitting here just as long waiting on some help but these bastards haven't helped me either," my gay shoe lover said.

I continued to say to the man in the black-rimmed glasses, "And I know I've seen her"—I pointed to the woman behind the desk—"go get two donuts from over there in that box. And she wonders why her behind is spreading."

The dark-haired officer looked at me, Mr. Gay Shoe Lover, and then down at the lady behind the desk. "Ms. . . ." he asked, waiting for my name.

"My name is Zacariah."

"Please step this way and I will see if I can help you," he said, gesturing for me to follow him.

"Can you help me next, Mr. Officer?" Gay Shoe Lover yelled.

Once we were in his private office away from the chaos he told me to have a seat, before closing the door and taking a seat behind his desk covered in files. "How can I help you today?" he asked, shifting papers and closing some folders, making a clear space for him to write.

"I would like to file a missing persons report," I said, looking down to see his name was Detective Wallace.

"And how long has this person been missing?"

"About three weeks now."

"What's her name?"

"Essence Clemmons."

"When was the last time you saw her?"

"I was in the hospital. She was visiting with me after . . ." I blurted, stopping myself from revealing anything about that horrid night. The look he gave me was one of curiosity as to the reason why I was hospitalized, but I didn't go into it.

"I was in the hospital three weeks ago. She visited me that night but I haven't seen or heard from her since."

"And why have you waited so long?"

"I wasn't sure if she was with her boyfriend, or visiting her parents. Once I contacted them and found out neither of them had heard from her I came here."

"Can you give me her description?" he asked.

"I can do better than that," I said, reaching into my purse and then handing him a picture we took eight months ago when we took a trip to the beach. We both were smiling like we hit the lottery. And in a sense we did. The entire vacation was paid for by Derrick. Damn I missed that man something terrible.

Detective Wallace looked at the photo and his expression changed from one of helping to one of distress. I could have sworn his eyes saddened a bit. His once upright shoulders slowly began to slump. He tried to hold his masculine demeanor together but I could tell something was wrong.

"Does she have any distinguishing marks, like a birthmark or tattoo?" he asked.

"Yes. She has a tattoo of half a heart on her right ankle that says 'best.' I have the other half," I said, showing him my half-heart tattoo, which read FRIEND.

"Will you excuse me for a minute?" he asked, getting up from his desk, and I nodded.

Once the door shut behind him, I began to look around the space at the file cabinets probably filled with cases. I also viewed many plaques of accomplishments on the ivory-colored walls this officer had achieved. A large window was to the right, allowing bright sunshine to spill throughout the room. The signature family portrait sat on a small table behind his chair, with him, a woman I assumed was his wife, and seven children. I had to count a second time to make sure I counted correctly and I had. This man didn't play around. If he solved cases like he took time to create so many kids, this case would be solved real soon. Little did I know how right I would be.

Chapter 21

Jaquon

That "anything" I said I would do to get my friendship back with Derrick was the worst thing I could have said, since he came up with the one thing I didn't want to do.

"Anything," Derrick said callously. Derrick's tone was like ice running down my back when he said it. I knew whatever he wanted me to do in order to continue our friendship would be exactly the opposite of what I wanted to do.

When he said, "I want you to stay away from Kea," I thought I would fall out laughing. *Stay away from Kea.* We were boys but not even he could keep me away from getting the love of my life back.

I pondered his suggestion just to make him think I was considering it, but then I told him, "I'm not going to be able to do that."

I didn't know if his ultimatum was due to a brother-sister bond, or him wanting to continue a love affair that he knew could never happen. If he thought things between them could be like they were, he was sicker than I thought. Regardless, it didn't matter because Kea was mine first. He would have to get back with Zacariah because he wasn't getting Kea back. Knowing Zacariah, she had already concocted a plan to make that happen.

"Well then I guess our friendship is a done deal," Derrick said unsympathetically.

"If that's the way you want it," I said, feeling my cell phone vibrate in my pocket. I pulled it out and, lo and behold, it was the devil herself, Zacariah.

Derrick looked at me and then at my cell. He said, "You can get that." He walked away and I answered the phone before it went to voice mail.

"What do you want?" I blurted, not bothering to say hello.

"Jaquon," she called out with her voice cracking.

"Zacariah, why are you calling me?" I tried to whisper, looking back to make sure Derrick wasn't listening. He was at the checkout counter.

"Please. Just let me get this out," she said seriously.

The fact that she said "please," I knew something wasn't right. "Okay, what is it?"

"It's Essence."

"You do know me and Essence are done. That's what you wanted, right?" I asked.

"Shut up, Jaquon, and let me—"

"Don't be telling me to shut up," I retorted.

"Jaquon, she's dead," Zacariah finally yelled.

I paused, thinking I heard her wrong. "She's what?"

"Essence is dead," Zacariah repeated as she cried hysterically into the phone.

"Who told you this? How do you know?"

"The police told me. I went to file a missing persons report because I hadn't seen her since I got out the hospital."

"So she's been gone that long and you just going to file a report?" I said, thinking back to the night I saw Essence with some guy at the bar.

"I thought she might have gone to her parents' house or, at least, was on her way there," she explained.

"Maybe the police got it wrong. How do you know it's her?" I questioned, hoping what she was telling me was a mistake.

"I took a photo of her with me to the station and showed it to the officer, and the next thing I know they were taking me to identify her body," she said, crying. "Jaquon, it was her. It was Essence!"

"Zacariah, you have done some cruel things in your life but this has to be the worst," I said, thinking she was telling me a lie. This had to be another one of Zacariah's sick and twisted ways of getting back at me.

"I'm not lying. For once I wish this was a trick but I swear on my life I'm telling you the truth," she pleaded. "If you don't believe me, go to the station and ask them yourself."

No matter how hard I tried to find an inkling of dishonesty in her voice, I couldn't. Zacariah was speaking through a pain that could only be represented by truth, which in this case was the death of her best friend.

"Where are you?"

"I'm at home. I mean Essence's place."

"Do you want me to come over?" I asked. I never thought I would ever be around Zacariah again, especially if I didn't have to be, but this was under unfortunate circumstances. I felt I had to be there regardless of what we'd been through. Essence would have wanted that.

Zacariah told me to come over and that's what I did. When I walked into Essence's place, Zacariah was in a heap of mourning on the sofa. She was in the fetal position with tissues surrounding her. Her eyes were puffy and her nose was running. I looked at her, feeling sorry for her for the first time ever. Again, this was a feeling I never thought I would have for her. I walked over to the sofa, sitting on the opposite end. It was quiet, too quiet for me.

"You okay?" I asked, thinking that was a dumb question.

She shook her head no. "I can't believe this, Jaquon. I can't believe my best friend is gone," she said with tears trickling down her face. She tried to wipe them before they spilled from her eyes but they were coming too fast.

"I can't get the image of her out of my head. When they pulled that white sheet back, I saw my friend lying on this cold metal table. Her eyes were closed and her skin was grey, looking like she was ashy or something. Her lips were cracked, and hair pushed back from her face. As much as it didn't look like her, it was her. No spirit. No anything."

Zacariah giving a vivid depiction of Essence, whose life had been stolen too soon, was unnerving. I couldn't bring myself to imagine the image she was describing.

"How did she die?" I asked, wondering if this was an appropriate question at this time.

"She was suffocated. They found her body in an alley with her hands duck-taped behind her. Then they put a plastic bag over her head and duck-taped it around her neck. Whoever did this to her then tossed her body out like she was trash," Zacariah said, breaking down again. "The police actually thought she was some hooker. My friend wasn't a hooker. How could they think she was a streetwalker?"

"Well, Zacariah, they did find her in an alley. There are so many women who die a horrible death. And unfortunately she got categorized wrongly."

More tears streamed as she thought about what I said. She asked, "Who would do something like this to her?"

I moved closer to her, wrapping my arms around her. Her feet fell to the floor as her face collapsed into my shoulder. Tears trickled, dampening my shirt.

"She didn't deserve to die like this," Zacariah cried out. She sat up, wiping her nose. She looked at the coffee table and I followed where her eyes went. There was a calendar opened to the month of November, which was two months away. Circled was the week of Thanksgiving.

"We were going to take a trip to Georgia to visit her family. She wanted to surprise them with a long visit. We were going to make it a friend and family time. She was so excited about going but now she can't go," Zacariah said.

"Have you spoken to her mother?"

"I can't bring myself to call her. The last time I spoke to her, Jaquon, I told Mrs. Clemmons Essence may be on her way to surprise her. I couldn't think of anything else to tell her. And I really thought maybe Essence was on her way there. I thought with everything that went down, she wanted to get away, pushing her time to visit with her family sooner than waiting until November. Oh how I wish she was visiting with them instead of being . . . being dead," Zacariah said, bursting into tears again.

"Someone has to call them, Zacariah," I said.

"I gave the officer her mother's number so they could contact her. I couldn't do it. I didn't want to be the one to have to tell them that their child has been murdered."

"But don't you think you can bring them some joy in knowing Essence was planning this surprise for them?"

Zacariah nodded, picking up the calendar. She brushed her fingers over the writing of Essence and then brought it to her chest. She shook her head and began to cry again.

"I'll call her but I can't right now. I need some time."

The both of us lay back on the sofa, taking in the space decorated by Essence. This was her home, which she put her heart and soul into. Pictures of her family and friends anchored a room encompassing her very spirit. It was now I realized the gravity of this situation. Essence was no longer a part of us and it was in this moment I knew I would never see her smiling face again. Yes, I hurt her and maybe even used her at some point, but there was a time I came to like her a lot. That's why I kept going back to her.

The night I saw her in that restaurant I should have pulled her out of there. I left the club without so much as a good-bye, leaving her vulnerable to whomever did this to her. I felt guilty now because I thought there was a possibility I could have changed this outcome. I could have changed her fate but now I would never know since she was gone.

Chapter 22

Zacariah

When I woke up I saw that Jaquon was gone. I guessed my state of sorrow sent me into a deep sleep. He was nice enough to put a blanket over me before leaving. I sat up and realized the reason why I woke up was due to a knock at my door. I swore I didn't feel like answering it. So I screamed, "Go away."

The person knocked again, causing me to get angry. Did they know I found out I lost my best friend today? When I got to the door, I whipped it open, saying, "Didn't I tell you to go . . ."

It was Fabian standing there dressed very nicely and holding one rose. He was smiling but I wasn't. Once he saw I wasn't exactly dressed, the smile left his face. For some reason tears entered my eyes again and began to run down my cheeks. Fabian pushed his way in, closing the door behind him, and walked me back over to the sofa.

"I'm sorry. I forgot about our dinner," I said sadly.

"It's okay. What's wrong, Zacariah?"

It took me a minute to talk. I felt embarrassed for crying in front of Fabian but the stress of losing Essence was causing my throat to feel like it was closing as I tried to hold back my emotions. I knew in order for my throat to open, I had to release this grief that was taking over me. I began to weep again. I wondered if this weeping would ever stop along with the pain I felt.

Fabian grabbed me and held me in his arms. He didn't bother to ask me anything else. He leaned back on the sofa and pulled me into his embrace. I had gone from lying with Jaquon to now lying with Fabian and I didn't even care. It felt good to have someone to be with even if that someone wasn't Derrick.

"I'm sorry," I said again.

"Stop apologizing. Whatever is going on has to be serious for you to be in this state."

More tears streamed because it was definitely something bad.

"You don't have to tell me if you don't want to. I'm here for you. I can stay with you or I can leave if you want to be alone."

I shook my head, saying, "I want you to stay."

He stroked my arm, saying, "Okay."

"And I want to tell you why I'm upset. I just can't get it out," I said sorrowfully.

"It's okay. Tell me when you are ready."

I sat up from his embrace and took in a deep breath. I felt my throat open up slightly. Now here was my chance to say what I had been trying to say.

"I found out today my best friend was murdered."

"What?" he asked, shocked, like he knew her. "I'm so sorry."

"It's still raw you know."

"Of course it is. It's going to be that way for some time. I know exactly how you feel."

"You do?" I asked, wondering what he meant by that.

"I wish I didn't. I lost my best friend two years ago. Call it him being in the wrong place at the wrong time."

"For real?"

He nodded, saying, "We were at this house party having ourselves a good time and he went outside to get some fresh air. He was standing on the front porch with some other people when a guy just walked up and started blasting."

"Are you serious?"

"Yep. The gunman was a jealous boyfriend after his girlfriend and her new man. Evidently he couldn't take it anymore and thought it was best that if he couldn't have her no one could. My friend took a bullet in the neck, which severed his carotid artery. When I got outside to see what had happened, my friend was lying on the porch. I've never seen so much blood in my life. That man ended up killing my friend, his ex, her new boyfriend, and two other individuals that night."

The charismatic, cocky Fabian who walked through my door was now an emotional, subdued man. His heartache was visible, as if the incident happened days ago.

"I'm so sorry for your loss. Did they catch the guy who did this?" I asked him.

"Oh they caught him. After he shot up the porch, he ended up shooting himself in the head," Fabian said.

"He took the coward's way out."

"I know, right?"

"Did you ever think you would get over the pain of losing your friend?" I asked.

"In the beginning, no. My best friend died in front of me. For a long time I kept picturing him lying on that porch with his eyes wide open, struggling to take his next breath. I knelt down to him and gripped his neck, trying to stop the bleeding. He grabbed me, looking at me like, 'please, help me.' But it was nothing I could do. I yelled for someone to call the ambulance. At that time I hadn't noticed the others who were shot. I just saw my boy. I remember his last couple of breaths the most. He died in my arms and it has freaked me out for a long time."

"I keep seeing Essence lying on that metal table. I almost wish I never identified her. I think it was better to remember her the way she was and not grey and lifeless."

"I wish I could say the road is going to be easy. Those images never leave you but you can change those views. Look at a picture of your friend every night before you close your eyes. Think about you all's happier times and I promise with each day that goes by it will get easier to deal with your pain."

"Right now I don't even think a picture of her would work. I'm so tired of crying. I know looking at her picture would cause me to weep even more."

"And do that. You have to grieve. Tears are natural. Even in my grown-man status I cried like a baby over losing my friend. And I didn't feel less than a man about doing so either," he said, smiling.

"I'm glad you are here with me. I know this wasn't what you had in mind when you planned our date," I said.

"Things happen. We can't control things. I'm happy to be here for you. And it's not like we still can't eat dinner. Have you eaten anything today?" Fabian asked.

I thought about it and realized I hadn't so I shook my head.

"Okay, I'm going to go pick up our dinner," he said, sitting up.

"You don't have to do that."

"But I want to. Besides, I'm starving," Fabian said, standing to his feet.

"Where are you going?"

"Let me surprise you."

I didn't have the energy to argue with him about it. I said, "Okay," and watched as Fabian went out the door trying to fulfill our dinner date anyway.

Chapter 23

Kea

I received another dozen roses from Jaquon with a card that read:

> To Kea, the woman I love with all my heart. I will send you flowers every day if I have to if that means getting you back into my life. You mean everything to me and I don't want to lose you. I love you. Jaquon.

I had to smile at the thought. He was definitely trying really hard to get me back. I knew that sounded crazy but the cocky Jaquon living with me weeks back was not the man sending me these flowers today. He was making it hard for me to forget about him. And it didn't help I still loved him.

I set the vase filled with the flowers down on the coffee table when I heard my cell phone ring.

I ran to my room to retrieve it from my tote. I searched the massive bag and couldn't get to my phone before it stopped ringing. The disadvantage of carrying a large bag was it took you forever to find what you were looking for. Finally finding my cell, I saw I had one missed call and a voice mail message.

I dialed in, and heard, "Hi, this message is for Kea Fields. I am calling from DNA Solution Center in regard to setting up another appointment for you to have your test done again. Please give me a call at 555-7171. Thank you and have a nice day."

Just when I thought my day of guilt couldn't get any worse, the nurse from the clinic called to remind me of Derrick being my brother. I sank down on the bed and reeled. How could I have allowed myself to be taken by him again knowing the information revealed to us was that we were kin? I slept with Derrick, my blood. In the heat of passion I didn't care. Was I bad? Was I trifling? What in the world would our parents say if they found out we were still intimate? Hell, what would people say? I didn't want any finger-pointing, saying we were committing incest. No one likes to be ridiculed and certainly not for what me and Derrick had going on.

I was supposed to see Derrick again today. Not for sex but to go back to the DNA center to let them know we were going somewhere else to have another test done. I knew it was easier to tell them this over the phone but Derrick suggested it was a good idea for us to do this in person so we could see if it was anybody we recognized. When we were there before, we were too caught up in everything to pay attention to anything. I thought a man could have run up in the center with a bomb strapped to his chest and we would have stood there, wondering what he was about to do. That's how emotional this situation was and had been. We'd been too blind to see anything lately.

I arrived ten minutes early and stood outside the facility, waiting for Derrick. I thought this was my way of preparing myself to be able to deal with him. But as soon as he turned the corner in his suit, I almost melted. The sight of him enticed me and guilt infiltrated me all at the same time. I hated these feelings I had for him and tried to control my urges, which were about to take me into an erotic state.

"What's up, Kea," he said, reaching out to hug me, and I stiffened when he embraced me. He smelled so damn good. My body wanted to mesh with his but common sense was telling me

I could never be this close to him again, even in the form of a hug. I guessed in my state of rationalizing everything, I forgot to speak back. Derrick withdrew from me, asking, "Are you okay?"

"Yeah. I'm cool," I stammered.

"It seems like something is wrong."

"Just nervous about this, that's all."

Derrick looked at me suspiciously. I thought he knew I was talking a bunch of BS but he let it go.

Trying to be myself again, I said, "You look nice."

He looked down at his attire and said, "Thanks. I'm finally getting back in the swing of things with my job. Work keeps my mind off of all this drama going on in my life now."

I nodded, still feeling nervous.

"Well, you ready to do this?" he asked in anticipation.

I nodded and he held his hand out for me to go first and we headed into the office. When we entered, the kind woman who helped us before was there to greet us.

"Hey, you guys, how are you?" she asked happily.

"We're okay," I responded, not saying it believably.

"Did you all come to set up another appointment?"

"Yes and no," Derrick said.

The woman looked puzzled.

"What I meant by that is we do want another test done. But we have decided to get a second opinion from another facility."

"You know we would love to assist you again. I hope it wasn't anything you thought we did wrong," she said sincerely.

"No, you guys were great and it's nothing against your office. We feel more comfortable going with another facility," Derrick said again.

"Is there anything I can do to change your mind? We can have another person retrieve and process you if you like."

Ms. Kind Lady is turning into Ms. Persistent, I thought.

"Again, you all were great but we just wanted to come together to tell you this. I know one of us could have just as well picked up the phone and done the same but we thought it was best to let you know in person," Derrick struggled to say. "Plus we wanted to thank you for what you have done."

"I appreciate this. Do you know which facility you are going with?"

"Yes, my mother found a place that's going to do it. We've scheduled the appointment already."

"And where is that?" she asked unrelentingly.

"I can't remember the name right offhand," Derrick said, playing it off really cool.

"Well I hope you get the results you are looking for. Our staff is good at what they do. I hate that you have decided to go elsewhere," she said, giving a phony smile. It was obvious she wasn't happy about out decision. What reason would she have to be upset anyway? She did her job, or did she? This didn't make any sense to me.

On our way back to our vehicles, I asked Derrick, "Did you think that was a little pushy?"

"I did. She kept on like she wished we would change our minds."

"Besides here, have you seen her or anyone else for that matter outside this place?" I asked. "Because I haven't."

"Not really, but that woman seems familiar to me. I can't place where I think I've seen her but hopefully it will come to me soon."

"I'm glad we got this done and out of the way."

"Now the two of us can grab a bite to eat," Derrick said.

"I'm sorry but I have something else to do."

"What's more important than me?" Derrick asked.

"My daddy," I retorted.

He held his hands up in surrender. "Dad comes first," he said, grinning. "So when do you think we can get together again?"

Uncertainty seized me. "I'm not sure. I don't know if it's a good idea for us to be around each other."

"Why? Is it because of what happened between us the other night?"

"Yes, you can say that."

"Do you regret it?" he asked.

"Yes. No. Yes." I twisted in confusion. "Derrick, what happened the other night cannot happen again."

"Are you saying this because you are thinking about taking Jaquon back?"

"Whoa! Where did that come from?" I asked, wishing Derrick would stop coming at me with all these complicated questions.

"I saw him in the video store the other day and he didn't hesitate to tell me how you two are getting back together."

"He said that?" I asked in amazement.

"In so many words, yes."

"Derrick, we are not back together."

"He seems to think so."

"I have nothing to do with Jaquon's thoughts. He's a grown man," I explained.

"When was the last time you saw him?"

"On my birthday. He sent me flowers and cooked me dinner."

"Did he spend the night?"

I didn't like this line of questioning and I could tell Derrick didn't like asking them. Those two had to get into a deep conversation and knowing the both of them, it couldn't have gone well. I knew Jaquon. He probably went into details letting Derrick know his chances were great. And to be honest, maybe they were. Especially since Derrick and I couldn't go any further until we got this second set of results. But I was not about to put my life on hold to see.

"What's wrong with you, Kea? It's that easy to get back with you? All he has to do is buy flowers and cook dinner to get back in good graces with you?" he asked angrily.

"Don't talk to me like that, Derrick," I said, perturbed.

"You need to open your eyes and see he's not good enough for you."

"Am I not supposed to be flattered he's trying to get me back? Because I am. I find it kind of cute."

"You shouldn't. The brother did cheat on you constantly."

"And if I recall, you supplied his alibi. What does that say about you?" I retorted.

Derrick shifted uneasily.

"Don't go condemning Jaquon when you were an accomplice to his wrongdoing. And let's not forget about the fact that you forgot to tell me he also slept with Zacariah."

"I didn't tell you because I knew it would hurt you," he said angrily.

"Hurt me. Derrick, I was already hurt. Don't you think that was information I needed to know? But I guess it was bros over hoes, huh."

"Don't be stupid, Kea. He's just going to hurt you again."

"Stupid. You calling me stupid," I said heatedly.

"Yes, if you are thinking about taking him back. Yes, I'm calling you stupid."

"You know what? I'm not doing this here with you," I said, throwing my hands up. We were on the sidewalk. Individuals were noticing our squabble. "I'm going to meet my dad," I said, walking past him to my car.

Following me, Derrick said, "You know you are all I think about, Kea."

I paused, turning to him. "Where do you expect for this to go?" I asked, pointing at him and me. "We cannot have a relationship."

"Yes, we can, baby," he said, walking up to me. He draped his arms around my waist. "I love you so much and it kills me that I can't have you and he can."

Pushing him away I said, "Hear me loud and clear, Derrick. We will never be together again as long as I know we are siblings. I'm tired of beating myself up for having feelings for a man I know I can't have. You are constantly on my mind and seeing you only complicates things for me."

"That's because you love me too."

"That may be the case but I can't be with my brother."

Those words caused Derrick's face to contort into a fractured soul. He said, "The results were wrong. I know it," he said confidently.

"And until it's proven, I can't be with you anymore. Not even as your sister. So please stay away from me," I said remorsefully.

"Is that why you are thinking about going back to Jaquon, so you can use him to forget about me?"

"If that's what it takes, then yes," I said regretfully. "My life must go on, Derrick. Maybe you should considering doing the same."

He was speechless now and shock was present on his face. I hated what I was saying to him but I knew it had to be said. I had to cut my ties or I would fall back into bed with him again and that couldn't happen. There were too many emotions building within me and seeing him only intensified my love for him. I needed to sort through them without him being around me. If he was right and we were not siblings then we could see where our relationship took us. But until then we had to go on with our lives and leave each other alone.

Chapter 24

Derrick

We had never argued before and it didn't feel good to do it now. I could not believe she was thinking about taking him back. We were so close to getting what we wanted but she was going to allow him to come in and ruin things before we had a chance to hash things out. I was so frustrated. I woke up excited about my day for the first time in a long while, only for it to end with the possibility of me never getting her back and losing her to Jaquon. *Should I listen to her? Should I go on with my life and move on to the next one?*

The smell of her herbal scents escaped her sanctuary as I waited for the door to swing open. This was unlike me to drop by unannounced but I needed to see her. My morning had started out rough and caused a domino effect on the rest of my day. It could be that my mood wouldn't allow me to enjoy the sunny day that awaited me but my happiness was eclipsed by Kea.

I knocked again since no one answered, and I was surprised that when the door opened, I was greeted by a man.

"Can I help you?" he asked somewhat rudely.

I looked around to see if I had the right place and came to the conclusion that I wasn't sure. With one fist clasped I said, "I think I may have the wrong place."

"Who are you looking for?" the man asked and I was unsure if I should say her name. Maybe this was her boyfriend. Not really caring, I told him.

"I was looking for Trinity." I knew I told her I didn't want to do names but on my way out from being with her the last time, I saw some mail on the table. My curiosity got the best of me and I saw that her name was Trinity Gordon. I thought, *what a perfect fit for such a unique woman.*

"She lives here," the guy said audaciously and not budging. I stood there in silence wondering if the six-foot-five giant was going to let me in, but he just stood there. Was he dense? Did he know to let me in or go get her for me? Was she even here? What?

I raised my eyebrow, hinting to him "what's next" but he never budged, gritting on me. My inner cockiness emerged. I bristled up, thinking who this punk thought he was thinking he could attempt to scare me? Fear was not in my vocab, especially when it came to another man. As much aggression as I had to relieve, I wanted to fight. All he had to do was jump wrong and it would be on.

Breaking the stare down I asked, "Okay, is she here?" pushing the conversation further. If this was her man we were already busted, so why walk away like I didn't know her? It was clear he was upset I was standing at the door but it was something he had to deal with, just as long as he didn't come at me stupid. I hoped he knew better. At this point I didn't care. I had already summed this dude up to the type who battled so I knew I had to bring my forcefulness forward also.

Right then Trinity came around the big, burly man. "Steven, I know you are not trying to intimidate my guest," she said, punching the man in the chest playfully. "Come in, Derrick," she said cheerfully. "I hope you weren't out there long."

I walked in, still watching the man who was eyeing me like he wanted to rip my head off.

Looking into Ms. Bohemian's face made the situation worth it. Dressed in some ripped jeans, a white tank top, and those wooden bracelets, with her hair pulled back from her face by a white wrap, she looked striking.

"Please excuse my brother's manners. I don't know where he gets his impoliteness from but Mama didn't raise us like this," she said, trying to lighten the air which was filled with two men's testosterone reaching peaks to clash if need be. Just the fact that she said he was her brother made me breathe a sigh of relief. I understood the nature of his threatening position now. He was a brother trying to protect his sister and I had to admire that. I knew if I had a sister, I would react the same way. *And come to think about it, I do have a sister, Kea, or that's what the test proved.*

"Steven, this is Derrick. Derrick, Steven," she said, introducing us.

"Nice to meet you," I said, not bothering to extend my hand to shake his.

"Likewise," he said unconvincingly.

"I'm sorry to just stop by like this," I said. "I would have called but I didn't have your number."

"It's not a problem," Trinity said. "We were about to sit down and eat some dinner. Would you like to join us?" she asked in this happy-go-lucky manner that made me feel right at home.

I looked at her brother, who looked none too happy at her invite, so I said, "I don't want to intrude."

"Come on, Derrick. I have more than enough. I made some chicken breast with a basil and garlic cream sauce, which I'm serving over pasta with a side of seasoned asparagus," she said, trying to convince me to stay. Really she didn't have to say anything because the smell of the food was alluring.

"Please stay. I really do have enough. Don't let my bully of a brother deter you," she said, swinging at him playfully again. "He's a big teddy bear underneath all those muscles."

And boy did he have muscles. Looked like he lifted houses for a living. His arms and shoulders were so big it looked like he walked intentionally pushing his shoulders to his ears. Dude was huge. He could play the black Incredible Hulk. Standing about six foot five I knew he had to weigh a good 300 pounds and it was all muscle. I wanted to ask him if he competed in those weightlifting competitions but I didn't want to offend him.

I ended up staying and dinner was great. In the beginning it was a little awkward with her brother trying to interrogate me.

"So where did you meet my sister?" he asked, stabbing at his food.

"I met her at a bar."

"Were you there to pick up women?" he asked, slicing at his chicken and tossing it into his mouth.

"Steven, don't be rude," Trinity said.

"I'm trying to figure out what this man's intention is with you."

"How do you know I'm not the one with the intention?" Trinity retorted.

"You know how I am, Trinity. I'm just looking out for you."

"I'm a big girl who can take care of herself," she said. The phone rang and Trinity excused herself from the table, giving her brother the evil eye to leave me alone. Once she was out of the room, he began speaking again.

"Derrick, right?" he asked.

"Yep."

"I love my sister and I'm going to always be here to protect her."

"I wouldn't expect anything less," I commented.

"She's special to me and I stay in her life because"—he paused, looking at the doorway Trinity exited through, before continuing to speak— "I'm involved because Trinity has some issues and I need to be here to look after her."

He said "issues" like she had something more serious than the problems we have in everyday life. Hell, I had issues. But I didn't comment, and continued to listen.

"She's been through a lot. I don't want anyone to hurt her in any way. If you are not serious about being with her then you need to leave her alone. I don't think Trinity is strong enough to deal with another heartache."

"I understand," I said, not knowing what else to say. Trinity and I were just friends at this point. She knew I was serious about another woman so right now we didn't have anything serious going on. I didn't think her brother needed to know all the details so I decided to keep that to myself.

"I don't ever want to see Trinity go down the rocky road she's already traveled. It was not pretty. It has taken her a long time to get back to this normal state."

Normal state. There he went again hinting around like something wasn't right. I wanted to ask what he meant by that, but Trinity came walking back into the kitchen. She was smiling and I couldn't help but think, *this beautiful woman couldn't have anything wrong with her, could she?*

"Who was that?" her brother asked.

"Some guy trying to offer me a credit card. I can't stand these telemarketers calling with all these bogus offers to get me in debt. If I wanted a credit card then I would go get one."

The rest of dinner went on without a hitch. I guessed Steven got what he wanted from me and told me what I needed to know. I was still a little curious as to what he meant by normal but I left it alone. He seemed to loosen up a bit. The rest of the conversation pertained to sports, politics, and reality shows.

Once it was time to clear the table, both I and her brother Steven jumped at the duty with the reasoning being, "It's the least I can do after such a wonderful dinner."

Steven backed off once he saw I offered too. He let me do the honors while he escorted his sister out of my presence to the next room. It didn't take me any time to get everything cleared away. Once every dish was loaded into the dishwasher, my job was basically done. All I had to do was wipe down the table, stove, and counters and it was a wrap.

When I entered the living room, I saw Steven wasn't there. She could tell by me looking around that I was searching for him.

"He had to leave," she said, sitting in the Indian position on her sofa.

"And he left without saying good-bye," I said, walking over to sit next to her. She laughed. "I guess I made a wrong impression on him, huh."

"Sort of. Stopping by unannounced is what threw him off. And it didn't help that I never mentioned you to him before. My brother and I are very close. I usually tell him everything. So seeing you standing at my door stunned him."

I didn't know whether to take that as an insult or her just being cautious. I mean we did only have one night together and that was also on the basis of us not knowing each other's names. Speaking of names I asked, "How did you know my name?"

She smiled and said, "When we left the bar the other night together, the bartender said your name."

I thought back and couldn't remember. Then it hit me. When I passed the bar with Trinity in front of me, my man Boe, who owns the place said, "Take care, Derrick." I smiled at the memory and looked at Trinity, thinking how observant she was.

"You acted like you didn't know my name that entire night but you acknowledge me today."

"I couldn't introduce you to my brother as the man whose name I didn't know. He had to know we were together somehow because you knew where I lived. Not saying your name would have sent my brother over the edge," she said, laughing. "You are sitting there acting innocent. I can't recall ever telling you my name."

She had me there and I felt embarrassed. I explained how I found out what her name was.

"That's pretty slick for a man who didn't want to make things official," she said, placing her hand on my knee, showing me her beautiful smile. "So what brings you by? I knew you had to be going through something in order for you to come by like this."

My entire time here I didn't once think about Kea. That was until now.

"This is about her again, isn't it?" she asked.

"Yes. We had a big fight today and it got to me."

"Does this woman not want to have anything to do with you?"

I nodded again, wondering how this woman could read me so well.

"It's her loss," Trinity said sincerely.

"It's more complicated than that. She wants to be with me too but she feels like we can't."

"She loves you, doesn't she?"

"Yes, and I love her."

"Is she involved with someone else?"

"Not really," I said.

"Then what's the issue?"

I looked at her, wondering if I should spill my drama on to her. Her eyes were so calming and welcoming as they made me settle into a comforted state of mind. My spirit led me to release the agony I had been going through.

"We are siblings," I said, not realizing how outlandish it sounded. Her expression never changed. I was expecting her to gasp or leap across the room in disgust but she just smiled. Her eyes accompanied by a smile made me want to explain further and I told her everything that transpired over the past few weeks. From our partners cheating on us to Kea being my best friend's girl. To how we got together one night after I kicked my longtime girlfriend Zacariah out, to us sneaking and getting caught. To getting ousted by my ex Zacariah in front of a crowd as she informed Kea and me we were brother and sister. To the death of the man I knew nothing about but was supposed to have fathered Kea and me. To the results ending a love I wanted to continue.

Trinity listened intently, never once interrupting me as my past soap opera inundated her serene world. A couple of times she gripped my hand, consoling me. Once my mouth stopped moving and no more words could be spoken, we both stared at one another. I wondered what she was thinking.

"Sounds like you have been through a lot," she said.

"That's an understatement."

"You will be guided in the right direction. Don't give up so easily. True love usually happens once in a lifetime and I don't think fate would interfere with the love you all have. I think it's more there. You just have to be patient and wait on it to reveal itself."

"But how long am I supposed to wait?"

"However long it takes. And don't get upset with Kea because she's protecting her heart. Remember we were not raised to procreate with a sibling. She's trying to stick to that belief."

"I appreciate you listening. And I appreciate all you have done for me. You are a good woman and I don't want you to get hurt by my problems. I don't want you to think I'm one of those brothers who only come over to hit it and quit it because that's not me."

"Derrick, I knew that the first night I met you. You didn't come across as a playa and I liked that about you. That's what drew me to you. That and the fact that you are so damn cute."

I smiled.

"I also saw your pain and I was more than happy to make you forget about it for just a little while," she said, gripping my hand again.

"You know I usually don't get down like that."

"Really?" she said, asking in a joking way.

"I don't. I'm a one-woman kind of man. I don't do one-night stands. I'm still trying to figure out where you came from."

"Well I was born . . ." she started explaining jokingly, but she knew what I meant.

"You are a phenomenal woman."

"I know," she said, causing both of us to laugh again.

"And you can let your brother know I'm not out to hurt you. I'm coming correct because I have that much respect for you."

"My brother doesn't have anything to do with me. If being with you is what I want, he can't stop that."

"I wish I met you before all of this happened," I said, looking at her earnestly.

"It would be a lot easier wouldn't it?" she said, leaning on the back of the sofa with her head leaned against her hand.

I nodded, saying, "I don't want you to get your hopes up about us. I can't turn my feelings for Kea off just like that," realizing I didn't say it quite the way I wanted.

"I understand, Derrick. You don't have to keep explaining. Maybe in another lifetime fate will guide us to one another."

"I hope so," I said.

"But until then I'm still here for you. The cards have been laid out for the both of us. And I tell you what," she said, reaching into the drawer of her coffee table, pulling out a deck of cards. "Let's take it back to the old school," she said, pulling a box of Uno cards out.

I smiled, saying, "Do you know I'm the champion at this?"

"Well I guess I'm getting ready to take your title," she said, shuffling the cards as I scooted back to give us room to play on the sofa.

"Bring it on then," I said, looking into the eyes of an angel. I did wish I met her months before my world got turned upside down. Then I wouldn't have to worry about going through the drama that would fill my days to come.

Chapter 25

Zacariah

The ride back from Savannah, Georgia was a quiet one. I was happy I didn't have to drive as I dozed in and out of sleep. Jaquon was speeding down the highway, heading for home, as I took in the scenery, thinking about Essence and how her funeral was the last time I would ever see her face again. I could still hear Essence's mother break down when they closed the casket, symbolizing the last time anyone would ever see her again. Yes, we had pictures and memories to remember her by but it wasn't the same as having her here with us.

Then my thoughts led me to think about Fabian. Suddenly I found myself smiling a bit at the thought of him and how he took care of me during my time of grief. When he came back that night of our dinner date, he brought back so many different dishes for me to choose from

that if I didn't come out the house for a week,
I still would have had enough food to last me
for a while. He even thought to pick up some
champagne, which helped alleviate some pain
behind Essence's death. We sat and watched TV
and talked and ate. We had such a good time. I
never thought I would have a good time with no
other man besides Derrick. Hell, Derrick didn't
even cross my mind when I was with Fabian and
I found that to be good for a change.

"Are you okay?" Jaquon asked, looking over at
me and then back at the road.

"Not really. I knew this was going to be hard
but not this hard, you know."

"I understand. I don't do funerals. I didn't go
to see my uncle who passed away years ago so
that should tell you something."

"It tells me you are a punk."

"I'm not a punk," Jaquon blurted.

I giggled, saying, "I'm just playing, boy.
I appreciate you going with me. It meant a lot. I
know we don't get along but for once we made a
weekend work."

"We did, didn't we?" he asked.

"Is the truce over once we get back home?" I
asked.

"You know it is. You can't ever let things go,"
he said.

"Me," I shrieked.

"Yeah, you. You are always causing drama with people," he said, passing this big rig.

"People should learn to mind their own damn business and leave me the hell alone."

"Zacariah, this world does not revolve around you."

"Yes, it does, and I'm going to make sure it does."

"How's that working for you? You couldn't control Essence dying. You couldn't control getting beat down by Kea. And you couldn't control Derrick not leaving you," Jaquon said.

I turned to Jaquon and wanted to smack him but I didn't since he was merging in front of the massive truck. I wasn't trying to cause a wreck.

"You want to hit me now don't you?" he said.

"Yes."

"The truth hurts, huh."

"Jaquon, can you please shut up the rest of the way home? Because I don't feel like hearing anything from somebody who can't keep his dick in his pants."

"You didn't mind when my dick was in you," he retorted.

I reached over and smacked him in the face anyway. The car swerved a bit but Jaquon managed to keep it in the lane. To my surprise he reached over and punched me in the arm.

"Keep your hands to yourself, Zacariah. I will pull this car over, push you out, and leave you to walk back to Virginia."

I stopped. Only because I was tired and wanted to get in my bed and get a good night's sleep.

About twenty minutes later I asked, "Would you have left me on the side of the road?"

"Yes."

"You would have left a defenseless woman—"

"Defenseless," Jaquon said, cutting me off. "Nobody would mess with you. The way your mouth runs would make the assailant run for his life."

"Funny."

"I'm serious. You are a beast."

"Why you got to be calling me a beast?" I asked.

"I mean that to say whoever messes with you is going to catch hell."

I paused again before asking, "Do you think Derrick will ever take me back?"

Jaquon sighed, saying, "Honestly I don't think he will. You've done your dirt way too many times for Derrick to look past that. I mean come on, would you take him back if he did all the things you did to him?"

"I may," I said, unsure.

"No is more like it. Then on top of that, Zacariah, you turned around and put his life on blast in front of a crowd of people. That has pretty much severed your ties to him forever, along with sleeping with me."

I heard what Jaquon was saying but I didn't want to believe that to be the case. Derrick loved me once and I knew he would love me again. It may take some time for us to get back to where our love was but I believed we could love again. After meeting Fabian I had to wonder if I wanted Derrick's love anymore.

"Zacariah," Jaquon said, snapping me out of my thoughts. "You need to start being nice to people and learn how to tell the truth. Stop all that conniving you be doing because it's only going to come back and bite you in the long run."

"So right now you are being completely honest with Kea. You are not lying and scheming."

"My lies only hurt her and I don't want to do that to her anymore."

"So you told her you were going out of town with me to attend the funeral of the girl you cheated on her with?" I questioned, knowing I was sitting beside the same trifling Jaquon.

"I didn't lie when I told her I was going out of town."

"You just avoided what would make her mad by telling her parts."

"You can say that."

"Sounds like scheming to me. What makes you think she won't find out about our trip?" I asked.

"The only person who could tell her is you," he said, glancing over at me.

I smiled devilishly.

"And you wouldn't do that, would you?" he asked.

"Not conniving Zacariah," I said lightheartedly.

"Why would you even want to? What has Kea ever done to you?"

"Have you been paying attention? Duh, she slept with my man, your best friend, and had the nerve to put her hands on me," I said, getting heated.

"Still, it didn't start with them, Zacariah. We did our dirt first. We got it back. What come around goes around," he explained.

"True but that's not helping me get over her ruining my life. I promise you she will never have Derrick again."

Jaquon looked at me and back at the road and then at me again. "Zacariah, what have you done?"

"Nothing," I said, never looking in his direction.

"You've done something."

"So what if I have? Do you want Kea to be with Derrick?"

Jaquon didn't say anything, letting the silence be his answer.

"We want the same thing. Neither of us want to see them two together because we want them back. You do still want Kea don't you?" I asked.

"Yes, but at what cost?"

"We've changed but we haven't fully embraced the honest way of life. Let me do what I'm doing and you do you," I suggested.

"I'm going to say this and then I'm going to be quiet. Your scheming is not going to work. Whatever you have done will come back to bite you. Take it from me. Life is too short for games. Look at where games got Essence."

My attention was drawn back to looking at the trees and miles of highway moving us closer to home as I absorbed his words. Not wanting to hear anymore I turned the volume up on the radio, which was playing "Thin Line Between Love and Hate." *How ironic,* I thought. There was that thin line and I had been standing on both sides of it. So was Derrick. I needed to erase the line so we could reconnect again. I hoped my plan worked, but where would that leave me and Fabian?

Chapter 26

Zacariah

The phone was ringing off the hook and I was ticked off because I was trying to get some sleep after a seven-hour ride from Savannah. Looking at the caller ID, I saw it was my cousin calling. I wondered what she wanted and at this point I didn't care. I was tired. My eyes were not ready to open and my body screamed "stay put" as stiff muscles screamed for relaxation. I turned to my back and placed the pillow over my face to fall back to sleep.

Once I willed myself up after sleeping for another four hours, I searched for my cell, finding it on the kitchen table. I saw I had seven missed calls and my voice mail box was up. Debating, I put the cell down. I was going to check it later. First, I had to get me something to eat before

gathering up Essence's clothing to send to her
mother. If I didn't do this now, I was never going
to do it. I told her mother I would send all her
personal items like pictures, jewelry, and some
childhood things Essence had. There was also
the issue with her clothes, furniture, and house I
had been staying in rent free for weeks now. Her
parents decided to sell the house but they were
giving me two months to find my own place,
which I thought was nice of them because they
could have kicked me out on my behind. Hopefully by then, I would be living back under the
same roof with Derrick.

They told me I could have Essence's furniture,
which shocked me. Most families fought over
things like this but they said they didn't have the
room for it since they had just remodeled their
own home. They told me I was more family to
Essence than some who were actually blood related so I could have it. They also told me I could
have her clothes. The only thing about that was
Essence was a lot smaller than me. I could wear
a couple of her jogging outfits but that was it. I
had more tits and ass than she did. We did wear
the same size shoes so I decided to keep them
but all the other things had to be shipped to her

family. I told them I would get the house ready to be sold. When I left this place would be empty, and the memories Essence and I had here would be gone, too.

Packing up about twelve boxes, most of which were items I would be taking with me, I set them in the living room. Exhausted, I decided to go back to sleep since I hadn't fully recouped yet from the long trip. Then I remembered to check my voice mail messages. Dialing, I heard I had four messages.

First message: "Hey, Zacariah. This is Fabian. Just calling to check and see how you were doing. I had a good time with you the other night and I hope there are more of those to come. Give me a call when you get a chance. I left my number on your fridge. Hope to hear from you soon. Later."

Hearing his voice soothed me and I found a part of me liking Fabian more and more. I didn't know if this was a good thing since I was still trying to get Derrick to take me back. I guessed time would tell.

Second message: "Zacariah, this is Susan. I think we have a problem. Call me when you get this."

Third message: "Zacariah, it's me again. Where are you? Call me back."

The other voice mail messages were the click of a phone hanging up, not leaving anything.

I called Susan and, like I thought, she wanted to come over. Whatever she had to tell me could have been done by phone but, no, she had to disturb my day with her presence.

It took Susan only fifteen minutes to get to where I was staying. As soon as I opened the door she started in with the mouth.

"Girl, it's about time I got you," she said, walking past in a white jogging suit that was actually cute on her. Susan wasn't one who knew how to dress but today she looked good.

"Hello to you too. Damn. You just come busting up in my place.

"A simple hello your damn self would have eliminated me leaving those messages. Where in the hell have you been? I've been blowing up your phone."

"I was out of town," I said, yawning.

"You should have told me you were leaving," she said.

"I didn't think I had to check in with you before making moves," I said with an attitude.

"Well you are going to wish you would've called me."

"What's so urgent anyway?" I asked, sounding perturbed.

"It's about Derrick and Kea."

"What about them?" I asked, all of a sudden feeling my heart race a bit.

"They are getting the test done again," she said.

I yawned again, wishing I could close my eyes. Walking into my kitchen to get something to drink, Susan followed. I said, "Just alter the test again."

"I can't. They are going somewhere else."

That halted me. Susan got my attention then. Any sleepiness I had was replaced with nervousness. "What?"

"You see why I've been trying to contact you."

"When did they let you know this?" I questioned.

"A few days ago."

"And you just telling me now," I blurted.

"Don't go there with me, Zacariah. I am not in the mood for this. You left town without telling anyone so don't get mad with me," she retorted irritably.

"Don't come at me like that, Susan. I'm the one who's been on the road for hours."

"Whoopty-freaking-do. Do you want me to hand you a trophy for being the most tired? Damn. At least your job is not on the line."

"Shut up and tell me where they are going."

"Which is it? Shut up or tell you—"

"Susan," I screamed, interrupting her. She was plucking my last nerve.

"Zacariah, I don't know."

"What do you mean you don't know? You didn't bother to ask them or try to persuade them to have it done at your facility again?"

"I tried but Kea wanted a second opinion from somewhere else," she said.

"Kea?" I questioned.

"Yes. She came by with Derrick."

"I should have known. It was probably her idea. She's always trying to mess things up. I can't believe this. Why can't they just take the results for what they are and deal with it?"

"I don't know. All I know is I don't want to lose my job behind this."

"How would that happen?" I asked.

"I was the one who administered the test. I swabbed their cheeks and sent the swabs to be tested and I was the one who altered the file to make it look like they were brother and sister. What if my job finds out? And what if they find out I'm your cousin? Derrick was looking at me like he knew me."

"Enough with the what-ifs. I don't feel like hearing all that right now."

"We might go to jail behind this, Zacariah."

"Ain't nobody going to jail. Technical things happen all the time, and who knows we are kin? You are not going to get into any trouble so relax."

"Easy for you to say, Ms. Living Off Men."

"I haven't gamed in a while now. And there is nothing stopping you from scheming if you want to."

"I love myself too much to pimp myself out like a common whore."

"First of all, I'm not a whore."

"The proof is in the pudding," Susan shot back.

"Just shut up for a minute and let me think."

"Why, so you can come up with something that's going to get us into a deeper mess than we are already in?"

"First of all, no one knows we are cousins. Did he recognize you in the office?"

"No. I don't think so. He did keep staring at me."

"I don't think he knows who you are. The one time he saw you, it was a quick glance, so relax."

"I knew I shouldn't have done this. My gut told me to leave things alone but I didn't listen. Tampering with medical records is grounds for dismissal and possible criminal charges, especially if Derrick or Kea finds out and wants to prosecute me. And what if they want to sue the facility? Then they could come after me, too, for the money. I never should have helped you."

"I didn't make you do this, Susan."

"Like hell you didn't. You practically begged me."

"So? You still didn't have to do it but I guess the two thousand dollars I paid you helped change your mind."

Susan was finally at a loss for words.

"Look at who's money hungry. The apple doesn't fall too far from the tree. Dangling money in your face made you do some unethical things yourself."

"I'm going to tell you one thing, Zacariah. If I go down, I'm taking you down with me," she said.

"How? It will be my word against yours. I wasn't the one who changed anything. And as for the money, I gave you that in cash. You can't prove that transaction ever happened. So as you can see, your threats mean nothing to me," I said confidently. The nerve of Susan thinking she could threaten me. Please. She forgot who she was dealing with.

"Like I told you, if this thing blows up in my face, I promise you I will take you down one way or another, even if it means telling Derrick everything you did in order to get him back."

With that Susan stormed out the house, leaving me dumbfounded for a minute.

Telling Derrick would ruin any chances of me getting him back so that couldn't happen. This was not going according to plan and I had no clue what I could do next. *Derrick and Kea cannot find out they are not brother and sister. Not now. Not ever.*

Chapter 27

Kea

When I saw her standing before me, I almost lost consciousness. It was Mother, Ms. Diva herself, standing in front of me with her nose in the air, wearing a cargo pocket-lined dress that showed off her long legs. She looked exquisite as usual.

"Well, are you going to invite me in?" she asked in her snobby tone.

I stepped to the side and let her enter. She looked around as she entered, of course, taking in her surroundings. She never came to see me for anything so I wondered what this visit was all about.

"What are you doing here, Mother?" I asked coldly.

"I wanted to stop by and see how you were living," she said, looking at the flat-panel TV hanging on the wall, one of the only things I had purchased since I received my money from Mr. Hanks's will.

"As you can see, I'm living fine, no thanks to you."

She whipped her head around and gawked at me. She then turned, sitting down on my sofa. I didn't think she was going to sit at all by the way she was looking at it like it came from a junk-yard.

Cutting to the chase I said, "You found out the man who raped you left me a bunch of money, didn't you?"

She looked at me, surprised, saying, "Well I did hear about it."

I knew it was a matter of time before she found out. As to how, I didn't know. But when it came to Mother, if there was anything she wanted to know, she somehow had the connections to find out.

"And you thought you would come see if your daughter would share the wealth," I said, again cutting to the chase.

"I mean it is my right. I am your mother."

"So you are playing Mommy Dearest now? The last time I talked to you, you couldn't stand to look at me, much less talk to me. Emory is your favorite and only daughter, remember."

"Emory is a fool."

"You mean she hasn't met the standard of what a good daughter should be," I said sarcastically, walking close to her but never sitting.

"She found out Aaron was cheating and has asked him for a divorce."

"Well good for her. She should leave him," I said proudly.

"No, she shouldn't. I told her she needed to stay with him. Emory has a good life and she should suck up his indiscretion and continue to be his loving wife. A little affair here and there shouldn't stop her from living well."

"You mean you want her to stand by his money and not her self-respect."

Mother didn't agree nor disagree.

"Why is it all about the money with you? When I needed you as my mother, you turned me away. When I didn't have a dime to my name, you acted as if I were dead. Now, when you hear about me coming into some money, you come sniffing around like a hound who has found its prey. Are you now trying to prey on me, Mother?"

"No one is preying on you, Kea. You are talking foolish. I figured you would want to share your newfound riches with me. After all I do deserve it," she said complacently.

"All my life you treated me terribly. You beat me, demeaned me, and made me feel worthless.

Now that I'm worth some value, you come running," I said, walking around her to the other side of the room.

"Kea, calm down before you disturb your neighbors," she said, looking around like one of them was going to come knocking at the door.

"I'm not going to calm down. How dare you come over here asking me for anything? You don't deserve a damn thing from me."

"I was raped," she blurted loudly now.

"So what," I said angrily. "You made me pay for that so I see that as you getting paid in full."

"I had to carry you for nine months knowing you were that monster's child," she yelled.

"And that made me a monster too, right?" I belted.

"I didn't say that."

"You didn't have to because the way you treated me represents the resentment you had toward me."

"Enough with the past. I didn't come here to rehash old demons," she said like she tasted something repulsive. "This is a new day and I'm here to collect for my troubles," she said boldly.

"Troubles," I said, giggling. "Are you going to pay me for mine?"

"Your payment came in the form of letting you be born."

Just when I thought my mother could never surprise me with more putrid behavior, she came up with something else that made me stand back and shake my head at her audacity.

"You self-righteous hypocrite. I wouldn't give you a dime if you were crawling in the gutters in the deepest of ghettos. How dare you come over here holding out your hand like I'm supposed to bow down and pay you for my birth? You can go to hell."

Mother stood abruptly, saying, "And you wonder why I never loved you, you little wench. Joseph never should have spoiled you like he did because it's made you into this disrespectful, selfish brat I see before me."

"You are mad because he loved me despite how I was created," I belted, pointing at her as my anger erupted.

"If he would have shown the same amount of love to me, then we may still be together," she retorted.

"You only wanted Daddy for his money. I don't think you ever loved him. The fact you treated him like your own personal ATM and punching bag mentally is the reason why he finally left you. You deserve to be alone."

"I deserved to have the best out of life, damn it."

"But why does it always have to be at everybody else's expense? Having the best also consists of love, family, relationships, and trust."

"None of that matters to me. No one ever showed me any of that so why should I?" she protested.

"Daddy did. He truly loved you. How could you have not seen that? For goodness' sake, he loved you enough to raise a child who wasn't his. He gave you the life you dreamed of. Talk about can't see the forest for the trees. Daddy adored you, Mother. He worshipped you and you used and abused him just like you did me."

"Abuse?" she asked, surprised.

"Abuse, Mother. You mentally made him feel less than a man. You whipped me and Emory to obedience. What else do you call it?"

"I call it getting my house in order."

"And how does that house feel now with no one in it but you?" I asked with tears beginning to form in my eyes. My words shook Mother for a minute. I noticed it but she tried hard to compose herself, like my words weren't affecting her.

"Mother, I know you have had a very hard life but we loved you. I loved you despite how you treated me. We could have been your riches. Now look at you. You have no one."

"I have friends," she retorted.

"What friends? How many of those friends stop by to see how you are doing? How many wrap their arms around you and tell you they love you? How many pick up the phone and talk about everyday life with you?"

Mother said nothing.

"That's what I thought. You are a miserable, stuck-up woman who will one day find out that happiness does not come in the form of money, and if it does, it's only temporary. But I don't have to tell you that because I think you already know that," I said, looking her straight in her eyes. This caused her to turn her head.

"So are you going to give me my money or not?" she asked coldly.

I shook my head and said, "Have a nice life, Mother. I wish you the best."

"Very well then. I shall be going since you want to act ungrateful."

I walked to the door and opened it gladly. She walked out into the hallway. Turning to me, she said, "No good things will come to you, Kea, for treating me like this. I'm still your mother."

"Just like you, Mother, I have already endured hell. So from this point things can only go up."

With that she turned and walked away.

I felt like years of torment were being lifted from my spirit. It felt good to finally tell Mother how I felt, even if my words didn't sink in.

Chapter 28

Jaquon

I knew I was taking a risk just stopping by to see Kea but I wanted to see her bad. She had been on my mind all day and I hadn't seen her since our night together. I was sending her roses trying to win her back but she hadn't called me to thank me or anything. I was kind of hurt by that.

Kea didn't say anything to me, but to my surprise she threw her arms around my neck to embrace me. I only hesitated for a split second before I wrapped my arms around her. I could tell she was upset.

Walking her backward into the apartment, I asked, "Kea, baby, what's wrong? Talk to me."

She buried her face in my chest and wept. I walked her over to the sofa, sitting her down. I sat down next to her.

"Baby, talk to me. I'm here. What's got you so upset?"

"Everything, Jaquon."

"Everything like what?"

"You, me, my mother, my dad, and my . . ." She paused.

"Your what?"

She looked at me before saying, "My relationship with Derrick."

I sighed at the mention of his name, hoping he was not a part of why she was so upset. I tried not to get upset and continued to try to comfort her.

"It's been so hard lately and I don't know if I'm coming or going."

"Take a deep breath, baby. Breathe," I said, sucking in air like I was her Lamaze coach. She stopped talking long enough to do what I asked.

"Feel better?" I asked and she shook her head. I leaned back on the sofa and drew her into me. She wrapped her arms around my waist as she laid her head on my chest. The moment felt good, having her close to me again. I was happy I chose to come over. Even if she was thinking about Derrick, right now she was here with me. I wondered if she could hear the pitter-patter of my heart racing. I closed my eyes and took in her fragrance, wanting nothing more than to envelop her. I missed this. I missed her and I didn't realize how much until this moment. I messed up and lost a good woman and knew I wanted to do anything to get her back, even if that meant talking about her relationship with Derrick.

Kea rose up and I let go of her reluctantly. She looked at me with dampened eyes and smiled. "I'm sorry I got your shirt wet."

"This old thing," I said, flicking it. "I got plenty of these. I would let you walk all over it if it meant being here with you again."

She lowered her head before asking, "What are we doing, Jaquon?"

"I thought we were . . ." I said, then paused, watching her head shake.

"I mean us. What is this?"

"I hope this is us becoming one again," I said honestly.

"But were we ever that?" she questioned with saddened eyes.

I felt bad, knowing some of the pain she was feeling was caused by me. I sat up, moving closer to her, if that was possible. I took her hands into mine and said, "Kea, baby, I know I messed up. I know I hurt you too many times to count but the one thing that stayed constant is my love for you."

"But—" she said.

"I know. If I loved you, I wouldn't have done the things I did. I know this. And even now I can't explain why I cheated on you. Immaturity played a large part in it."

"And maybe me being willing to deal with it."

I nodded reluctantly, saying, "Kea, I was wrong. I would scream this from the Empire State Building, the Great Wall of China, and Mount Everest if this would prove to you how much I love you. I want you back in my life," I said, looking at her lower her head again.

"I'm scared, Jaquon."

"I completely understand why."

"I don't know which direction to go. One thing I do know is that I don't want to go back into this with you not knowing where I stand, or you lying to me. Lying creates distrust and right now I can't say I trust you."

"Again, I understand but I'm willing to gain your trust back."

"But it's not that simple," she said above a whisper.

"You do still love me, don't you?" I questioned. I was almost afraid to hear the answer.

She said, "Yes."

I felt an instant relief.

"I also love Derrick."

She said it all in the same breath, halting my joy.

She finally lifted her head for our eyes to meet. "I know that sounds crazy but I have to be open with you. Derrick feels like something isn't right about the test and I'm starting to think the same thing, which is why we are having the test done again."

"Maybe you should accept the fact. Getting your hopes up on someone who you may never be able to have will only leave you with a broken heart," I said, hoping I wasn't coming across as being cold. But I meant it. It killed me that she still had feelings for Derrick, and the fact that she admitted she loved him crushed me. I guessed this was my payback for hurting her but I was still willing to be with her.

"When are you having it done?"

"Soon, and that's why I'm hesitant about us," she said sincerely.

"What if the test proves you and Derrick are not related, then what?" I asked, again not certain if I wanted to hear the answer.

"I don't know, Jaquon. There is a possibility I will go back to him."

"You know I'm going to fight for you regardless," I said, wishing they wouldn't do this. If

Kea found out they weren't siblings, I could lose her forever and I didn't want that to happen.

Kea smiled and said, "I see that. You are determined."

"How about we just go with the flow and see where this thing takes us again? I guarantee you the journey will be a lot smoother. Whatever happens, happens. I know going into this again that you may change your mind about being with me, but I'm willing to take that chance. So how about it? Can we be roommates again? Can I be your man?" I said jokingly, but was as serious as a heart attack.

"I don't want to hurt you," she said.

"Don't worry about me. I'm a big boy. So can we try this thing to see where it takes us?"

Kea hesitated, twiddling her fingers.

"You know you scared me straight," I said, giggling, causing her to smile. "I never thought you would leave me, but you did, and it was my wake-up call to treat you like the queen you are, so take me back, please," I said.

Still Kea hesitated.

"Do you want me to get down on one knee and beg? Because I will," I said, moving to the edge of the sofa to do just that.

"No, don't do that," she said, grabbing my arm, but I dropped to one knee anyway.

"I love you. Can I come back home?" I hung on for her answer as the silence between us made me a little uncomfortable.

"Okay, we can do this," she said, and before she could say another word I planted my lips on to hers. It was slow, soft, and meaningful. I savored the flavor she left as we pulled away from each other. She was biting her bottom lip and it turned me on so much.

"I can't believe I'm doing this again with you," she said.

"Believe it, baby, and I promise to love you wholeheartedly."

With those words I kissed her more intensely this time. Our lips parted and our tongues found one another moving in a rhythmic motion. I wanted to devour her, and hoped our evening would end with us making love. But before we could get to that point, there was a knock at the door. *Damn.*

Chapter 29

Kea

I swore I thought Terry could sniff out when Jaquon was at my place. Just when I was about to get me some for real this time, and it wasn't going to be another wet dream, here she came stomping into my place, dressed like she was going to the club.

"Are you serious, Kea? I mean again," she said, looking at Jaquon, who was slouched down in my sofa with a hard dick and head leaned back like he wanted to make Terry vanish.

"You have to be a hound from hell to constantly know when I'm here," Jaquon said abruptly.

"Call it knowing when a punk ass like you is trying to get my friend back in your life. I'm trying to save her from making the biggest mistake of her life."

"Terry, please. Jaquon is not a mistake."

"Come again?" she said, tossing her cream-colored tote on my chair. She placed her hands on her hips and with major attitude she said, "Mistake is the least of what he is."

"Can you leave please?" Jaquon asked.

I looked over at him as he eyed me and I knew what was up. There was that seductive look letting me know he was ready to give it to me good, and I wanted it. "Terry, I'm busy."

"Busy doing what? Ain't nothing y'all need to be doing up in here. You need to get it together and let me take you out for a night on the town," she said, sitting down next to her tote and making herself at home. She looked at Jaquon like "What?" and I knew my friend wasn't about to budge.

"Please, Terry. I don't feel like going anywhere tonight. I've had a rough day," I said, making my way over to sit beside Jaquon.

"More of a reason to go out and have some fun, girl," she said happily.

"I don't feel like it."

"You heard her, Terry. Put your bat wings on and fly up out of here," Jaquon said.

Terry shook her head and said, "Why don't you crawl back under the slums from which you came?"

Here they went again. I swore these two hated each other and I knew each of them had valid reasons why.

"Enough you two. I have a headache. I can't deal with you two bickering tonight."

"Well can you deal with these?" Terry said, pulling out two tickets from her purse.

"What are those?" I asked curiously.

"Girl, these are two tickets to go see R. Kelly."

I perked up then. "Are you serious?" I asked with excitement now fueling my adrenaline.

"Hell yeah. Front-row tickets at that."

"How in the hell did you manage this?"

"It pays to have my job sometimes. To start this night off right I even got us a limo."

"For real?" I asked, not believing her.

"Look outside. It's taking up all the parking spaces on this side. You better hurry up before some of your neighbors get upset and be knocking at your door."

I got up off the sofa and went to the sliding glass door, peeking out. Sure enough, a black stretch limo was taking up at least three spaces.

"You are serious."

"Now you believe me? Girl, go get dressed." Terry told me.

I looked back at Jaquon, who knew then I was going. I didn't think he would bother stopping me since we were trying to get the relationship thing popping again. Telling me no would not look good right now.

Jaquon got up off the sofa and said, "Go have fun with Terry."

Terry smirked because she knew this was another battle she had won and Jaquon's attempts wouldn't come to pass tonight.

I went over and hugged him and moments later Jaquon was gone.

"Good riddance," she said with her legs crossed and fumbling in her purse for something. "I don't know why you insist on being stupid."

"I'm not stupid. Why does everybody feel the need to call me that?"

"Because it's true when it comes to that dog."

"We are not getting serious. Maybe I just want to have some fun."

"You mean have him play with your kitty-cat again."

I laughed and couldn't respond.

"Girl, go get dressed so we can get this night started."

The concert was everything I expected it to be. R. Kelly was off the chain. He was a musical genius and his performance didn't disappoint.

The place was packed. The crowd was hype and the vibe in the air was electrifying. I was so glad Terry got me to go out with her because we had a ball. From the limo ride to going to a restaurant to eat after, the evening was so much fun. The night flew by and when it was time for Terry to drop me off, she was two sheets to the wind after having way too many drinks.

"Are you going to be okay going home by yourself?" I asked Terry.

"Of course I am. I'm tipsy but I know how to defend myself." She reached in her purse and pulled out her gun.

"Terry," I belted.

"What?"

"Put that thing away before you shoot yourself."

"The only person who's going to get shot is the person who's thinking about attacking me. People are crazy."

"Is it loaded?" I asked as she moved it around, making me scared to be around it.

"Of course it is."

"Is the safety on? Because I'm not trying to catch a bullet."

"Girl, you good. The safety is on."

"How did you sneak it past security?"

"Oh, I didn't take in the place. I have it for after. You know that's when people get to acting crazy. I would have made a special trip to this ride to let whoever know I'm not to be messed with."

I shook my head and opened the door to get out. Before exiting I reached over and hugged Terry.

"Thank you again, girl. I had so much fun."

"Anytime, girlfriend."

I got out of the limo, saying, "Call me when you get home." I watched the limo pull off before I made my way up the steps. Reaching the top floor I pulled my keys out to enter when I felt a hand on my shoulder. I twirled around in panic.

Standing there was Jaquon.

"Are you crazy? You scared me to death," I said with my heart beating fast.

He smiled and said, "I'm sorry. I didn't mean to scare you. I couldn't figure out how to get your attention any other way."

"Putting your hand on a woman at three o'clock in the morning is not the way," I said, turning back to the key dangling in the lock. I turned the key and we entered together. "What are you doing here anyway? It's late."

He smiled and said, "I came to finish what we started."

Jaquon approached me and didn't give me time to put down my things. He kissed me deep. Coming up for air, Jaquon picked me up and carried me to my bedroom.

He placed me down and lay on top of me. We groped one another through our clothes as the strapless dress I was wearing slowly made its way around my waist. Both of us wanted this. The alcohol I drank earlier had me on fire. It was sending me into a frenzy, making me so horny, and Jaquon was ready to douse my fire.

Next thing I knew Jaquon slid his way down my body. He was between my legs. He lifted them in the air, spreading me wide. He licked me one good time long and slow. Surges shot through me. He rose, looking at me, as I looked down to see what he was waiting for.

"I'm going to play with you first," he said seductively. Jaquon slid two fingers inside me. In and out he went, wiggling his fingers to touch all sides of my walls.

I quaked and yearned for him to put his mouth on me. I reached down and gripped his hand, assisting him in his strokes. He smirked at my urgency and played with my wetness until I was panting loudly. Jaquon must have gotten turned on more. He lowered his tongue to join his fingers but replaced one for the other. His tongue flicked while his fingers pushed in and out of me, causing me to cum immediately. One thing Jaquon knew how to do was eat the punany. For just a split second I had to wonder if he had done any of his other women like this. It would explain why some were so damn crazy over him.

I shivered from my climax as Jaquon made his way back up my body. I heard his belt buckle jingle and knew he was pulling out his johnson. I knew it was throbbing to enter me. I considered leaning forward to return the favor by sucking him dry but he was trying to get me back. Why do him any extra favors when this was favor enough for him?

Jaquon lifted one of my legs over his shoulder and pushed himself inside me. His rhythm was slow, almost like he was teasing me, but he didn't need to do that because after a few strokes I was cumming again. My body trembled beneath him. He looked at me like he enjoyed seeing me satisfied. He leaned down and kissed me on my lips. I reached around and grabbed his butt, pulling him deeper into me. The weight of his body collapsed as he gave me what I wanted. Deeper was where he went.

I moaned as he ground his johnson inside my saturated womanhood. After cumming about four times, I stopped counting because I was ready to fall off into slumber. I didn't think my body could take another orgasm but just when I didn't think another one would come, my body quivered to the reaction of peaking again and again and again.

Jaquon was right on time tonight because I needed some bad. He was giving it to me right. After he climaxed, he rolled off of me.

I felt like I could sleep for a week. Curling up in his arms, Jaquon lay on his back, wrapping his right arm around me.

"I love you, Kea," he said, slowly drifting off to sleep.

"I love you too, Jaquon."

Chapter 30

Derrick

The past few nights had been great with me spending a lot of my time with Trinity. I enjoyed being around her so much that it got to the point as soon as I got off of work, I felt like I needed to be near her. She helped keep my mind off Kea. Any time I got alone consisted of the what-if's until we got this paternity test done. Unfortunately for me, the new diagnostic center we found couldn't schedule an appointment until October Twenty-first. Today was October Eighth. In the meantime, my waiting would consist of being with Trinity.

Trinity and I were in the grocery store gathering some items for her to cook dinner for us tonight. She was spoiling me with her many splendid dishes. I told her I needed to get away from her before I started putting on weight.

We were in the rice aisle when the last person I expected to see was looking at something on the shelf and had not noticed us. She must have felt my eyes staring at her because she looked over and made eye contact with me. She looked at me with a smile until she laid eyes on Trinity. I almost made the decision to turn and walk in the opposite direction when Trinity noticed me looking in her direction.

"Derrick, are you okay?" she asked, looking from me to where my eyes were. Like the lady I knew Kea to be she started to approach. I never answered Trinity's question because moments later Kea was standing right in front of us.

"Hey, Derrick. It's good to see you."

"Good to see you too," I stuttered, trying to figure out what to do next. Kea looked at me, then Trinity, but I was at a loss for words. I guessed both women felt my awkwardness and Kea stuck her hand out to introduce herself.

"Hi, my name is Kea. I'm a friend of Derrick's."

"Hi, I'm Trinity. It's nice to meet you," she said, playing it off well.

Kea said, "I don't know what's gotten into Derrick. He acts like he's seen a ghost."

It felt like I had. Trinity nudged me a bit, trying to bring me back to reality.

I said, "I'm just shocked to see you here, that's all."

"I have to eat like everyone else. It looks to me from your cart you all are going to be eating well," she said coolly.

"Yes, I'm thinking about making curried goat with rice and peas, and cassava bread. For dessert I think I'm going to do a rum cake. Have you had it before?" Trinity asked.

"I've only had curried goat once and I didn't care too much for it."

"Well you haven't had good goat until you've had mine. I have mastered cooking it. Maybe I can make it for you sometime," Trinity said kindly.

That really impressed me.

"That would be great," Kea said.

I couldn't believe how smoothly the conversation between the two of them was going. Here I was uncomfortable and they were getting along like they had known each other forever. I was making this situation worse than it had to be. It was because I wanted Kea and here I was with another woman. I wondered what she was thinking. I didn't want her to think I was playing her because I wasn't. Trinity and I were just friends. Well, friends who had sex together, but friends. Kea didn't need to know that.

"I'm going to let you two catch up a bit. Derrick, I'm going to the next aisle to pick up some sugar because I'm out," Trinity said. She held her hand out again and said, "It was nice meeting you, Kea."

"Nice to meet you too, Trinity," Kea said as Trinity left. Kea looked at me, smiling.

"It's not what you think," I said, feeling like a guilty man who had been caught cheating.

"Derrick, it's okay. You don't have to explain anything to me. I'm just your sister."

"Come on, Kea. You know we are more than that."

"We were," she said grimly.

"Why won't you let us be together?"

"You seem to be doing well without me," she said bluntly.

"She's just a friend."

"A very beautiful friend at that. Have you had sex with this friend?" Kea asked.

Her question caught me off-guard and I looked at her without answering.

"I see. Was this before or after we did what we did?" she asked, pointing back and forth between us.

"It was before. It happened the night we found out the results."

"I'm glad you have decided to move on. She seems perfect for you."

Just when I was about to say something else to her, Jaquon walked up. I watched as his free hand met the center of Kea's lower back and she looked over at him, smiling. What the hell was going on? This couldn't be happening.

"I found the ice cream you wanted," he said arrogantly. "Butter pecan, right?" he asked her happily.

I wanted to smack that smile off his face.

"You got it," she said.

Jaquon looked at me with a slight smirk on his face. I guessed that was his way of letting me know, "I got her back. Now what?"

"What's up, Derrick," he spoke.

"You back with this fool?" I asked Kea without acknowledging Jaquon.

"We are working on a relationship."

"A relationship. What does that mean?" I asked, confused.

Kea looked at Jaquon and said, "We are seeing where things are going to take us. We are not officially together. I guess you can say we are reestablishing our friendship."

"Does this friendship include you having sex with him?" I asked, since she asked me the same question.

Kea shifted and gave me the same silent answer I gave her.

"I can't believe this. You are so unhappy with yourself that you choose to go back to the one man who brought nothing but misery to your life," I said, pointing at Jaquon.

"It's what I want, Derrick."

"You heard her, Derrick," Jaquon said, stressing the K sound in my name. "She wants me."

I swung on him and hit him dead in his mouth. Jaquon tumbled to the floor and I pounced on him, punching him over and over again in the face. He was flat on his back and struggled to sit up but my punches wouldn't allow him.

"Derrick, what are you doing?" Kea yelled. "Stop it, Derrick," Kea screamed.

Jaquon tried to hit me but I was on him, hitting him again in the face, causing him to tumble back down. Somehow he managed to twist his way free, throwing me off of him. He jumped up, grabbing me around the waist and slamming me into the shelves. Items went flying everywhere as Kea screamed for us to stop.

I saw Trinity turn the corner and run in our direction. She pushed past Kea and tried to grab me off of Jaquon.

"Stop it," Trinity and Kea shouted, but neither of us was giving up. It was not until two men who heard the commotion came over to break us up that we stopped.

"Don't be mad because Kea chose me," Jaquon roared with blood spewing from his nose and mouth.

"She settled until she could get the right man," I shouted.

"She is with the right man," Jaquon countered.

"Shut the hell up before I punch you in your mouth again."

"You caught me one time. You won't get me again," Jaquon spat.

"I'm calling the cops," someone said as Jaquon and I glared at one another, waiting for the other to make the next move.

Kea went to Jaquon as Trinity stood in front of me, pushing me in the chest. Trinity and Kea thanked the guys for helping as each of them held our arms to escort us out the store.

Trinity asked Kea, "You got him, right?" She nodded as she tugged on Jaquon's arm, pulling him away from us.

"Derrick , we have to go," Trinity demanded.

I didn't move. I stood watching Kea pull Jaquon, who was walking backward, glaring back at me.

"Derrick, let's go before you get arrested," Trinity belted.

I didn't care about being arrested. My world collided once more with the fact that Kea was taking Jaquon back into her life. Why? Why, when she had me? Couldn't she wait until the results came out before she decided to give him another chance? I was devastated.

Wanting to slump to the floor, Trinity wouldn't allow me to. She threw my arm around her shoulder and basically carried me to the car. Kea and Jaquon were long gone by the time we got outside.

I had to wonder if Kea was going to be there to doctor his wounds. Why couldn't she be here for me?

I guessed that didn't matter now since Jaquon was who she was with.

Chapter 31

Zacariah

Many people call what I was doing stalking. I called it checking up on my man. I had been sitting outside his house a little ways down the street in my new ride for about two hours when I saw him whip into his driveway. I was not happy when I saw a woman get out of the passenger side and follow Derrick into his home. This was not Kea and I wondered who in the hell this was. When did he find time to get another woman when he could have chosen me?

I was on fire and had to know what was going on. As soon as his door closed, I pulled up in front of his house. I went to the door, knocking like a woman on a mission, and my mission was to find out who this woman was. No one came to the door. So I pounded on the door harder, wondering what was taking him so long to answer. They had just walked in and I knew they didn't have time to get into anything sexually in the amount of time it took me to come to this door.

When I raised my fist to pound again, this woman answered the door.

"Can I help?" this blue-eyed woman asked.

"You can help me by telling me who are you?" I asked without speaking and her eyes stretched.

"Excuse me," she said, flabbergasted.

"You heard me. Who the hell are you and why are you in my man's house?" I bellowed.

"So you supposed to be Derrick's girlfriend?" she asked impishly like she didn't believe me.

"Yes, I am. Where is he?" I asked, getting ready to walk in, but Ms. Thang held her hand up to stop me. I looked at her hand and her like, "Bitch, please. You better get out my damn way."

"Can you wait right here while I go get him?" she asked, leaving the door open like I was supposed to stand here and take orders from her.

I barged into the house behind her.

She turned to me and said, "I'm sorry. I thought I asked if you could wait outside."

"And as you can see the answer is no. This is my house."

"Look, sweetie—" Blue Eyes began to say.

"I'm not your sweetie," I said angrily, ready to snatch her wild hair from her head. Look like she had tumbleweed for hair. She needed a relaxer.

Derrick came walking down the stairs. His shirt was ripped and his hand was bleeding.

"What happened to you?" I asked, running up to him.

He stepped back like I had some contagious disease. "I thought I told you I never wanted to see you again," Derrick said furiously.

"But I was in the neighborhood—"

"And why are you always in this neighborhood? If I didn't know any better I would swear you were stalking me."

And what if I am? I thought. "I'm not stalking you, boo."

"I'm not your boo."

I looked over at Blue Eyes, who was standing a couple of feet behind Derrick, watching vigilantly.

"Are you going to introduce me to your little friend?" I asked, gesturing toward Blue Eyes; probably were contacts anyway. Everybody wanted light eyes so it helped them get a man or woman. Me, I went with what was given to me. Besides my hair and nails everything else was real.

"No, I'm not introducing you. Now get out," Derrick said, pointing to the door.

"How long have you two been seeing each other?"

"I see I'm going to have to call the police and have a restraining order put on you for real," he said.

"What happened to Kea? Are y'all over now? I thought you were getting another DNA test to see if you are indeed brother and sister. I thought she was the one you wanted to be with."

Derrick tilted his head to the side and then crossed his arms in front of him, frowning. His hand went to his chin like he was thinking and he asked, "How do you know we are getting another test done?"

There I went again letting my mouth run faster than my mind. This always happened when I got mad and now I had stuck my foot in it again.

"Don't worry about how I know," I said, trying to play it off.

"Zacariah, I think you have somebody feeding you information. Who is it?" he asked, shifting his weight.

"Nobody is telling me anything," I said as he gaped at me.

"No. Somebody is telling you something and I get the feeling the person has to work for the paternity office we had our test at," he said, rubbing his chin as he thought about it harder. "Only Kea and I knew, along with the woman who we spoke with, about taking another test elsewhere."

That person has to be my cousin and, yes, she was the one who told me, I thought.

"You know what, Zacariah, thank you for coming by today because you have helped answer a question that's been bugging me for a while now," he said, grinning with confidence.

"What are you talking about?" I asked nervously.

"I knew I had seen that technician somewhere before but I couldn't put my finger on where."

I listened, hoping he would just forget about this whole thing, kick Blue Eyes out, and decide it was me he wanted. But by his demeanor and the squinting of his eyes, I knew that wasn't going to happen. Derrick was figuring out my scheme. I wanted to run like hell but my feet wouldn't budge.

"That technician is your cousin right?" he asked like I was going to confirm.

But, I said nothing. I stood still.

He said, "I was so caught up in everything that was going on that it never occurred to me until now."

"I don't have a cousin who works at a DNA center," I retorted.

"Yeah, she's your cousin all right. It's all coming back to me now. I met her in the very beginning of our relationship," he said, giggling. "You decided to get your cousin to help you somehow. It all makes sense. That's why she kept trying to convince us to retake the test there. Did she alter the results for you, Zacariah?"

"No. I wouldn't do anything like that," I said fearfully.

"Oh you would. You would do anything to get us back together or, rather, keep Kea and me apart."

"Don't hype yourself up that much, Derrick. You act like you are the only man on earth," I spat.

"I know I'm not but to hear you tell it, I'm the only man for you. That's why you were here that night I didn't come home, so you could console me, thinking I would be so upset that I would fall back into your arms and we would live happily ever after," he said, giggling again. "What you didn't count on was me meeting Trinity here," he said, gesturing toward Blue Eyes, "and that she would be the woman to help console me."

I peered at the woman and she smirked. I wanted to rip her face off, eliminating that condescending look. He turned to look at her as she watched my demise.

"You are one conniving woman. To stoop as low as to make Kea and me think we were siblings. You good," he said, clapping. "Finding that picture in my father's apartment was like you hitting the lottery. I bet you even knew the results before we did."

I said nothing. I just thought, *Yes.* Because my cousin did call me to inform me they were not kin. That's when I told her to change the results. What else was I supposed to do? I couldn't stand to see them together and have Kea live the life I was supposed to with Derrick. He was supposed to take me back like before but she interfered and got him mixed up.

"The cat is out of the bag so you might as well come clean."

"I have nothing to come clean about," I said, standing my ground.

"You are a stubborn one. You are going to deny it to the end. Well you can leave now. Thanks for making this bad day now turn into a good one. I can't wait to tell Kea."

Derrick turned to Blue Eyes and asked, "Can you make sure she leaves? I have to make a phone call real quick."

"Certainly," she said.

I watched as he went over to her and kissed her on the cheek. He peered at me, shaking his head before going back upstairs, leaving me standing there speechless.

Chapter 32

Derrick

I couldn't wait to get Kea on the phone and tell her what I just found out. As soon as I got upstairs I picked up the phone and dialed her number. The first call went to her voice mail. I hung up and dialed her number again. Again the call went to voice mail and I dialed it again. Kea was going to answer my call if I had to lock her phone line up trying to get her to answer. After about the seventh call Kea answered.

"What, Derrick? Haven't you done enough?" she bellowed.

"Kea, just hear me out. I found something out today."

"I don't feel like dealing with you right now."

"If you hang up, I'm coming over there and you know you don't want that. So please listen to me for a second."

The line went silent. I waited a few seconds to see if she had hung up on me but there was no dial tone. I heard a slight sigh and knew she was still on the phone.

"I know who the technician is. It's Zacariah's cousin."

"What?" she asked.

"Yes. The woman who administered the test is her cousin. I didn't remember until Zacariah came by today."

"What was she doing at your house?"

"Stalking me of course."

"So do you think she had anything to do with the results?" Kea asked.

"I wouldn't put it past her. By her behavior when I was talking, she looked guilty."

"But the technician didn't seem like the type of woman who would do anything like this."

"I thought that too, but what better way to get over on us than to be cordial? You do remember how persistent she was, especially when we told her we were having the test redone somewhere else? And this is Zacariah's blood."

"True," Kea agreed.

"If she altered the results and we had it done somewhere else, then she knows the outcome will be different," I said, excited that my gut was right.

"So where do we go from here?"

"Tomorrow, I'm going to call and see if we can move up our appointment. Maybe there were some cancellations or something. You do still want to do this right?"

"Well yes, but—"

"But nothing. Kea, look. I'm sorry for what happened earlier. Jaquon just made me so angry and I was already mad that you were there with him."

"You had no right to hit him," she said.

"You are right. I let my anger get the best of me."

"And how could you get mad when you had your friend with you? You didn't see me flipping out," Kea said.

"I'm not you, Kea."

"Trinity seems like someone you can get serious with."

"She's a friend. Trinity knows everything going on, including the fact that I love you."

"You told her everything?" she asked.

"Yes. She's been my sounding board lately when I couldn't come and talk to you. Every time I would see you, all I visualized was being wrapped up in your arms and making love to you. I miss that so much." She didn't respond so I continued. "Do you hear me?"

"Yes, Derrick. I hear you."

"Let's get this test done so we can hurry up and be together. You do still want to be with me, don't you?"

Kea hesitated.

"Baby, please don't give up on us. I don't care that you are with Jaquon now but once those results prove we are not siblings, can you come back to me?"

"I have to go, Derrick," she said.

"Kea, please don't get serious with him again. I'm going to call tomorrow with our appointment time, okay?"

"Okay," she said.

"Baby, I love you," I said, and it was met with a dial tone.

I didn't know whether to feel happy at the idea of finally being with Kea or hurt because there was a possibility she still loved Jaquon. I couldn't fathom that and lowered my head onto my thumbs as my elbows met my knees.

"She's gone," Trinity said.

I heard her and lifted my head to see her standing in my bedroom doorway. "How long have you been standing there?"

"Long enough to know you are determined to get Kea back. She's a beautiful woman and I see why you want her back. She's got a good vibe."

"She's one of a kind."

I turned to face Trinity and said, "I'm sorry for getting you involved in all my drama. Today's events would have made an average person run for the hills."

"It's okay. I'm used to being pushed in fights and harassed by ex-girlfriends," she said light-heartedly.

"I totally ruined this day for you."

"I told you it's okay. It was nice to finally meet the key players in your drama-filled past."

"And present," I said, giggling.

"I know right," she said.

"I will make it up to you. I'm going to take you to the new jazz club that just opened up. We can listen to some soothing music and grab a bite to eat."

"No, I think I'm going to go home and chill by myself for a while."

"You don't have to go," I said, reaching out to her.

She walked up and grabbed my hand. She said, "You may need time to think through some things, Derrick."

"Right now I don't feel like thinking at all. I really could crawl under these covers, flick the TV on, and call it an evening. And you know it would be better with some company. I think a marathon of *Twilight Zone* is on."

"Color or black and white?" she asked.

"Black and white of course. You know those are the best."

We both laughed and I said, "The calm of your eyes in combination with your smile always makes me feel good."

Trinity walked up to me and pulled me up. I stood in front of her as she draped her arms around me and placed her head on my chest. She felt so warm and I took pleasure in her being next to me.

"I don't want to hurt you," I told her. "You are too good of a woman to deal with all the things I have going on. I fear things could get serious between us and I don't want to hurt you by going back to Kea," I said, caressing her back.

"I knew what I was getting into when I got with you, Derrick. So don't feel bad."

"But I do."

"I would do anything for you. You needed me and I was happy to be here for you. I'm always here for you, even when our friendship ends," she said tranquilly.

"Why couldn't I have met you years back before I ever got involved with Zacariah?"

"Fate didn't want it that way. It wanted us to meet just like we did and we should enjoy each other's presence while we can."

"I'm going to miss you."

"Don't completely write me off. Not yet," she said, pulling me into her. She looked up at me and there were those blue eyes hypnotizing me again.

"How about one last tryst?" she suggested, pecking me on the cheek. I began to wrestle with whether I should do this but once she started unbuttoning my shirt and planting soft kisses on my exposed chest, I was drawn to her. I tilted my head back, enjoying her lips on my breast, and looked down when I felt her hands moving south. Trinity sat on the edge of my bed and began to unbutton my pants.

"You don't have to do this," I whispered.

"But I want to."

She reached inside my pants and pulled out my johnson, which had grown to its maximum capacity. With no hesitation, Trinity took me into her mouth, causing instant tingles to come over me. I had to wonder what type of guy was I becoming when I knew what I was doing was wrong. But it felt so right. And for an instant I understood why Jaquon was the dog he was. If a woman was willing to give it to you any kind of way and it felt this good, then why not go for it? Still, that wasn't the type of man I wanted to become.

I looked down at Trinity giving me everything she had and I couldn't resist her. My heart knew to stop this now but my body urged me to let her do what she was doing. Regardless of the battle I was having within myself, it didn't take long for her tongue to bring me to a brink of discharging. Trinity never pulled back as she sucked up every drop of my semen, which surprised me.

Who was this woman really, and could she let me go as easily as she claimed she could?

Chapter 33

Kea

I was so glad it was a new day and that yesterday was just that: yesterday. After Derrick and Jaquon's altercation, our evening was ruined. For me it was, anyway, but Jaquon was on cloud nine. He was so happy that Derrick had seen us together. He thought that would finally keep Derrick away from me, but if he only knew the truth.

When Derrick called to let me know the information he had found out, Jaquon was taking a shower. When he came out and asked who called, I told him it was my father calling to check up on me. I knew it was wrong to start lying when we were trying to start this relationship on the right foot but I didn't feel like talking about it to Jaquon. I knew he would have been mad at the fact that Derrick had the audacity to call. His anger would be further fueled by me choosing to still find out whether Derrick and I were siblings. Somehow you'd have thought by Derrick sucker-punching him that it helped me see Derrick's true colors and I wouldn't have anything to do with him anymore. The fact of the matter was, I knew Derrick punched him because he was hurt seeing me with Jaquon. His love for me turned to rage so, yes, I still had major feelings for Derrick. Maybe more now than ever. So I lied to Jaquon's face about talking to him.

Derrick's words kept resonating in my mind. *"I love you, Kea."* And I knew he meant it. I loved him too and wondered why I took Jaquon back. In my moment of emotional breakdown, I fell right back into his arms. It wasn't until I saw Derrick with Trinity that I knew I wanted to be with him. I truly loved him with all my heart and it crushed me to see him with her. I was getting so tired of this circle of emotions. I couldn't wait for it to end. I wanted some peace in my life and if I didn't get it soon, I swear I was going to lose my mind and admit myself into a mental ward.

Jaquon snuggled up behind me and I could feel his morning hardness against me. He threw his arm around me and it reminded me of both of us having sex despite the feelings I had for Derrick.

Jaquon kissed the back of my neck and I knew he wanted a repeat. He caressed my stomach and brought his hand up to my breasts, squeezing them.

"Good morning, baby," he said groggily.

"Hey," was all I could say. I tried to think about how I could get out of doing this again. I was just going to have to tell him I didn't feel like it; whether it made him mad or not, I was not about to fall back into my old ways of doing it just because he wanted to. It was about time I stood up for myself, even with him.

"How about a quickie?" he whispered, breathing hard on the back of my neck as he pulled me closer to him. Neither of us had on clothes and his johnson was knocking at my back door.

"Jaquon, I really don't feel like it," I told him.

"Come on, baby. I'm ready. Don't you feel me?" he said, thrusting his hips forward.

Before I could deny him again the phone rang.

"Don't answer it. Let the voice mail pick it up," he said.

"But it might be important," I said, moving from his clutches.

"What's more important than this?" he asked, sounding disappointed, but I picked up the phone anyway.

"Hello."

"Kea," Daddy said in a tone I didn't like.

"What's wrong, Daddy?" I asked, struggling to sit up in the bed now.

"It's your mother. She's been arrested," he said, sounding panic-stricken.

"For what?"

"Conspiracy to commit murder."

"Murder!" I belted. Jaquon sat up now, looking at me.

"Yes."

"Conspiring to murder who?" I asked with panic in my voice now.

"Your real father, Otis Hanks."

I almost dropped the phone when he said it.

"Look, I don't have time to explain. Meet me down at the police station. I'm leaving the house right now."

"After I get dressed, Daddy, I'll meet you there."

With that Daddy hung up. I dropped the phone down on the base and jumped up to get dressed.

"What's going on?" Jaquon asked.

"I don't know. Something with my mother. I'm going to meet Daddy at the station."

"Let me go with you."

"No. You stay here. Daddy doesn't know we are back together and I don't want to make him more upset than he is already. I'll call you when I know more."

***

When I walked into the station, I was met by Daddy standing there with a weary look on his face. I ran up to him and embraced him. He was trembling and I could tell this situation was tearing him apart. Even though he and Mother were separated, he still loved her deeply.

"Daddy, sit down," I told him.

"I never thought your mother would do something so vicious. Not this. Not murder."

"How did you find out?"

"I was her one and only phone call. Can you believe it? She called me."

That figures. Mother had no friends so who else was going to see about bailing her out at this point? Again this was her using Daddy to get what she wanted. I didn't know whether to get mad or feel sorry for the pitiful, unhappy person she'd become. I knew Mother was cold and evil but not to the extent of murder.

When the cops led us into a room with a single table, chairs on either side and windows covered with bars, I thought about *Law & Order* and wondered if we were about to be interrogated. What I didn't know was they were bringing Mother in through another door to talk with us. She was handcuffed and looked worse than I had ever seen her before. Daddy went to her, giving her a kiss on the forehead, but the cops commanded him to stay away from the prisoner.

My mother is a prisoner now, I thought.

"Are you all right?" Daddy asked.

She still was cold as usual.

Was she serious? She called him and now she acted like she didn't care he was here. I controlled my anger and watched.

"Why haven't you bailed me out of here yet?" she spat.

"I don't have that type of money, Frances," Daddy responded.

"But she does," she said, looking at me. "Why haven't you asked her? She will do anything for you."

"Because it's not my place. You got yourself into this situation, so you need to be the one to ask."

Mama looked at me before turning her nose up. Unreal, she still had the audacity to think I was supposed to do whatever she wanted. Here she was, sitting here, facing murder charges and she acted like we owed her. What was this woman's deal?

"Did you have him killed?" I asked point blank.

"My lawyer informed me not to discuss the case," she said.

"I thought it was some juvenile delinquent and it was you."

"Are you going to accuse me all day, or get me out of here? I'm tired. I'm hungry and I want to take me a nice hot bubble bath."

"Who says I was getting you out?" I asked arrogantly.

"You will get me out of here. This is no place for a woman like me."

"You mean a woman who had someone murdered," I retorted. "They have a young man in custody who's ready to testify against you, Mother. You acted like some mobster putting a hit out on somebody."

"That young punk is lying on me."

"Why would he? Out of all the people he could have blamed this crime on, Mother, he chose you specifically. He describes you from head to toe. Everybody knows you two don't travel in the same circles. You had to have something to do with this."

"Like I said, he's lying."

"He said you paid him ten thousand dollars."

"Where's the proof?" she asked matter-of-factly. "It's my word against his. Who do you think a judge and jury will believe when they put someone like me against the word of a common thug?" Mother asked, glaring at me confidently. "Now either post my bail or get the hell away from me."

I looked at Daddy, who appeared defeated. He knew there was no reason to get out such an ungrateful, sanctimonious witch.

"Baby girl, I'm with whatever you want to do," he said sadly.

I pushed my chair from the table and said, "Find another sucker dumb enough to bail you out because I'm not doing it."

Mother shook her head, smirking, and said, "You are just like him."

"Like who?"

"Your Daddy always took from me too and you stand there thinking I'm going to beg for something that's rightfully mine anyway." Mother stood and said, "You think you are all that, flaunting your money in my face like it's a bone and I'm some dog who you want to take a bite. I will die first before I beg you to help me. I'm glad he's dead. I can't wait to meet the young man who took him out so I can shake his hand. They need to give him a medal of honor for taking out a child rapist instead of trying to lock him up for life."

Her words hurt because the Mr. Hanks I knew was nothing like the man who altered her life. And I wasn't trying to make excuses for his actions, because they were horrendous, but how long could someone live in the past? Here she was playing the victim like I was supposed to step up and help her when she never bothered to love me. I never asked my mother for anything, knowing the outcome was going to be a tongue-lashing or a smack. The only thing I ever wanted from her was love. I would have tried to give Mother the world now if she only loved me but she was too busy keeping up a wall that was obviously crumbling. Life as she knew it was over if she was convicted of this crime but she was too atrocious to grasp the situation. She didn't have to let what happened to her plague her continually but she chose to let it bombard her, leaving a trail of wounded hearts behind. And still she was too blind to see her imperfections.

I looked at my mother with a smile and said, "Have a nice life. I love you and I wish you all the best."

I knew this would probably be the last time I saw my mother and I cried tears of sorrow as I walked out with Daddy. If felt like I was burying her. Not in the form of a coffin being covered up with soil but in the form of recapturing my own life. I had to get past the hurt she caused me in order to continue on a path of virtue. I chose today to not be like my mother. Through all this pain I could hear the saying, "Everything happens for a reason." It hurts so bad while it's happening but once the storm has cleared, a newfound understanding emerges, making you into a stronger person than you ever thought you could be.

Chapter 34

Derrick

I was experiencing déjà vu, sitting here, waiting for this technician to read me the results of this second paternity test. This time Kea and I were alone waiting for the result. No parents accompanied us and neither did Jaquon or Trinity. A little over a week had passed since we had our samples taken and Kea didn't have much to say to me then. We were both in and out without much conversation. Now Kea sat again with very little to say to me and I wondered why she was giving me the cold shoulder. I knew she couldn't still be mad about me punching Jaquon; he deserved it and I gave it, and now it was time to move past it.

These results we were about to receive were going to change our lives forever. I just hoped that change for me would include Kea being in my life. We were destined to be together and after today I had no doubt we would.

Then Trinity crossed my mind. Even though we said we were going to stop seeing one another, we hadn't. Our friendship continued but that changed last night when I was at her home.

"Derrick, can I tell you something?" she asked.

"Anything. You know we can tell each other anything."

"You sure you won't act all weird toward me when I say this," she said, looking up at me.

"Are you serious? After all the crazy things I've brought your way. Give it to me," I said, waving my fingers in the "come here" motion at her.

"Okay, Derrick. I'm just going to come out and say it. I think I have fallen in love with you."

I was taken aback by her words. I sat there in silence as I stared at her like I was still waiting for her to tell me whatever she had to tell me. But she just stood there and I knew then I had heard her right. She was in love with me.

"Did you hear me?"

"Umm. Yes, I heard you."

She sat up, saying, "I don't expect you to feel the same way, because I know the situation. You are still in love with Kea. But all this time we've been spending with one another, the dinners, the talks, the movies, the lounging around and acting crazy, I've never been able to be *myself with another man like I have been with you."*

I still said nothing. I looked at her, still astounded that she was admitting to loving me.

"I know your equation doesn't include me but I felt like if I didn't let you know how I felt, I would regret never telling you."

"I'm . . . I'm glad you told me."

"I hope this doesn't change how we've been around each other. Love tends to make men back off and treat women like they have the plague."

"I'm not going to do that. Not now anyway," I said jokingly, thinking I did need to step back from Trinity for a while.

"I know you get your results tomorrow and in my heart I feel Kea and you are not related. With that I know I'm going to lose you but I had to try to see how you felt about me."

"You know I care about you, Trinity."

"But you don't love me, not like you do Kea."

"Yes. You and I, we have a different type of connection. It's hard for me to explain. I think what we have is more like a friendship-type thing."

"It's okay. You don't have to explain. I already got my answer from you," she said with the same cool, calm demeanor she always had. She

didn't look hurt, or annoyed, or even mad about it. Any other woman would be up in the floor showing her behind by now but Trinity was stately. She truly was an amazing woman and I wondered again why I couldn't have met her sooner.

When the technician came in with the results, I began to tremble a bit. This was it. This would determine my future. After some meet and greet and a little bit about what was going to be revealed, the doctor gave us the results. And they were that Kea and I were not related.

"Yes," was all I could say as I looked over at Kea, who was smiling. Her reaction was calmer than mine was but I was so happy. One, I hadn't slept with my sister, and two, this could result in Kea and me picking up where we left off.

The doctor went on to reveal Kea was in fact Mr. Hanks's daughter but I was not his son. The news excited me but also made me question who my father was. Why did my mother tell this man I was his son if she knew there was a possibility that I wasn't? I wasn't familiar with my mom's past like that. I knew relationships happened in life but I was finding it really hard to not see my mother as a woman who got around.

After getting the results in hand Kea and I left the center with the proof. She still seemed standoffish and I wondered why. This was the news we were hoping for, which should have brought elation to her.

"Kea, what's wrong with you?" I finally asked once we were standing outside the building.

"What do you mean?"

"You, being quiet and acting like you still don't want to have anything to do with me. Are you still mad I punched Jaquon?"

"Well it didn't make me happy."

"I understand that, but isn't the news we just got enough to bring joy into your heart for me? This means you and I can continue where we left off," I said.

"Derrick, I don't know. A part of me thinks it's too late. A lot has happened," she said.

"It's not too late. We still love each other. You do still love me don't you?"

"Derrick, I think we need to move on with our lives and forget about what we did have."

"Is this because of Jaquon? Please don't tell me you are still in love with the dude."

"I do love him," she said confidently.

"But do you love me?" I asked.

"This is not easy for me," she said with a cracking voice.

"It can be if you choose me," I said, moving close to her. I grabbed her hands and pulled them to my chest. "Baby, I love you. Don't do this to us."

"Derrick . . . I . . ."

I kissed her hands. Then I leaned in and kissed Kea. At first she was hesitant but I didn't back down. I kissed her until she relented.

Breaking our connection, I said, "Come with me."

She shook her head without saying anything.

"Baby, please just come with me."

"I have to be somewhere."

"I won't keep you long."

I stared into her eyes until she nodded, and I felt a slight victory approaching. If she wanted to truly be with Jaquon, I knew she wouldn't have agreed to come with me. This let me know she loved me more than even she knew.

I was happy she agreed to ride with me, leaving her ride at the medical facility. When we pulled up at my place, where both of us knew that maybe we had something, Kea dropped her head. I didn't know if this was a result of sadness or happiness. It didn't matter because I still had her with me. I got out of my ride and went around to open the door for her.

"I can't believe you brought me here," she said, getting out.

"We can't go up to the balcony because it's a wedding going on but we can still take in this spectacular view."

The sun was going down and I couldn't have timed it more perfectly. Leading her to the spot beneath a tree, we peered into the sky as the sun slowly submerged. We could hear the music playing in the background as another couple celebrated their coming together in marriage, which was the same place Kea's sister Emory had her reception.

"Do you remember when we stood out here together?" I asked.

"Yes, I remember."

"We knew what we wanted then even though things weren't quite the way we wanted them to be. Now we've got our chance back."

Kea looked at me longingly before turning her attention back to the beautiful sky. The sun was losing its battle with the day as the orange hue illuminated the horizon. There was something about this moment that made you feel blessed to be alive to witness God at work, in more ways than one.

After standing for what seemed like an eternity, I asked again, "Kea, do you still love me?"

Without turning her attention away from the sky she said, "Yes. I still love you, Derrick."

Joy filled me as passion came in as a close second. I gently turned Kea's face toward mine and planted my lips on to hers. Her lips were so soft. Each soft peck led to another one and another until I found myself pushing my body into Kea's as she leaned against the massive tree. Our bodies became entangled as I yearned to be in her. If I didn't have a fear of having the cops called on us for indecency I would have taken off my clothes and made love to Kea right under the tree.

Coming up for air, I said, "Please come home with me, Kea." My eyes begged for her to agree but hers were questioning if this was the right thing to do.

"Please, baby, come with me," I said again.

"It's getting late," she said.

"You know you want this. You know you want me. Come home with me."

"Derrick, I don't think it's a good idea."

"Really you don't have a choice because you are riding with me," I said jokingly, causing her to laugh. "I asked because I'm a gentleman but you know I will drive you to my house."

She smiled and said, "I knew I should have driven my car."

"Too late now. So will you come with me?"

Chapter 35

Jaquon

I called Kea six times and she still didn't answer her phone. I knew she had to have the results by now. I wondered why she hadn't called me with the results, or come home with them for that matter.

I paced the floor in our place and hoped she wasn't where I thought she was. What if the test proved they weren't related? Would this mean she would now leave me for Derrick? I didn't think I could handle that and I really didn't think I could handle if she was with him right now.

I dialed her cell number again.

"You have reached Kea. Please leave a message and I will get back to you as soon as possible."

"Kea, where are you? Why haven't you called me? Baby, I'm worried about you. Give me a ring when you get this, okay?"

I hung up and began pacing again. My concentration was broken when someone knocked at the door. I rushed to it, swinging it open.

"Dag. Is there a fire or something? You look like you about to rush off somewhere," Shelia said from across the hall.

"What do you want?" I asked, mad that it was her instead of Kea.

Holding out a cup she said, "Can I get some sugar?" trying to look at me seductively.

"Don't you buy groceries? Why are you always borrowing from Kea?"

"I haven't gone to the store yet."

"Then I suggest you take your skank ass up the street and get you some sugar."

"Who you calling a skank?"

"You," I yelled.

"Well you weren't calling me a skank when you were hitting this not even a month ago. I bet your boo don't know I was one of the plenty you planted your seed in."

I snapped. I mean I lost it. I stepped out of the apartment and wrapped my hands around Sheila's throat. The cup in her hand fell to the concrete, shattering. I pushed her back into her apartment, which was easy because her door was open with some music coming from it. Once in her apartment, I slammed the door along with slamming her against the wall.

"Let me go," she whispered. My hand remained clamped around her neck.

"You were a past mistake I regret to this day!" I yelled.

"Let me go, Jaquon. You're hurting me," she tried to say, pulling at my hands wrapped around her neck.

I let her go and Sheila fell to the floor, sucking in as much air as she could.

"I can't believe I allowed myself to sleep with you," I said, walking deeper into her place, pacing wildly. "I've changed," I said, wondering why I felt the need to explain anything to this woman.

Shelia was finally on her feet. I thought she was going to come at me and be mad about me putting my hands on her. But this trick was smiling. She was actually smiling.

I looked at her, frowning because I didn't get it. Why in the hell was she smiling?

"If you wanted to come in my place, Jaquon, all you had to do was ask." She smirked. "I would have let you enter in more ways than one."

"What?"

"You know I like it rough. That was foreplay for me. I was waiting for you to whip that puppy out and pummel me with it."

"Sheila, I will never sleep with you again."

"A dog can't change, boo boo. Not you anyway. You are the infamous Jaquon Mason. You've hit more women than that basketball player Wilt Chamberlain back in the day. You know that man claimed to have slept with over twenty thousand woman."

"I need to get out of here," I said, trying to walk to the door, but Sheila stepped in my path.

"I'm surprised your dick still works," she said, walking toward me. Then she grabbed my johnson and I backed away from her gentle caress. Just that one touch made me rise right there in front of her and I hated it.

"Oohh, baby. It looks like it's ready to have some fun."

"Not with you," I said blatantly.

"Come, Jaquon," she said, stepping closer to me. "You remember how we used to get down, the way you used to take it from the back. You used to punish me something fierce."

Sheila was a skank but she was a hell of a woman when it came to her skills in the bedroom. Her reminiscing took me down memory lane with her and I remembered the way she used to sex me. The more I thought about it, the harder my johnson became.

She reached out and grabbed it again.

This time I didn't step back from her grasp.

She smiled and said, "You are very good at what you do, Jaquon, and I wouldn't mind having another go at this nice thick cock."

Her words, along with the way she was caressing my johnson, sent shivers through my body. My mind wasn't strong enough to overcome the feelings my body was having at this moment. I closed my eyes, enjoying her caress, and wondered how I went from trying to choke this trick out to enjoying the rubs she was giving me.

"Why don't I remind you what you been missing?" she asked, attempting to unzip my pants.

I opened my eyes and saw Sheila looking at me seductively. Skank entered my mind but Sheila was very attractive and had a body that couldn't be denied.

"Bring your A game, baby. Teach me a lesson. I'll get on all fours like old times, boo," she said, letting go of me and stepping back with a smirk. She lifted the tight tee over her head, revealing her plump melons.

"I always come with my A game," I told her and wondered why I was not running out of there.

"Then show me. Remind me of what I've been missing all this time." Sheila proceeded to unhook her bra and let her breasts be freed. Damn she was sexy. She gripped one in her hand and began licking her nipple as she peered at me. She was performing and Sheila was definitely good at this.

The dog in me wanted to do her. I was hard as titanium right now. Anger mixed with lust was not a good combination to be in, especially when my anger was directed at the woman who didn't have the decency to call me back.

Sheila was pulling her shorts down, exposing her bright pink G-string. She walked over to a chair and draped each of her legs wide open over the arms of the chair. Spread-eagle, Sheila proceeded to lick her fingers before plunging them into her warm center.

"I'm so horny for you, Jaquon. Come and give me what my body's been craving. I'm all yours to do whatever you want, so come get it, baby."

A call from Kea right now before I did something I would regret would be right on time, but there was no ring of my cell. Sheila continued to push her fingers in and out, moaning as she pleasured herself.

I didn't know what to do. I knew what the right thing to do was but the offer had been laid before me, and what type of guy would I be to back down from this offer? I had to do what I had to do. I started walking toward Sheila, who was smiling at my approach. when I heard footsteps coming up the stairs.

I began to panic. What if it was Kea? I ran to the door and peered out the peephole, seeing that I had left my door standing wide open. In my rage I forgot.

"What's wrong, baby? Come over here and give mama what she wants," Sheila purred, but I wasn't trying to hear that now. I was trying to figure out a way to get out of this apartment without getting busted by Kea.

I peeped out the hole again to see a woman standing there this time. By her wild mane, I knew it wasn't Kea.

Who was she and why was she at our door?

Chapter 36

Jaquon

The woman started to enter my place. Since I didn't know who she was, I opened the door to Sheila's place and stepped out in the hallway.

"Can I help you?" I asked, admiring her blue eyes when she turned in my direction. She looked familiar to me but I couldn't remember where I had seen her before.

"I don't know if you remember me. I met you the day you and Derrick got into your little altercation."

"Oh yeah. I remember you now," I said, looking at the broken mug still in the hallway. "Damn. I meant to get that. My neighbor dropped it. When she was picking up the pieces she cut her hand. I was making sure she was okay."

Blue Eyes nodded. "If you have a moment, can I speak to you about something? It shouldn't take long."

"Sure," I said, stepping over the broken mug and leading her into my place. Before we continued I got the dustpan and went back in the hall to sweep up the glass. Once back inside I went to Blue Eyes.

"So what's up with this visit?" I asked, sitting down. "So you are the one who tried to break Derrick and me up that day?"

"Yes."

"So am I to assume the two of you are together?"

"We're friends."

"Did he send you over here to apologize?"

She giggled, saying, "As a matter of fact he doesn't know I'm here."

"Okay."

"Jaquon, right?" she questioned.

"Yes, and your name is what again?"

"Trinity."

"Nice name."

"Thank you. But getting back to why I'm here . . . And please don't take what I'm about to say the wrong way. I'm here to tell you that you need to straighten up."

"What?" I looked at her like she had lost her mind.

"Jaquon, you are a dog. You are a trifling man who can't keep his dick in his pants. You sleep with anything with a pulse and I find you a bit repulsive."

"Excuse me," I said with surprise. *Is she serious?* I thought.

"I'm going to need you to restrain your urges and learn to be the man Kea wants you to be. It's time to grow the hell up and stop being this playa. Just because you are using women to cover up something that possibly happened to you in your past doesn't mean you can't fly right now and take Kea as your own."

"You came all the way over here to diss me?"

"Yes," she said callously.

"Don't take what I'm about to say the wrong way, but you need to mind your own damn business and stay the hell out of mine," I said, getting up from the sofa. "And if you know what's good for you, you will get the hell out my place," I said furiously, after letting what she said sink in.

Trinity began to laugh. I mean she was really tickled about something, and her laughter angered me more.

"Get the hell out," I yelled.

She whipped her head around to me and said, "Sit down, Jaquon. I'm not done yet."

"Like hell you aren't."

Her laughter turned quickly into a look of dare. "You must think I'm stupid. If you think I believe you were checking on your little friend to see if she was okay from a cut hand, you got another think coming."

Homegirl was stepping up to her dare with a poise that seemed unfazed by my anger.

She went on to say, "You choked your so-called friend up and slammed her into her own apartment. Honestly I believe you came close to sleeping with her."

I was stunned into silence.

"Now sit down before I make another trip over here to tell Kea that you have been screwing the neighbor."

I was in a rage. I stood for a minute before doing as she requested, and sat down.

"That's a good boy."

"I'm not a boy," I countered.

"Well your actions are not that of a man," she retorted. "Jaquon, you weren't in that apartment long enough to sleep with that woman but I know in a matter of minutes your conclusion would have been to be deep inside her. The scent of sex seeped into the hallway as soon as you opened her door so ain't no telling what homegirl was doing to urge you to cheat on Kea yet again."

Scowling, I asked, "Can you get to the reason why you are here? Because you are pissing me off."

Again she smiled and said, "You want to be with Kea and I want to be with Derrick. If you cheat on her then that's going to leave her free to be with Derrick. Do you get it now?"

"Kea doesn't want Derrick anymore. She made her choice in the store that day."

"Poor little Jaquon. All that body and no brains."

"Yet you were the stupid one who allowed a man in love with another woman to fuck you," I countered.

This comment caused Trinity to flinch. I found her weakness.

"For somebody so quick to call everybody else out on their flaws, how have you allowed yourself to fall in love with a man you can't even have?"

"Oh, I can have him," she bellowed.

"Not without my help, it seems. That's why you are over here isn't it, to get me to stay faithful so Kea can never leave me?"

"Don't sit there and act like you would be happy for Derrick to have her."

"I'm not but I'm not threatening you either. I'm getting Kea back all on my own. Now I know your threats don't hold water, especially if telling Kea about my indiscretions is going to make her leave me and send her running into the arms of Derrick."

Trinity seemed to be losing her power in this conversation. She was so quick to shut me down but now it looked like the tables were turning.

"So you want Kea to become Derrick's wife?"

"Wife?" I questioned.

"I found a diamond ring in Derrick's console table. He doesn't know I found it but I did. And I know he's going to ask Kea to marry him."

"And how do you know the ring was for Kea?" I asked incredulously.

"It had an inscription inside the ring. 'To Kea with love' is what it said."

"I'm going to hurt him," I said, jumping to my feet.

"Jaquon, please sit down. You are such a silly boy."

"Is your hearing bad? Because I thought I told you don't call me a boy. I'm a man."

"Whatever. Look, Jaquon, I'm sure of what I want. I'm paying attention to what's going on around me. You, on the other hand, have let the seduction of loose women cloud your mind to not see a good thing when it's in front of you. So not only are you going to straighten up, you are going to ask Kea to marry you."

Was this woman serious?

"Two proposals will confuse Kea more and with you being with her the majority of the time, I think she will eventually accept yours."

"He's probably asking Kea to marry him now. Where the hell am I supposed to get a ring on such short notice?"

Trinity reached into her tote and pulled out a velvet box. She had to be kidding me. The woman came with an engagement ring in tow.

"Ask her tonight," she said, handing me the box.

"You really do love Derrick, don't you?"

"I'm willing to do whatever it takes to make him my man."

Trinity got up to leave, saying, "I'm glad we had this little talk." She went to the door, opening it to leave, only to find Sheila standing there looking like she had her ear to the door, eavesdropping.

"You see what I'm saying. You need to handle this," Trinity said, looking at Sheila in disgust.

"Who the hell is she, Jaquon?"

Trinity looked back at me and said, "Please, from now on think with the head on your shoulders and not the one between your legs. Get your woman back and drop these skeezers." With that she sauntered past Sheila, who was ready to go off now at the fact that Trinity called her a skeezer.

Chapter 37

Kea

There was no talking when Derrick and I got to his home. Our passion for one another had been extinguished and now a fire had been ignited again. All of the time we missed being away from each other came down to this moment. I still questioned myself as to why I was here. When Derrick dropped me off at my car to come back to his place, I could have driven myself home to Jaquon. But my love for Derrick wouldn't allow me to. I knew I was in trouble when he kissed me under the tree and now I was here with him. As much as Derrick wanted me was as much as I wanted him inside me.

Derrick came to me, caressing my face in his hands. He pulled me into him and placed a soft kiss on my lips again.

"I've wanted you so bad and now I can finally have you with no worries or hesitation," he said passionately.

I wanted to concur but thoughts of Jaquon entered my mind.

"I want to make love to you," he said, pulling my body into his. Our embrace allowed me to feel his erection and I craved him in that moment. My inner thighs throbbed to have him inside me. Then my cell phone rang.

Derrick let go of me. I tried to struggle to get into my purse and answer it. I wasn't fast enough before the call went to my voice mail. I saw that it was Jaquon. In fact I had several missed calls from him. I knew he was waiting for me to get home so I could tell him what the results were.

"I need to make a call real quick," I said, attempting to dial Jaquon's cell.

"Please don't," Derrick begged. He took my phone and my purse out of my hand and placed it on his console table.

My body shook with nervousness. I didn't know why I was so nervous. I had been with him numerous times before but this time it felt different. It felt real. All of our secrets were out and we could be with one another with no inhibitions stopping us. But I had one that should have been stopping me. I had Jaquon. How would I now play the hypocrite when I went back into our relationship agreeing to start off on a clean slate? Here I was playing the cheating girlfriend again.

Before, I felt I had every right to sleep around on him but now I had no excuse to do what I was doing. I knew deep in my heart Jaquon was with me for all the right reasons, his main one being the fact he loved me. But still I had doubt if he could remain faithful to me.

"I can't do this," I said with tears filling my eyes. This was too much for me. My mind was cluttered with which decisions I should be making. Part of me wanted to dive into Derrick's arms but the other part wanted me to go into my relationship with Jaquon doing things right. I was so confused. *Which one of these men do I choose?*

"Derrick, I really can't do this," I repeated, hoping he would step back and give me a minute to think about this, but he kept coming at me. With all his love and all his grace, Derrick kept touching and caressing me, bringing exhilaration to my body and I loved it. I wanted it. I craved him and yet I felt so bad for feeling this way.

I stepped out of his path and walked to the other side of the room. "I'm serious, Derrick, I can't do this," I said with tears streaming down my cheeks. "This isn't right. I'm with Jaquon now. I love him too."

"But you love me more," he retorted as he crossed the room to meet me again, and I was met with more caresses and kisses to my weak spots.

"Please. Can't you just let this go? Let me go."

"I can't, Kea. I love you too much to see a good thing get away from me."

"Why are you making this so difficult for me?" I asked as Derrick began to lift my shirt over my head. He then took off his own shirt, revealing this magnificent body. Damn I forgot how good this man looked. Derrick kissed me deep as he gripped the back of my head and pulled me into him. When we came up for air, I realized this man had unbuttoned, unzipped, and dropped my pants. I was so caught up in our infatuation that I didn't even comprehend what was happening.

"I want you so bad," he said, undoing his pants now.

When his manhood sprung out his boxers, I knew there was no turning back now. But I continued to try. I turned away from him and attempted to pull my pants back up but Derrick came up behind me in that instant. His body was so hot when it made contact with my body. His energy immediately transferred to me. I felt his hardness on my behind as Derrick reached around my waist and stooped a bit to insert his fingers into my center. With the first entrance, I sighed with pleasure. As much as I wanted my body to combat his cravings, my own were beginning to take over. His fingers gently stroked me deep. I dripped my satisfaction as my juices saturated his hand. Damn this felt so good.

He kissed my neck and gripped my breast with his other hand as he continued to plunge his fingers in and out of me. I was so close to cumming as he stroked my clit and pinched my nipple. I leaned my head back in the crook of his neck as he pleased me to no end. Gripping his hands, I could not resist the urge to climax any longer and I pushed his fingers deeper inside me, causing more friction to release my nectar onto his hands.

As my body jerked from exhaustion I could feel my center quiver around his fingers as tingles invaded me. Derrick kissed my cheek several times, allowing my body to calm itself from such a massive eruption.

Removing his fingers slowly, my body shuddered. I watched as Derrick brought his drenched fingers to his lips and began sucking my wetness from them. Just when I didn't think I could get turned on anymore, I was. Derrick smiled a seductive grin and I knew it wasn't over. Hell, I didn't want it to be over. He bent me over the back of his couch. He then rubbed the tip of his manhood against my center, sending more tingles throughout my body. Moments later Derrick was inside me.

"Oh, Derrick," was all I could say as he filled every nook and cranny I had in me. His strokes were slow and steady, like he was teasing me, and it was working.

"Harder," I told him and he gripped my hips and pushed himself deeper, causing me to scream his name.

"Yes, Derrick, like that. Give it to me, baby," I demanded and Derrick graciously obliged.

His strokes sped up and his power deepened within me. As hard as he was pounding into me, he was beginning to push the couch forward. Pulling himself from inside me, Derrick gripped my hips to stand and led me around the couch and sat down. He reached out for me to climb on top of him and I did so. I helped guide his massive tool inside me and slowly sat down onto it. With his hands around my waist and me gripping the back of the couch, our bodies slowly became in sync as I began to grind into him. He met my grinds with his thrust. I leaned my head back, enjoying this, and before long found myself climaxing yet again. But this time Derrick never stopped his stride, causing my body to be met with multiple explosions back to back.

"Not another one," I caught myself saying, but Derrick never halted. It was like he was trying to make up for all the time we lost in between all this drama and he was delivering.

One after another my climaxes were coming as Derrick deepened his strokes and pounded into me. I too bounced up and down onto him until his grip became even tighter. I knew it was a matter of moments before he was about to release. Leaning forward, Derrick pushed himself to the edge of the seat and gripped my shoulders, pulling me into him. He laid his head on my exposed breast as he stroked me. This caused me to have yet another climax and Derrick was exploding with me.

Once it was over, he leaned back. I laid on top of him in exhaustion. Both of us panted like dogs in heat as our bodies attempted to calm down. You would think after his climax he would be limp but he wasn't. His manhood was still hard as a rock inside me. One false move and I thought I could climax again.

I slowly gained the strength to climb from on top of him. I collapsed next to him, instantly thinking about what I had done. Here I was again cheating on Jaquon and the bad part of it was, I enjoyed every minute of it.

Derrick began rubbing my legs and we continued to lie back without saying a word. My eyes were closed and I knew if I allowed them to stay this way, I was going to fall asleep. Gaining the energy to get up, I slowly got up from the couch and picked up my clothes, which were scattered about. I then went to the restroom to clean myself up because I didn't want to go home with Derrick all over me. Knowing my luck, that would be when Jaquon asked to make love to me. This would have to be a time I would say no. I had enough orgasms to last me a few days.

When I emerged from the bathroom, Derrick had his pants on and was putting on a tank top instead of the shirt he took off.

"I have to go," I said nervously, somehow feeling weird about what had just happened between us.

"You know you don't have to go."

"Derrick, this was absolutely amazing but it was also a big mistake."

"Really."

"This should have never happened."

"I'm glad it did and from your reaction it looked as though you were glad too."

"I never should have come. I should have driven home instead of coming here. I never should have let you talk me into this," I said, finding myself backpedaling.

"Whoa, Kea. Wait a minute, babe. I didn't force you here. You came at your own free will. You know you wanted this just as bad as I did. So stop fighting this. We are destined to be together. You are destined to be my wife."

His words caught me off-guard. I stopped breathing for a minute and struggled to gasp for air.

Finding my voice, I manage to say, "Your wife?"

Derrick walked over to the console table, pulling the drawer open. He retrieved a black box from it. I knew what he was about to do and I began to weep.

He walked over to me and said, "I have had this for a while now. The night all of these made-up secrets came into our lives, I was planning on asking you to marry me later that night. I knew we were meant to be together."

Derrick got down on one knee, kneeling before me. "Kea, I love you and I would be honored if you would become my wife. Will you marry me?"

I tried to choke down emotions I knew I had no control over anymore. "I . . . I . . . I . . ." I stuttered, still not knowing how to answer.

"Say yes." He tried to sway me.

"But what about—"

"Shhh. This is our moment only for you and me. No one else deserves to invade this juncture, Kea. Please say yes. Tell me you will be my wife."

"I can't give you an answer right now, Derrick. I just can't," I said.

Derrick's head dropped. The two-carat diamond that was staring me in the face was now hidden as Derrick closed the velvet box. He stood to his feet and walked to the other side of the room, rubbing his face with his hands. He was upset and had every right to be, but I was not going to say yes to something when I wasn't sure if it was him I wanted to be with.

"I'm sorry, Derrick. It's just—"

"You know what? You are sorry," he blurted, surprising me with his outburst. "I've tried to fight for you from the first time we made love to one another. I've lost my best friend for you. I was willing to do whatever you wanted." He looked at me intensely. "I was willing to give you the world. And you stand here not giving me an answer to a proposal I knew you would say yes to."

I didn't budge. I let whatever frustration he had come out.

"Yet you still are considering being with the man who cheated on you constantly."

"Derrick, he's my—"

"Your what? Your man? Your provider? Your love? Your what?"

I couldn't say anything.

"What type of hold does this dude have on you?"

"I . . . I . . ."

"I can't understand why you insist on being treated like a second-rate partner. We both know his first love is other women."

"But he's changed."

"Are you sure about that? I mean really." Derrick looked at me questioningly. "If he's done all this changing, then how long do you think it's going to be before he sleeps around on you again?"

I couldn't say anything because he did have a valid point. And it was one I had been asking myself as I became closer to Jaquon.

"I'm a living witness to his dirt. Dude stayed at my house using me as his alibi. You know it."

"Derrick, I can't help the way I feel. Jaquon was my first love."

"So, that means you are supposed to spend the rest of your life with him?"

"No."

"Then why are you staying? Did I make another mistake falling in love with the wrong woman?"

"That's a low blow, Derrick. I'm nowhere near being like Zacariah."

"Are you sure about that? Zacariah cheated on me and you basically are doing the same thing. Hell, I just pulled my johnson out of you minutes ago. Yet you claim you still love Jaquon. I mean who's playing who here?"

"Go to hell, Derrick," I said, searching for my shoes.

He continued to ramble on. "You kept going back and forth between Jaquon and me. You can't stand here and say it wasn't a point you weren't sleeping with the both of us at the same time," he said, looking at me like he was waiting for an answer. I wasn't about to tell him he was right.

"Derrick, that's enough," I said, wishing I could find my other damn shoe.

"The only difference is with you, Kea, I allowed it to happen. I loved you enough to know when you got with me, you were still with Jaquon. You needed to figure out who you wanted to be with until we got the results. And honestly I thought you were going to choose me. At least when I got with you, you were the only woman I was sleeping with. Can you say that?"

"Just like you said, Derrick, you knew where I stood when you got with me so don't stand there now and put me down for it."

"Kea, I'm hurt. I'm hurt you can't decide. Jaquon's proven to you a hundred times over why you shouldn't choose him. Yet you stand here wanting him. You must like being dogged."

"I guess I do."

"The truth hurts, doesn't it?" he said coldly.

"No! The truth is you are a hypocrite too. Yes, I have never held anything from you or Jaquon about how I feel about either of you. If anything, I've been the one hurt this entire time. Yes, Jaquon hurt me by cheating but don't stand there and act like you didn't lie to me either."

"How did I lie?"

"You lied by omission. You didn't tell me about Zacariah and Jaquon."

"I told you I was protecting you."

"No. You were protecting yourself. You standing here mad because I didn't accept a proposal a few hours after I found out you weren't my brother and you made love to me. I mean come on. Couldn't you have given me some time to wrap my mind around all these different changes happening in my life?" I asked with more tears streaming. "Don't stand here and act like you didn't find someone to occupy your time because I don't think Trinity is someone we imagined. She is real. And in my gut I know you slept with her so don't criticize me about something you are doing too," I said, finally finding my other shoe and sliding them both on my feet.

Derrick leaned against the arm of the sofa as his knuckles dug into the cushion.

"I do love you, Derrick. There's no doubt in my mind about that but I also love Jaquon. I can't help my feelings. I can't help that I'm confused like this. But you know what? I'm making my choice now. No, I'm not sure if it's the right one, but it's going to be one that's going to end all of this going back and forth."

I picked up my purse and cell phone and walked to the door to leave. Putting my hand on the knob, I turned and said with every morsel of my being, "I choose Jaquon."

Opening the door, I heard Derrick say, "I'm telling you now, Kea, if you walk out that door, I'm not sure I'm going to be here when you figure out he wasn't the man you should have chosen."

I looked at Derrick for a moment and said, "Then it's a choice I'm going to have to live with, isn't it?" slamming the door behind me.

Chapter 38

Derrick

I couldn't deny that Kea's not saying yes to me hurt like hell. I really wanted to make her my wife. I put myself out there for her and she basically dissed me. As far as I was concerned, I was done with Kea. She made her choice when she walked out that door. I thought today with us finding out the results would solve everything but instead somehow it got twisted, and destroyed the very thing we both were trying so hard to regain.

Now, I had just woken up from a nap after I finished having sex with Trinity, wondering how I even allowed myself to sleep with this woman knowing she confessed her love to me and only hours after I had slept with Kea. Looking at the spot where Trinity was lying before she exited my room, I knew Kea was right. I was a hypocrite for calling her out on her actions when

I was doing the same damn thing. I thought I had it together but lately I was turning into this person even I didn't recognize anymore. I stood and put on my pants because I wanted to go see where Trinity had disappeared to. I went down the hallway and heard her talking to someone.

"Just do this for me . . . Please, I'm begging you, I'm okay. Yes, I'm sure. Just pick up the merchandise and take it back to your place. Stop arguing with me . . . I'll deal with it when I get there."

I wasn't sneaking up on Trinity, nor was I trying to eavesdrop on her conversation, but the mere fact that she was whispering puzzled me. Taking a few more steps, I thought Trinity sensed I was behind her because she turned around.

"Yes. Just do that for me, okay? Bye," she said, cutting her conversation short and hanging up abruptly.

"Is everything okay?" I asked.

"Everything's good. Did you get enough sleep?"

"I did, but who were you talking to on the phone? And why were you whispering?"

"Oh, that was my brother. I asked him to pick up some things for me. I was whispering because I didn't want to wake you," she said, walking over to me and wrapping her arms around my waist. "You were sleeping so peacefully, I didn't want to disturb you."

Somehow I didn't quite believe everything she was telling me, but who was I to argue?

Trinity let me go and pulled her floral pink robe tighter around her body. She said, "I'm starving. You want to go out and grab a quick bite to eat? You want burgers, Chinese, Italian, what's your preference?"

"I really don't feel like going out."

"Then let me go pick up something and I'll come back."

"You don't have to do that."

"Will you stop it and let me do this for us?" she said, smiling.

"Okay," I said, giving in.

"And you still haven't told me what you feel like eating. I don't want to go pick something up and you decide that's not what you have a taste for."

"You can't go wrong with some good old-fashioned soul food."

"How about some chicken with greens, mac and cheese, and a slice of corn bread?" she suggested.

"Sounds good," I said, getting hungry thinking about the food. "Do you have some hot sauce?

Because I can't eat my chicken without hot sauce," I said.

"A sister keeps some hot sauce up in her house," she said, laughing. "Just let me throw something on real quick and I'll go out to pick it up."

Trinity left and I wondered why I couldn't allow myself to just fall for this woman. She had openly poured her heart out to me and here I wanted someone who didn't want me. Why did life have to be this hard? I guessed I was making it that way. Maybe Trinity was the woman I should be putting all of my time and energy into. It wasn't hard. She was fun to be around, very attractive, and I hated to sound trifling but she was good in bed, too. Still, there was something about her. I couldn't quite put my finger on it. And from past experience, when my gut told me something, it usually wasn't wrong. So what was she hiding from me?

Did I even have the right to question when we hadn't been together that long? We weren't officially in a relationship so it wasn't any of my business. I guessed I would play this thing out and see where our friendship would take me. I had more important things to do, like work, and finally getting my nerve up to talk with my mother. Finding out Mr. Hanks wasn't my father made me question who was. And why didn't she know? *And does Daddy know?* With these questions I felt like some hard answers would come. I knew it was going to be something I didn't want to hear. Still I had to know and the root of my revelations had to come from Mama. It was time to prepare myself because I didn't know what type of drama was going to happen to me next.

Chapter 39

Zacariah

When I woke up, I was startled to see I was not home. Where in the hell was I? I squinted my eyes and tried to focus on my surroundings and was immediately drawn into a dark, cramped space. Without thinking I rose up and hit my head on something. I couldn't sit straight up. I couldn't stretch my leg out. Where was I? I reached forward and felt metal. It was warm. And I was moving. I realized I was in the trunk of a car.

Panic set in as I hit the metal, trying to get someone's attention, but it was no use. The vehicle was maneuvering down the street. But where was it going? Who had me? Why was I here?

"Can somebody help me?" I yelled. "Please! Can somebody please help me?"

I began kicking and pounding on the metal, thinking I could somehow bust my way out of here.

"Please. I'll give you whatever you want. Just please let me go," I begged, which was something I never did but desperate times call for desperate measures.

The car stopped and I thought maybe, just maybe whoever was behind this was going to free me. I waited to hear the car door shut, or even some footsteps approaching the back of the vehicle but, to my dismay, the car took off again. I figured maybe the driver stopped due to a stop sign or light, which meant I wasn't anywhere secluded. But I knew if I didn't get out of here soon, secluded could be my next location and death would be inevitable.

I began kicking and using my knees to push up on the top of the trunk, but it wouldn't budge. From the feel of the vehicle, it wasn't old. As a matter of fact it still had a new car scent. Then it hit me. I'd just seen on the news where the trunks had this safely release due to children thinking it was fun to hide in trunks. The release would allow them to free themselves.

I began searching blindly for this emergency latch but didn't feel anything. The car came to a stop again and I froze, thinking maybe the person had me where they wanted me. But when the car took off again I knew I didn't have much time. Frantically I continued searching as my hand ran alongside the back of the car in the dark space. I felt something that felt like it didn't belong. The more I moved my hand over it, the more excited I became when I realized this could be the release. Had I finally found it? I pulled and tugged, hoping I would be freed from this nightmare, only to realize this wasn't the lever to release me at all. Evidently I was in a car made before they invented the latch I was so desperately searching for.

I began to kick, pound, and punch as hard as I could, hoping this trunk would open miraculously, releasing me. I thought back to how I got here and remembered I was in a club. I was so frustrated with Derrick and him not taking me back and having the audacity to get involved with another woman that I needed to get my mind off of him for a moment. I needed to loosen up and enjoy a night full of fun even if it consisted of me sitting at the bar and having a few drinks by myself. I thought about calling Jaquon but knew that was a lost cause since he was stuck so far up Ms. Goody Two Shoes' behind now. He claimed he was faithful now. For a while I didn't believe it, but so far I hadn't heard or seen Jaquon stepping outside of the boundaries that would make Kea dump him again.

So now everybody was happy except me. Kea had Jaquon and Derrick had his little trick. Realizing their happiness only made me sad.

I went to the bar Essence and I had frequented on so many occasions. Just being in this place reminded me of her and I almost started to cry because I missed her so much. I needed her here. She was my only friend. What was I going to do now with no friends, no family, and no place to stay? I felt like life was screwing me again. Why did my life have to be so hard? Why couldn't I be happy?

I turned the wine glass up to my mouth when this attractive man approached me. In my nature I sized him up as having some money and was pleased at having an attractive, well-off man stepping to me again. It had been awhile since I had played this game. But my skills were still sharp as a tack, or so I thought. I remembered us talking and laughing but I didn't remember too much after that.

Was it this guy I met in the bar who had me? Did he spike my drink when I wasn't looking only to drag me out of the club like I was intoxicated? Talk about irony. I used to be the one who drugged men to rob them but now the tables had been turned. I was now the victim.

I wanted to cry. I wanted to give up on life and let whatever was going to happen to me happen. I was convincing myself that this was it. Whatever this man was going to do, I knew in the end he was going to kill me. I wept like I hadn't before. Knowing your time was coming was one thing but knowing it was going to be at the hands of someone else was even worse. I didn't know if he was going to shoot me, or stab me, or strangle me. All these demented forms of death recycled through my mind. Was he going to rape me? He could even torture me for days if he wanted to.

Then Essence entered my mind. Did she feel just like I did in this moment, knowing it was the end for her? Did she give up like I wanted to now? An even better question could be, the person who had me, was it the same person who was responsible for murdering my best friend?

I couldn't give up like this. If this man was going to take me, he was going to have to fight me to the death because I wasn't a punk. I sucked up my tears and began to scream. I punched and kicked and pushed as hard as I could.

It must have been heaven giving me another chance because my last few kicks and pushes caused the trunk of the car to pop open. I couldn't believe it. It was open. Fresh air entered, letting me know I was free. This was my opportunity to get away.

I didn't think twice before jumping to my freedom. Asphalt met my skin as I tumbled to the pavement. Pain shot through my body as I rolled but I didn't care because I was free. I had gotten away.

The car all of a sudden stopped. He must have figured out I had escaped. I saw the backup lights of the car appear, indicating he was about to back up. Was the perpetrator backing the car up to run me down now? I didn't know. I couldn't move because my legs felt like jelly. Was this my end? Did I escape only to get run down by a car?

Chapter 40

Derrick

I was about to do something I didn't want to do but knew it had to be handled. Out of everything I had been through in the past few months I never knew it would come down to this.

I stood in the doorway, looking through the screen, hesitating to go in. I didn't know if it was fear I was feeling or anger. I hoped it wasn't anger because I had never been angry at my mother. This was the woman who brought me into this world, giving me life. But whose seed helped determine my existence?

"Why are you just standing at the door like that, son? Come on in here," Daddy said, entering the room.

I guess in my hesitant state I didn't realize they could see me standing here. I opened the door and entered.

"What's wrong with you, and why were you standing out there looking like some lost puppy?"

"I got a lot on my mind, Pop."

"Well, son, you know I'm here if you need to talk."

"Right now I need to talk to Mama. Is she here?"

"No, she had to go to the store and pick up something. She should be back any minute. You can sit down and wait, can't you? It's not often you and I just get some father-son time."

Father son-time, I thought.

"Son, you know I'm not one to beat around the bush so, tell me, what's got you so upset?" Pops asked, looking over his black-rimmed glasses at me.

I wanted to chuckle. You would think by now he would get some glasses he could push up on his nose, but he kept these because they saved him some money.

"Talk to me, son," he pushed.

"I found out yesterday Kea is not my sister."

"That's great news right?" Pops asked.

"It is, but the test also revealed that she was Mr. Hanks's daughter."

"Oh I see. Which means you are not his son?"

I nodded.

"And now you are wondering who your real father is?"

I nodded again, saying, "Pop, I don't want you to think I don't appreciate everything you have done for me. You have been the best father but . . ."

"But you want to know your true blood," Pop said.

"Yes. I feel lost in a sense. I mean, I have you and Mama, but who is this other man walking around who carries the same blood as I do, and why didn't he love me like you did?"

"Well, son, I can't answer that question for you. All I know is that I love you. I see you as my own, as if my blood was running through you."

Water began to form in my eyes and I tried to hold it back. Pop's words were so powerful right now. No, I wasn't some young teenager finding out that the world he knew was not true, but I was this grown man who had a chance to live a great life. I was happy with the world I had months ago. But after one thing began to tumble, it seemed like everything around me tumbled with it. Now it was like the world I knew was a past dream. Everything I knew to be true was false to me now.

"Son, don't let this bring you down. Don't let these skeletons ruin the wonderful blessings you have."

"Nothing feels wonderful anymore, Pop. As blessed as I know I should feel, I'm questioning God right now, asking Him why would He allow this to happen to me? Everything is wrecked. How could my life change so drastically?" I asked with a tear rolling down my cheek.

"Son, I hate to say this, but you sitting here saying you asking God why you. Why not you? Why do you feel like no troubles should ever come your way? As hard as things may seem, the one thing I do ask of you is to not be angry with God, for He is good. You really shouldn't be questioning Him, if you want to know my honest opinion, but you are human and we've all done it at some point in life."

"I'm hurting right now," I said, looking at him solemnly.

"I know you haven't known much turmoil because your mother and I have tried to make your world as easy as possible for you. Doing that is bad in a way because you don't know how to handle trouble when it does come your way. Unless you have walked in tragedy and mayhem, it's hard to know how to come up from it."

Mama walked in with bags in her hand, cutting short the conversation me and Pop were having. I swiped at my tears and leaped to my feet to help her. "Let me get those for you, Mama."

She looked at me strangely. Her beaming face turned to confusion. She looked at Pop, asking, "Is everything okay?"

I stood there holding the bags, and then I proceeded to walk to the kitchen. Pop motioned for Mama to follow me and she did.

"Derrick, baby, what's wrong?"

I put the bags down on the table with my head hung low. She put her hand on my back and I turned to her. Without a second to reconsider, I blurted, "Who's my father, Mama?"

"Wha . . . What?" she asked, bewildered.

"I want to know who my father is."

"Mr. Hanks is your—"

"No, he's not," I said, cutting her off. "Kea and I took the test again and it was determined she was his child, not me."

Mother was dumbfounded. She stopped touching me, like my negative energy shocked her to step back from me. I could see her mind racing as past years flashed through her mind. "But . . . this . . . can't be true."

"It is. I have the papers at home if you want to see them. To my surprise, in the midst of finding out what I wanted, I also learned he wasn't my father, which got me to thinking who is? You told me Pop wasn't my biological father."

"Derrick. I don't believe this," she said, grasping at her chest. She clinched her shirt like it was going to bring answers to her.

"Believe it, Mama."

She stumbled over to the chair at the table and sat down, still stunned.

I was wondering what was taking her so long to answer my question so I decided to ask her again. I needed to know this and the more time I allowed to lapse between these quiet moments was making me angrier.

"Who is my father?"

She looked up at me but turned abruptly, like she didn't want to answer me.

"Mama."

"Derrick, I can't do this right now," she said, sounding upset. Why was she upset? I was the one who didn't know my heritage.

"Mama, I'm not leaving until you tell me. I have the right to know my existence."

"Not today!" she belted.

"Mama, I have never disrespected you—"

"So don't start now," she retorted.

"I want to know the truth. Who is my father?" I said louder.

"And I said not today!"

My anger rose to a level I knew would cross the lines of a son disrespecting his mother, and I couldn't contain the beast that raged within me.

"Tell me, Mother, who is my father?" I yelled.

She turned and looked at me fearfully, but at the same time like she didn't recognize the child standing before her. This wasn't her sweet Derrick yelling at her. No, not Derrick who came by to see how she was doing and gave her money whenever she needed. No, this was the son who lost who he thought he knew weeks back. The Derrick before was sure of himself. The Derrick standing before her now was lost in a heap of lies.

"If you don't know, then say so. Is it that you can't remember who you slept with? Did you sleep with that many men that you can't recall which one helped in developing me?"

"Enough," Pop's voice rang out from behind me. "You will not disrespect your mother like this."

"Then she should give me the answers I need."

"I don't care if she never answers you, boy. You better not ever, as long as you living, yell at your mother again," Pops said sternly.

"You are not even my real father so how can you tell me? How can you know how I feel?" I blurted. The words left my mouth before my tongue could hold them back. I closed my eyes in regret as the look on the man who loved me my entire life showed more hurt than I had ever seen.

Pop paused. If I didn't know any better I could have sworn water started to develop in his eyes.

"Son," he still called me, regardless of my disregard of his status, downgrading him. "That is my wife and that is your mother. If you are not sure of anything else going on in your life, the one thing you are sure of is the woman sitting before you is the one who has been here for you always. She is the one who birthed you. She is the one who has raised you and she's the one who's loved you your entire life. And as long as I have breath in my body, I'm going to stand by her side. I will not have you or anybody else disrespect her in the manner you just did."

I knew Pop was right but I knew I deserved answers. And I wasn't sure if I could talk to her until she was ready to give them to me. So I looked at the both of them: Pop with his wounded expression, and Mama with tears running down her face. I took in their emotions. But I had some emotions to deal with myself that I felt trumped theirs.

"Are you going to tell me who my father is?" I asked Mama as calmly as I could.

"Baby, I just can't do this today."

With that I nodded. I looked at the both of them before brushing past Pop and leaving their home.

Chapter 41

Kea

"Yes. Yes, Jaquon, I will marry you," were the words I heard come out of my mouth, but I couldn't believe I was saying them to him. Jaquon jumped to his feet and pulled me to him, lifting me up in his arms and twirling me around.

"You have made me the happiest man ever," he said with his face buried in my neck.

Two proposals in less than a twenty-four-hour span. What was going on? What had I just done and why did I say yes to Jaquon and not Derrick? I confused myself. I thought all of this as Jaquon kissed on me with happiness, still twirling me around like I was some kid.

Jaquon put me down and slipped the diamond on my left hand.

I couldn't stop trembling.

He took my hand into his to steady my fingers and slipped the diamond on. "I can't believe you said yes," he said.

"I can't believe it either," I found myself mumbling, but I said it loud enough for him to hear.

"What?"

"I'm just joking," I said, playing it off.

"I can't wait until you become my wife, baby. Maybe we don't have to wait. Maybe we can go to the justice of the peace and make it legal tomorrow."

"Are you serious?" I questioned.

"Yes. Why not?"

"Because you just asked me," I said with my heart racing now, not wanting our marriage to come to pass so quickly. He had already caught me off guard with the proposal. Now he wanted to marry me immediately.

"Who cares? We love each other."

"We don't have witnesses or anything."

"Get Terry. Well, scratch that. Get your dad to come and witness it."

"We usually need more than just one witness."

"Then we'll pick up a bum on our way," Jaquon said.

"A bum," I said, giggling. He had truly lost it now if he thought I was going to let a bum help represent our union.

He laughed and said, "I don't care if it is the mailman, the butcher, the hooker standing on the corner, I want to be your husband. You have made me the happiest man ever."

"Jaquon, give me some time to let this sink in first. I haven't had the ring on my finger five minutes yet. And besides I always wanted a big wedding. Not some guy in a robe downtown who couldn't care less. I want it to be like our marriage is going to be. I want happy memories for us to cherish a lifetime to come."

"You really want a wedding?" he asked, looking at me meaningfully.

"Yes. It's every little girl's dream."

"Well if it's a wedding you want, then it's a wedding we shall have." Jaquon leaned down and kissed me. "Can we start the honeymoon now?" he asked, grabbing my butt.

"Maybe we should wait until the wedding," I suggested.

"Wait to make love. Are you serious?"

"Yes. You know, let the fire build between us. That way when we finally do it, it will be intense."

"Kea, I promise you whether it's today or months from now, a brother is going to be intense," he said, smiling.

"You are crazy."

"Crazy about you," he said, kissing me again. "Come on, baby. Let's go to the room. It's been awhile."

"Awhile to you is one day."

"I can't help it if I want my woman every time I see her."

"So you are really serious about this?" I asked.

"Yes, I'm serious."

"Don't think me becoming your wife is going to change the fact you still supposed to be faithful. I'm still going to demand respect and fidelity."

"And I'm going to give you that and more."

Jaquon did seem serious about this and had proven to me his dedication so far. Still, I did fear his words were just that: words. What if Derrick was right and this was all a ruse to get me back into his life? Then this would be the biggest mistake I would ever make. I truly did fear not choosing Derrick could be my downfall to a broken heart again.

I looked at Jaquon, who was beaming, happy to have me as his fiancée. I hoped the ring wouldn't make him think he had me for life, because I would divorce him at the drop of a dime if he cheated on me again.

"Since you don't want to give up the goods, let's go celebrate. I want the world to see my future wife."

I agreed to his suggestion. I needed to get out of here and get some air and wonder why in the hell I had said yes to this proposal. And the one thing I couldn't help but think was, what would Derrick think when he found out this news?

Chapter 42

Jaquon

On our way out of the door, Sheila from across the hall came stepping out of her apartment too. As soon as I saw her, I wanted to push Kea back in the crib and wait for Sheila to get where she was going. But Sheila saw us, so I didn't have a choice but to play this thing out.

"Well hey, Kea," she said like she hadn't seen her in a long time.

I swear she is so fake, I thought.

"How you doing?" she asked, being noisy. For once she was dressed pretty casual in a pair of jeans, sneakers, and blouse, which hugged her tight.

"I'm good," Kea said.

I shut the door behind me and locked it.

"You two going out on the town?" Sheila asked.

"Yes. We are celebrating," Kea said.

"You pregnant," Sheila blurted.

"No. Jaquon proposed to me today," Kea said happily, showing off the ring.

Sheila walked closer and took Kea's hand into hers, looking at the one-carat diamond.

"Dag, Jaquon. I didn't know you had it in you."

"What is that supposed to mean?" I asked.

"Not a playa like yourself. You sure you want to settle down with him, Kea?" she asked, and I wanted to push her over the balcony platform. "You know Jaquon has a reputation."

Kea didn't look pleased with Sheila's comment, but said, "Well he's a changed man now."

"I hope so for your sake, because I don't want to see you on *Divorce Court* talking about, 'I left him because he's been cheating on me again.'"

"That will not happen," I concluded, putting my hand on Kea's back to lead her down the stairs. When I looked back, Sheila was smirking at me. I grimaced and hoped she would leave us alone. To my dismay she followed.

"Well I wish you two the best," she said with her heels slicking against the steps as we all made our way down. "It's good seeing young love coming together. I wish I could find a man to settle down with."

I wanted to say, "If you stopped spreading your legs for every man with a hard dick then you would have one." But I thought better of it, knowing this woman could blow my spot up any second. So I played the nice, innocent neighbor and proceeded to keep my mouth shut.

"You two have fun," she said, smiling at us as I opened the door to my car for Kea. Sheila just stood there like she was waiting for us to pull off.

I hurried up and got in the car to leave. Oh how I wished I could go back in time and erase ever sleeping with that woman. And to think I came so close the other day. I guessed I could thank that blue-eyed lunatic. I didn't know who was the more evil of the two: Sheila or Trinity. Right now I couldn't worry about either because tonight was all about being with my baby Kea.

I knew today had to be the beginning of being a changed man for good. I didn't know what's been going on lately but it seemed like every woman I came in contact with had some sort of psychological issue. That alone was enough to make me turn in my playa card. It was best to settle down with Kea because my luck lately had not been good. Besides, I had a good girl who made one mistake messing with Derrick but I had her now. She chose me. She said yes to being my wife regardless of Derrick asking for her hand in marriage. I was indeed the happiest man ever.

When we arrived at the restaurant, the waitress led us to a cozy table in the heart of the restaurant. I knew I looked good dressed in a black suit. And Kea was stunning in her knee-length, kimono-style, multicolored dress. The waitress took a drink order after handing us our menus and then left to get them.

"We haven't done this in a long time," Kea said, looking down at her menu.

"It has been awhile. But once you become my wife I will make sure to wine and dine you more often."

Kea smiled, making my heart fill with joy. But that joy was soon cut short when I looked around to see Derrick and Trinity. I swore, in that moment, I felt like moving to another city. Was this area so small that every time I turned around I was bumping into people I didn't want to see? What was next? Was some female from my cheating days going to come up to Kea in the midst of our dinner to further ruin my evening? I sighed with annoyance.

"What's wrong?" Kea asked.

"Nothing," I said, hoping she would leave it alone.

"Jaquon, I can tell something's wrong. What is it?"

My eyes went to Derrick and Trinity's table. Kea turned to the direction I was looking and saw what troubled me.

She nodded, saying, "I see."

"Would you like to go somewhere else?" I asked, hoping she would agree.

"No, Jaquon. I'm not leaving. This is our night to celebrate. I'm here with you, the man I'm going to marry, and no one is going to ruin this evening for us," she said, reaching out and taking my hand into hers.

I knew then that Kea was mine. I smiled with satisfaction and thought she was right. I gripped her hand in approval and asked, "So what are you ordering?"

Kea and I drank. We ate and talked like we hadn't done since the first time we met. It felt good laughing with her and seeing how happy she was. Knowing I was the one bringing smiles to her face made this more special. I tried to see, if at any point, she wanted to turn and stare in the direction of Derrick and Trinity. But Kea never looked. All her attention was on me. She talked about the colors she wanted in our wedding and the month she thought we should have it in. If it was up to me, I would elope. I would fly her to Vegas to marry her, but I knew Kea wanted a traditional wedding with the church, flowers, bridesmaids, and the whole nine yards. And if that's what she wanted, that was what I was going to give her.

During our dessert, Trinity thought it was appropriate to make herself present amid our happiness, without Derrick in tow. I guessed he didn't want another fight to break out. The only difference with this one would be I wouldn't let him get by sucker-punching me again.

"Well hello. It's nice to see you again."

"Same here," Kea said, looking like she didn't mean it. I wondered if she was upset because Trinity was with Derrick.

"I didn't mean to interrupt. It seems I'm saying that to you a lot lately," Trinity said to Kea.

"It's quite all right," Kea said, looking uncomfortable all of a sudden.

"I mean here, and the other day at Derrick's place."

"Oh really," I said, looking at Kea. I didn't know what game Trinity was playing but she knew she told me this already. She probably also figured Kea didn't tell me. So what was her deal? Was she purposely trying to make Kea uncomfortable?

"Derrick and I needed to talk about some things," Kea said uneasily, taking a sip of her water as she looked to me.

"Baby, it's okay. I trust you," I told Kea, easing her mind.

Trinity looked at Kea's finger as Kea set her glass back down on the table. Trinity then looked at me. I ignored her stare and turned my attention back to Kea. I took her hand into mine and asked, "Should we tell her?"

Kea smiled, but before we could say anything Trinity came to the conclusion herself. "Please. Don't tell me you two are engaged," Trinity said, looking at the ring she gave me sparkling on Kea's finger.

Kea nodded and smiled as she tried to swallow down some more water.

"Congratulations," Trinity said happily to Kea and then me.

This woman was good and conniving.

"Thank you," Kea said.

"I can't wait to tell Derrick the wonderful news."

"I bet you can't," Kea mumbled.

"Excuse me?"

"I was going to tell Derrick myself."

"Oh okay. Do you want to tell him now?" Trinity pushed.

"No. I'm in the middle of dinner with my fiancé. I can talk to Derrick another time. I think it will be better coming from me and Jaquon. I hope you understand."

"I do," Trinity said.

"So if you don't mind, let us break the news to him. I really don't think it's a good idea him hearing this from a stranger," Kea said blatantly.

Trinity shifted from one foot to the other. I could tell she didn't like Kea's comment but she let it ride. Instead she breathed in much air like she was trying to deal with Kea's attitude and said, "Very well. I'll let you break the news to him. I'll leave you two to continue celebrating your evening."

"We would appreciate it," Kea said with a phony smile.

Trinity did the same and left our table.

"You are funny," I said, laughing at Kea rolling her eyes as Trinity left.

"It's something about that woman that isn't right. I didn't feel it about her the first time I met her but that could be due to your fight. But when I was leaving Derrick's place, she was standing on the other side of the door like she just got there. She tried to play it off but I think she was listening to our conversation the entire time."

"If your gut is telling you to feel that way about her then you should."

"And, Jaquon, nothing happened like that with Derrick and me. We just needed to hash some things out."

"Baby, I believe you. You don't see me tripping."

"It was like she was trying to cause some tension between us or something."

"Baby, it doesn't matter. She did not spoil our evening. We are going to continue to celebrate." I poured us the last bit of champagne and held my glass up to Kea. "To us, baby," I said. "May our future be as bright as it is now."

"To us," she agreed happily.

"I love you, baby."

"I love you too, Jaquon."

Our glasses clinked as a symbol of our love blossoming as we drank to our future. I hoped we had one, especially with secrets still floating around us.

I wanted to tell Kea how right she was. I wanted to tell her Trinity came to see me, but then I would have to explain why. Looking at Kea's finger I knew that conversation would not go over well. She would believe I only proposed because Derrick asked her first. Then our engagement would be over. Hell our relationship probably would be over, too. It would be hard to explain I really did want to marry her after such a portrayal and I wouldn't blame her.

So, I kept yet another secret to myself. I just hoped these secrets would stay buried for my sake.

Chapter 43

Derrick

After seeing Kea and Jaquon together, I didn't want to stay and have dessert. I told the waitress we wanted it to go as I watched Trinity talk to Kea and Derrick. Why she wanted to go speak was beyond me. They weren't her friends, so why did she have to leave our table to see what was going on with them?

It didn't take her long before she was walking back to our table. She seemed a bit perturbed about something, but when she noticed I had our dessert brought out in boxes, this made her perturbed mood even worse.

"What's this?" she asked.

"I'm ready to go," I said flatly.

"Why?"

I looked over at Jaquon smiling at Kea and said, "I'm just ready to go."

Trinity turned and looked at them and then back at me. "Don't tell me you are leaving because of them," she said.

"Are you coming with me, or are you going to sit here and enjoy your dessert alone?"

"Don't let them affect us," she said.

"Are you coming or staying?" I asked, getting up from my chair and grabbing my box, leaving hers in front of her just in case she decided to stay and enjoy it.

Trinity stood, angry that I didn't relent to staying and having our dessert, but I didn't care. I walked out with her following closely behind. We had to pass them and I wished we didn't. When I walked by, Jaquon eyed me and neither of us spoke. Neither did Kea and I. Seeing them happy only angered me more and I needed to get away from them before I was pummeling Jaquon again.

When I got home, I put my food in the kitchen and went to my bedroom to get more comfortable. A long sleep would suffice to help me forget about my life and what was wrong with it. I was so caught up in my mood that I didn't notice Trinity was in the room with me. I thought once she got out of my ride, she had gotten into hers and left.

"Talk to me, Derrick," Trinity demanded.

"I'm tired," I said, taking off my watch.

"You didn't say anything to me all the way here."

"I didn't feel like talking and I damn sure don't feel like talking now."

"Why do you let Kea get to you like this? It's evident she doesn't want to be with you," Trinity blurted. "If she wanted you then she wouldn't have accepted Jaquon's hand in marriage."

I snappishly turned to her and asked, "What did you just say?"

"They are getting married."

"Stop lying."

"It's true. I saw the ring on her finger tonight. She confirmed it. That's why they were there in the first place, to celebrate their engagement."

I took my shirt off and threw it across the room. "She can't marry him. I want to marry her."

"Well it's true, Derrick, and you need to accept she's made her choice. She told me I could tell you because whatever you two had was over."

"Why didn't you tell me when you got back to our table?" I asked.

"So you could possibly cause a scene? Look at you now, throwing your shirt and temples throbbing. You know you would have gone over to confront them."

I took in what Trinity was saying and sat down on the edge of my bed. She came to sit beside me. "Maybe that's why Kea wanted me to tell you."

"She looked so happy," I said, hurting because it was supposed to be me who made her happy.

"Hopefully, she wasn't trying to make you jealous, or rub their love in your face."

"She's not like that."

"If she cared about you, she would have told you herself," Trinity said, making a valid point. "Kea could have walked over to the table with me and told you herself. Or better yet she could have called you to tell you so you wouldn't have found out this way. Derrick, Kea doesn't care about you. Not like you cared about her."

I listened to Trinity and wondered if what she was telling me was true. It did seem that way. She had to know I was there and when I walked past, she could have stopped me to tell me. But she didn't.

Trinity caressed the back of my neck, massaging it gently. Her touch was easing some of my pain and anger. I didn't know if I could take anything else at this point. There was the drama with my ex, Zacariah, tension with my mother, Kea not accepting my proposal, my father who I didn't know, and a life I didn't even recognize anymore. I wanted the life I had months ago. I wanted to be happy.

Trinity's soft hand moved from my neck to my exposed back. I closed my eyes because it really did feel good. The more she rubbed the more I began to relax.

"It's okay. I'm here for you," Trinity whispered.

"I just can't understand why my life has spun out of control."

"Then grab control of it, Derrick. Grab the happiness that's right in front of you."

I turned to look into her blue eyes and saw that tranquility again.

"I told you regardless of anything, I'm here for you. Have I lied to you yet?" she asked.

I shook my head. She got down on her knees and crawled between mine. She took my face into her hands. "It's going to be okay. I'm going to make it okay for you."

"Why are you still here for me like this?" I asked.

"Like I told you before, Derrick, it's because I love you." Trinity leaned in and kissed me. Her lips soothed my aching heart. She crawled closer to me, her lips never leaving mine. She began to undo the buckle of my pants until she was reaching into them, pulling my now erect johnson free.

"You know I can make you forget about all your troubles," she said softly.

That's when she leaned down and lubricated my dick with her tongue and tried to suck all of my troubles out of me.

Chapter 44

Zacariah

Here I was recovering from a trunk ride from hell last night and the same officer who revealed to me that Essence was dead was standing here asking me the same damn questions over and over again like I was going to change my story.

"Look, for the fifteenth time already, I don't know what happened. I was having drinks at the bar and the next thing I know I'm rolling down the road, trying not to get hit by a car as I managed to get away from whoever thought it fit to kidnap me."

"Miss, I know you are upset."

"Don't you think I should have a right to be?" I said, looking down at my bandaged arm and knee.

"Yes, but—"

"But nothing. Look, please just file this report the way I told you and let me go home."

I guessed he figured he wasn't going to get anywhere else with me so he had a patrol officer drive me home. It was damn near four o'clock in the afternoon when I walked through the door. I should have been sleepy but I wasn't. I guessed the drug whoever slipped in my drink had me sleep enough to not need any right now. Besides feeling sore from my near escape, I was okay. I knew one thing: I was hungry and felt like eating some breakfast food.

Scraping the egg I just scrambled from the pan onto my plate, which had two pieces of bacon and wheat toast, I set the pan in the sink. I poured myself a glass of orange juice and headed to the living room to watch some television. Just when I was about to take my first bite, there was a knock at the door.

"Damn it," I said. "Who is it?" I screamed.

"It's me, Susan."

"Come back later. I'm eating," I said, putting a forkful of eggs in my mouth.

The knocks persisted with Susan saying, "I'm not leaving, so open up the damn door before I kick it down."

No, this trick isn't getting ready to kick my door down. I put the plate down on the coffee table and made my way to the door.

"What?" I yelled when I opened it. Susan brushed past me like I told her to come in. "I didn't tell you to walk up in here."

"Guess who came to see me today?"

"Susan, I don't have time for no guessing games. I'm hungry. I'm a little evil right now and would appreciate if you left me—"

"Derrick."

That got my attention. I shut the door and walked deeper into the living room asking, "When?"

"I just told you, today. Dag, are you listening?" she said, finally noticing my bandages. "What in the hell happened to you?" she asked.

"It's a long story I care not to share right now. Tell me why he came by to see you."

"He came by to confront me."

Susan paused like I was supposed to figure out what Derrick said. She just stood there, looking at me with her arms crossed.

I asked, "So, what did he say?"

"He asked me did I know you."

"And?" I said, getting frustrated because I wished she would just spit this story out her damn mouth.

"I denied knowing you. He told me I looked familiar and he thought he seen me somewhere before."

"We did attend a cookout," I said, going over to the sofa to sit down and proceed with eating my food before it got cold. *Nothing worse than cold eggs.*

"Yes. You even introduced me to him," Susan said. "Maybe he didn't recognize me because then I had short hair and now my hair is long."

"So why are you worried? He didn't figure it out did he?"

"Zacariah, I don't think it's going to be that simple. Something about the way he approached me didn't sit right with me."

"Well you still have your job don't you?"

"For now. But look, he also told me that the test they had redone came back proving he and Kea were not brother and sister."

When she said that, I was sipping on my orange juice and spit it across the coffee table. "What?" I belted.

"Zacariah, I think he knows something. What if he's figured out who I am and is thinking about going to the higher-ups on what he thinks happened with that test? Zacariah, I'm scared."

"Scared of what? Girl, please. Just sit back and let things fall. Besides, Derrick can't prove you did anything. He doesn't even know who you are," I said, picking up my toast and taking a bite of it. With my mouth full I said, "Sit down for a bit and rest your feet. I'm about to watch this movie."

Susan walked over to the chair and plopped down in it like her life was over. "I've worked so hard to get where I am in my career. I love my job."

"Damn. You act like you can't get another one or something."

"Zacariah, I know you don't have to work, but some of us do, and when we find a job we love, we tend to stick around for a long time. Plus the money is good. I'm blessed right now."

"Then stop complaining," I said, taking another bite of my toast only to get interrupted again by another knock at my door.

"Oh my goodness. I mean can a girl get her eat on and rest from her near-death experience? Most days nobody wants to see me and now I got a revolving door of people tapping at my door."

I got up, placing my plate down on the coffee table for a second time, and went to the door. I swung it open without asking who it was or peeping through the hole to see who it was. This was one time I wished I had.

Chapter 45

Derrick

I could tell I caught Zacariah by surprise, which was my intention. Little did she know I followed her cousin over here. I knew I was taking a chance and could have been wrong in this instance, but the look on Susan's face when I confronted her let me know she was scared to death at what she thought I knew. Being lied to lately had given me a sense to recognize when something wasn't right, especially when I looked for it. Today I was searching for answers. I may not have known who my real father was, but I could find out exactly how that first paternity test came to show me and Kea as brother and sister.

"D . . . D . . . Derrick. What are you doing here?" Zacariah stuttered as she looked back at her cousin sitting on the chair.

Susan's mouth was wide open when I stared her down. "Can I come in?" I asked politely.

"Um . . . Um . . . I'm in the middle of something."

"I know. That's why I'm here," I said, entering Essence's place.

Susan stood to her feet and started walking farther away from me as I got deeper into the space. I walked over to the television, since it was the focal point in the room, and stood where I would be able to see both ladies' faces when I spoke. "So what do we have here?" I asked, looking at Susan.

"It's not what you think," Zacariah said.

I shook my head at the irony. "It feels like déjà vu to me. I can remember you saying something like that to me a few months ago when I found out you cheated on me. You do remember, don't you, Zacariah? I did the 'hand between the thighs' test."

Zacariah shifted nervously from one foot to the other before she said, "That was then, Derrick. And this is now."

"So are you saying you are a changed woman?" I asked.

"Yes," she said.

I giggled at her lies.

"What's so funny?" she asked.

"I'm laughing at you. You think you have changed but you haven't." I walked over to the plate on the coffee table, figuring it was Zacariah's, and picked up a slice of bacon off it. I took a bite of it and sat down in the chair. "Since when did you decide to play God and bring your little cousin in on the fun?"

"I don't know what you are talking about."

I giggled again, surprising myself at how calm I was. "You paid your cousin to change those results to make it look like Kea and I were brother and sister."

"And why would I—" she started to say.

I held my hand up. "Please. Don't patronize me. You did it because you wanted me back in your life."

"Derrick, I didn't do what you think I did."

I looked at Susan and asked, "You tell me, Susan. Did she get you to change the results or not?"

Susan nervously moved from foot to foot and opened her mouth to speak, but I held up my finger to stop her. "And please don't lie like you did to me earlier, because I don't know how I'm going to react if you do. As we can see, you do know Zacariah. I mean you are standing in her house."

Susan stared like she was scared to death. It wasn't like I was going to smack her around until she admitted the truth. But I knew she took what I said as a threat, which was what I wanted her to think.

"Speak up, Susan. Did she threaten you, blackmail you, or did she pay you to tamper with the paternity test?" I looked at Zacariah, who was gawking at Susan intensely. I guessed she was trying to send some subliminal message to her to keep her mouth shut. "Susan," I called out.

"Okay, okay. I did it."

"Susan," Zacariah blurted.

"Come on, Zacariah. He knows. Why continue to lie?"

"I appreciate you being honest with me, Susan. It tends to go a long way."

"Does it go long enough for you not to have me fired?" Susan asked.

"Let me think about that for a minute. I need to talk with Zacariah first."

"What is there left to say? The truth is out. I did all of this to get you back into my life," she said, defeated. "Now what? I did it because I miss you. I know I messed up."

"You damn right you did."

"But how long do I have to live with the repercussions?" she asked sadly. "Can't you tell by everything I'm doing that I want you back?"

"You didn't want me when you had me," I retorted.

"I didn't realize what I had until I didn't have it anymore, Derrick. I know now and that's why I've been fighting so hard to get you back."

"Susan, I know what I'm going to do now," I said, never turning my attention from Zacariah. I could feel the air get thick as the tension of what I was about to say suspended itself.

"I'm not going to have you fired."

I could hear Susan sigh with relief. She almost fell to her knees with gratitude as tears began to form.

"But," I said, looking at her, "if I hear of anything else like this happening again, you best believe I'm going to be the first one turning you in. What you did ruins lives." I turned to look at Zacariah and said, "It has ruined mine."

"I'm sorry, Derrick," Zacariah said.

"But there's one good thing about this whole thing."

Both women looked at me, asking the question, "What?" with their eyes.

"Your plan worked, Zacariah. I'm willing to give you a second chance."

"What?" she asked in surprise.

"I'm willing to take you back if you want us to work on our relationship."

Zacariah ran over to me and plopped down in my lap. She kissed my neck, my cheeks, my forehead, and then my lips.

"Thank you. Thank you. Thank you, Derrick. I promise I will never betray your trust again."

"But wait, Zacariah."

"What?" she asked, stopping her forms of affection.

"This relationship comes with some stipulations."

"What stipulations?" she asked, frowning.

"You said you are willing to do anything to get me back into your life, right?" I asked.

"Yes, Derrick, anything."

"Then you are going to have to share me with another woman."

"What?"

"You heard me."

"Share you. Another woman. Who?"

"Trinity."

Chapter 46

Trinity

"Where have you been?" my brother asked me when I walked through the doors of my place.

"And whose father are you?"

"You were gone all night. You have been gone many nights, for that matter," my brother said frantically.

"I was at Derrick's. Damn, can a sister get some lovin'?"

"No," he said loudly.

"And why not?"

"You know why," he answered.

"Steven, I'm a grown woman."

"You are a grown woman with a whole lot of issues."

"Steven, don't go there," I said, walking to the kitchen to grab myself some yogurt.

"Trinity, you know this is too soon."

"Love doesn't have a timeframe to happen, Steven. It comes when it does and right now Cupid's arrow has struck again because I love Derrick. Besides, I have things under control," I spat.

"For now," my brother said.

"Look, Kea and Jaquon are getting married. Derrick knows this and understands what he and Kea had has ended. Kea has chosen to move on. Derrick also knows I love him so he's going to choose to be with me."

"There you go getting your hopes up again. Trinity, this is what got you in the predicament before."

"But it's different this time," I said, peeling the foil seal off the yogurt container and licking it.

"You know how you are, Trinity. So why do you insist on putting yourself in a situation that could possibly take you back to a place neither of us want to see you go ever again?"

"My life does not stop because of . . ." I paused, not wanting to think about my past. "Steven, I'm fine. Look at me. Does anything seem wrong?"

"It never does in the beginning, Trinity."

"Is this how you are going to be as long as I'm with Derrick?"

"So you plan on being with him. You know I checked up on him. Not only does he love this woman named Kea, he also has some crazy ex-girlfriend who's been trying to get him back."

"I see you've been doing your homework."

"I have to know what you are getting yourself into."

"Well, I told you about Kea. And Zacariah, well, Derrick's done with her. Everything is working out for the good. Derrick and I are going to be together."

Steven sat down at the kitchen table, shaking his head in frustration. "You see what I'm saying?" he asked. "It's starting again."

"No, it's not."

"Does this man love you?" I paused too long and my brother said, "You see. He doesn't even love you."

"He will."

"How do you know?" Steven asked.

"I just do."

"Trinity, I love you but I don't know if I'm going to be here to help you this time. If you . . ." he said, and paused. "If you resort to your old ways, I'm leaving you to deal with whatever repercussions come about."

"But you are my brother."

"I know this, and I have been through the thickest of situations that should have landed us both in jail. But I will not go through this again with you. If you insist on going further with your involvement with Derrick, I'm leaving."

"I love you, Steven, and I know you love me. You will not leave me."

He got up from the table and said, "Yes, I will." He walked out of the kitchen.

"You can't do this to me. Why can't you just be here to support me? You know you are all the family I have."

Steven looked at me longingly and said, "Trinity, I want to live a normal life and we've been doing that for the past few months."

"And we can still do that."

"No, we can't if you get involved with another man. My life has been put on hold because I'm too busy trying to look out for you. I want to get married. I want to have children. How can I, when I feel like I have a child already in you to take care of?"

"I'm taking my medicine."

"Every day?" he asked.

"Every day."

"Because I counted your pills and you have skipped several. You couldn't have taken it last night because you stayed with him and your medicine is here."

This angered me. *How dare he track my pills like this?*

"You see what I'm saying. The lying has already begun. Who knows what's going to happen next?"

"Nothing," I screamed.

"Go take your medicine now."

"I will."

"Now," he demanded.

I stormed to my bedroom with him closely on my heels. "I don't need you to make sure I take them."

"I know but I want to see for myself."

I reached into the bottom drawer of my dresser and pulled out the bottle of pills. I poured one into my hand and popped it into my mouth, swallowing it dry.

"Open your mouth," my brother demanded.

I sighed, doing what Steven asked, moving my tongue around so he could see the pill was not hiding anywhere in my mouth.

"Are you satisfied?"

"I am now, but I meant what I said, Trinity. If troubles begin again, I'm leaving you by yourself to deal with it. And if I see things getting really bad, I will tell Derrick about you."

"You wouldn't," I spat.

"Oh yes, I would. He needs to know anyway."

"Then I will tell him. I don't need you butting into my affairs and blabbing my business to him."

"Tell him, and do it soon, or I will."

My brother left my room and my place as I heard my front door close. I sat down on my bed looking at the pills that had me by the throat. If Derrick knew about my condition, it could cause him to leave me forever. Hell if he knew about my past he could leave me. I hated to start our relationship off with secrets but I couldn't risk him not wanting to be with me.

No, Derrick couldn't find out. Not now, not ever. And if my brother considered telling him then he would need to be dealt with, just like the others who stood in the way of what I wanted.